"Edgy enough to push a timeworn formula from the basement up to the balcony. Dumas adds just enough zany to her mix to have readers lining up for more."

– Kirkus Reviews

"*Murder at the Palace* has great characters, including Trixie. It's a delightful book, and...the movie summaries just add to the appeal."

– Library Journal

"*Murder at the Palace* is a downright hoot. Fans of classic films will love this smart tale of travail starring Nora Paige...Rest assured that although the films involved are old, the story is witty and fresh. Especially enjoyable is watching the thoroughly modern Nora attempt to explain computer passwords to ghostly Trixie, whose idea of modern is a Duesenberg Model X Boattail Roadster."

– Mystery Scene Magazine

"This story immediately grabbed my attention...I could not put this book down...And Trixie...oh my goodness, I love her and...had me laughing on the subway...boy I'm excited for the next book in this delightful entertaining debut series."

– Dru's Book Musings

"Old movie buffs, fans of San Francisco, and lovers of well-done mystery series debuts will shout huzzah and encore at author Margaret Dumas."

– Criminal Element

"Stands with the best modern cozy mysteries and reminded me a lot of the Lily Ivory series by Juliet Blackwell. I'm adding this to my list of must-read series. Recommended."

– It's All About The Book

**The Movie Palace Mystery Series
by Margaret Dumas**

MURDER AT THE PALACE (#1)
MURDER IN THE BALCONY (#2)

MURDER IN the Balcony

A Movie PALACE MYSTERY

MARGARET DUMAS

HENERY PRESS

Copyright

MURDER IN THE BALCONY
A Movie Palace Mystery
Part of the Henery Press Mystery Collection

First Edition | September 2019

Henery Press, LLC
www.henerypress.com

This is a work of fiction. Any references to historical events, real people, or real locales are used fictitiously. Other names, characters, places, and incidents are the product of the author's imagination, and any resemblance to actual events or locales or persons, living or dead, is entirely coincidental.

Trade Paperback ISBN-13: 978-1-63511-535-2
Digital epub ISBN-13: 978-1-63511-536-9
Kindle ISBN-13: 978-1-63511-537-6
Hardcover ISBN-13: 978-1-63511-538-3

Printed in the United States of America

For Dolores and Marge,
The Glamorous Salviola Sisters

ACKNOWLEDGMENTS

One of the best things about writing this series is all the wonderful conversations I've had with people about classic movies since the first book came out. Thanks to everyone who cares enough about their favorite movie to tell me about it!

Many thanks to the amazing team at Henery Press, especially Maria Edwards, Art Molinares, Christina Rogers, Kendel Lynn, and a bunch of people I still haven't met who create art I could only dream of.

Huge thanks to trusted first readers Denise Lee, Erick Vera, and Anne Dickson for your insightful comments and encouragement, to Martha Paley Francescato for your great catches, and to Claire M. Johnson and Michael J. Cooper for your let's-try-for-every-other-week critiques and support.

I owe a lot to a multitude of film scholars and critics who have written brilliant books and made gorgeous documentaries about classic films. Particular thanks to Mick LaSalle, whose *Complicated Women: Sex and Power in Pre-Code Hollywood* was essential reading.

My very first film scholars were my family. This series owes a lot to Dolores, Keith, Richard, and John. So do I.

Author's Note: Spoilers Ahead!

When someone loves classic movies, and loves talking about them, they're bound to eventually share some spoilers about them. The characters in this book are gleefully guilty of that.

If you don't want spoilers, you may need to avert your gaze when the following movies come up: *The Divorcee, The Women, Roman Holiday, The Letter, Mildred Pierce, Born Yesterday, Mata Hari, Born to Dance,* and *Now, Voyager.*

Look away if you must, but you could also solve the spoiler problem by watching the movies. I'm just saying...

"Haunted! How perfectly fascinating!"

The Ghost and Mrs. Muir

CHAPTER 1

"I've been ghosted!"

This announcement got my attention. It was hardly proclaimed with the bold theatricality of Bette Davis telling the room to buckle up for a bumpy night, but still. Coming from Callie Gee, the film student who worked for me at the Palace movie theater, it was an unexpected greeting.

The lobby door closed behind her, cutting off the blast of chilly wet-pavement scented air coming in from outside. Her hair, normally a mass of dark tangled curls, was even wilder than usual due to the drizzling rain. Her voice was a mixture of disbelief and indignation as she made her statement, underscoring it with the implied *this doesn't happen to me.*

So, yes, it got my attention.

It also got the ghost's.

Trixie's blonde curls bounced under her jaunty little gold-trimmed cap as she switched her gaze from me to Callie and back again. "She saw a ghost? Where?"

"That's not what she means," I murmured. I didn't speak too loudly because I didn't want to be locked up as a delusional lunatic, something that would not be out of the question if it became general knowledge that the ghost of an usherette who died in 1937 was keeping me company while I refreshed the stock of licorice whips in the candy counter.

"What happened?" I asked Callie.

She crossed the lobby, unwrapping herself from a lengthy scarf and shaking droplets onto the worn blue carpeting. "Warren."

The level of revulsion in that one word called to mind the way

Humphrey Bogart had shudderingly said "leeches" in *The African Queen* (1951, Bogey and Katharine Hepburn.) Whatever Warren had done must have been bad.

"He hasn't answered a text in three days." She tossed her scarf and backpack on the ticket-taker's stool. "Or called or anything. I mean, how messed up is that? He gets his license and then ghosts me? I'm good enough for him while he's a lowly intern, but now that he's all Mister Real Estate he disappears?"

"Ooh!" Trixie hopped off the counter and followed Callie as she went to the coffee machine beside the popcorn maker. "That makes me so mad! What kind of a fella would do something like that? And I thought he was so nice. Didn't he seem nice?"

This last was directed at me. Callie, of course, didn't hear any of it, as Trixie only appeared to me.

"He seems so nice," I said to Callie.

This earned me one of her more withering glances. "Seemed." She tilted her head up and took a breath, regarding the enormous chandelier that graced the high ceiling, a glittering reminder of the long-distant glory days of the Palace. "He's dead to me."

The lobby was huge, and at the moment empty except for the two (or three) of us. A grand staircase swept up to the balcony on one side, and the vintage concessions counter stretched along the back wall, entrances to the main auditorium on either side of it. The carved wooden details everywhere were ornate and original, and the gold stars that patterned the carpet were based on the theater's 1927 designs. But on a drizzly January day, with the lights at half power to save on the electricity bill, I had to admit to a certain eau de shabby.

I'd made some progress since I'd taken charge, but I still couldn't describe the Palace as thriving.

"You'll hear from him." I slid the counter door closed and turned my attention to the popcorn machine. I'd been managing the place for almost three months, but I still hadn't quite gotten the hang of the antique beast. "Trust me, he'll show up with flowers and a million apologies."

I knew a little something about men showing up full of apologies. My wandering husband had done just that not too long ago.

"You bet he will," Trixie agreed. "Why, he'd be crazy not to."

"He better be in the hospital," Callie mused. "Or somebody better be dead."

"That's the spirit. Have you asked June?"

June Howard was my realtor. Warren was an intern at her firm, learning the business while studying for the state exam to get his license. Callie had only met him because he'd been shadowing June when she'd come to the theater to show me some listings back around Thanksgiving. When Callie had glanced up from her phone to point the way to my office, the world had stood still. The heavens had opened, and choirs of angels had sung. Or, as Callie put it, "I died. I literally died."

Now she looked at me like I was deranged. "I can't ask his boss. It's like asking his *mommy*."

I was sure June would beg to differ, but there you go.

"He'll call," I assured Callie. "Or text. The guy's crazy about you."

"Right?" she said. "I mean, he quit Tinder and everything. We both did."

"Well, then."

"What's Tinder?" Trixie asked. "Is it like reefer?"

I laughed and turned it into a cough when Callie looked over at me.

"Something in my throat," I said, shooting Trixie a glance. She shrugged and hopped back on the counter again. I'd explain later.

"Do you think he actually is in the hospital?" A tiny line appeared between Callie's brows. "He's been offline for days. Even his Insta."

"Which means he hasn't just ghosted you," I said. "He's probably taking a phone break."

"What? Why?" She clasped her phone to her chest.

"People do," I told her.

"Not normal people." The phone in question chirped and Callie instantly focused on it.

"I'd love to get my hands on one of those thingamajigs." Trixie eyed Callie's phone wistfully. "'Course, I'd like to get my hands on just about anything." She swooshed her manicured fingertips through the top of the cash register to make her point.

When I'd first met Trixie, after getting conked on the head by a faulty light in the balcony back in October, the whole swooshing through objects thing had admittedly freaked me out. She looked so solid, like any other young woman. Or at least, any other petite blonde bombshell in a vintage usherette's uniform, complete with gold braid, wide-legged trousers, and row upon row of gleaming buttons. But now that I knew her better it just broke my heart a little. How frustrating it must be for her to never be able to touch anything.

That wasn't quite true. If she concentrated very hard and made a superhuman effort, she could occasionally knock something over or even make herself seen. I owed my life to that ability. But it took all her energy, and she couldn't do it often.

Callie had fallen silent. I glanced up from the popcorn maker. She was immersed in her phone.

"Anything?" I asked.

"Nothing from my man." She held up the screen so I could see it. "But I just got something about yours."

"REUNITED!" The headline blazed over a photo of my husband—ex-husband—almost ex-husband—probably—and a woman who was not me.

This woman was an internationally gorgeous movie star with sultry dark looks and curves for days, while I could most charitably be described as "athletic." The only curves I had were modest and push-up assisted. At thirty-nine I was also a good decade older than her.

I'd retreated upstairs to my office after Callie showed me the picture. The office, along with a staff break room and the projection booth, was located down a hallway accessed from a hidden door at the top of the balcony stairs. I needed a hidden refuge before I could face the article. Even Trixie tactfully disappeared.

It was hardly an article. Just a gossipy blurb, really.

Ted Bishop and Priya Sharma are reuniting at Sundance to promote their upcoming movie *Catalyst*. Last year while filming the action thriller, both stars blew up their marriages, then spectacularly split. Sharma is now linked with industry mogul Otis Hampton, and Bishop is reportedly reconciled with his wife, a former TV writer. But who knows what will happen at Sundance? It can be pretty romantic in front of a crackling fire, and friends say Sharma's new bae won't be on hand...

I was the wife in question. And the reports of our reconciliation were...well, it was complicated.

My phone rang. I didn't need to see the caller ID to know who it was. When I hit the Answer button Robbie began talking, not even waiting for a "hello."

"Are you okay? I can't believe he's doing this. Did you know? Are you okay?"

"I'm fine."

Robbie—Roberta Prowse—was a massively successful TV show runner and my best friend in the world. She lived in LA and was responsible for me being safely removed from the Hollywood mayhem surrounding Ted's poor choices. She co-owned the Palace, and had sent me north to San Francisco and a haven of classic films when I'd needed a haven the most.

"Girl, don't tell me you're fine."

"I am," I said, and I was surprised that it was true. Mostly. "I didn't know, but I should have. It makes sense."

"Nothing that fool does makes sense. Nothing except his crawling back to you."

"He didn't exactly crawl." He'd arrived in a Tesla, which he promptly gave me, along with a diamond bracelet I'd never worn and a shower of "never agains" I didn't quite believe.

Particularly when looking at a photo of him with his arm around Priya Sharma's willowy waist.

"It's an old picture," Robbie said, reading my mind from her LA office.

"Yup." I'd seen it before. The world had seen it before. But it still had the power to make my stomach heave.

Robbie waited.

"I told him to get a manager," I said. "I told him to get an agent. He probably did and they probably told him this would be good for the movie. And no doubt it will be. My point is, I'm done with taking care of Ted's career for him."

"Right."

"I'm done with taking care of him, period. And we're not back together."

"Right." Pause. "But you're not not together, either."

Which pretty much summed things up.

"Is he there?" she asked.

It was a reasonable question. Ted had spent the last few months hanging around San Francisco whenever he wasn't contractually obligated to be somewhere else. Hanging around in a suite at the Ritz, I should underscore. Not in the little guest house behind Robbie's second home a few blocks from the Palace, where I was staying until I found a place of my own.

"Here in the city? I think so. But here in the theater? No." Only because I'd banned him. He'd spent the holidays flashing his megawatt smile at the customers and charming the staff with his movie star anecdotes. I had found this enormously irritating. I already knew he was charming. But he was also a lot of other things and I didn't need everyone looking at me like I was crazy for not instantly taking him back.

"What are you going to do?" Robbie asked.

"Well," I glanced at the clock on the wall. "The first show starts in forty-five minutes. I think I'll go make some popcorn and watch it."

"Good plan," she said. "A movie is always a good idea. You can do some good thinking in the dark."

"Right." Especially while watching this particular movie. From 1930, staring Robert Montgomery and a completely unleashed Norma Shearer. *The Divorcee.*

CHAPTER 2

I didn't make the popcorn after all. By the time I headed back down to the lobby the rest of the Palace team had arrived and everything was humming along. Their smooth efficiency never failed to surprise me, especially since the main team, in addition to Callie, consisted of a high school student, a nonagenarian, and the grumpiest man who had ever run a projector.

I knew the projectionist was in because he had blared his opening salvo, the drum-and-trumpet fanfare of the 20th Century Fox overture, through the sound system upon entering the theater. It was Marty's signature, how he started every day, and the way it rattled the coffee cups didn't bother me anymore.

"Hey, everyone," I greeted them from the stairs.

"Do *not* start with me." Marty was slumped on a stool behind the concessions stand, an unshaven tower of flannel and corduroy slurping down a soft drink and reading a newspaper. An actual newspaper. A paper paper. He claimed to prefer them simply on their luddite merits, but I suspected what he really liked was the ease with which he could hide behind the pages.

"Hi Nora. Latte?" This was offered by the student, Brandon, who had taken charge of the new espresso machine with something approaching religious devotion.

"I'm okay for now."

"Are you?" The look Callie shot me was layered with meaning.

"I'm fine," I said. Strenuously.

"Well, you'd better be, because I can't keep going through this." Marty ruffled the paper for emphasis. "*Will they or won't they* was a tired plot before talkies, and I refuse to be a party to any more of your angsty soul-searching over the highly untalented Ted Bishop." He turned a page forcefully and buried his face in the Arts section.

To be clear, Marty had never been a party to my soul searching, angsty or otherwise. Not that I hadn't been indulging in increasingly elaborate "what if" scenarios ever since Ted's dramatic attempt at a return to my life. My friend Robbie had probably heard enough to fuel multiple plotlines on any one of her hit TV shows. But Marty? He didn't exactly invite confidences.

Albert, the incredibly caring relic of the Palace, placed a gentle bony hand on my shoulder as I reached the bottom of the stairs. He peered at me from behind his round silver glasses. "We're all behind you, Nora, no matter what you decide."

Marty snorted and turned a page.

"All of us," Albert said firmly, shooting the rumpled projectionist the kind of glance that probably made Albert's many grandchildren sit up straighter.

"Of course we are." Marty stood and gathered his things. "We're behind you if you take that needy little weasel back, and we're behind you if you come to your senses and kick his magnificent ass to the curb." He crossed the lobby, pausing briefly to stare down at me. "But whatever you're going to do, do it. No one likes a waffler."

"Marty," Albert said reprovingly.

"It's fine," I said. "I prefer to think of myself as *considered,* but—"

"Ha!" Callie said, possibly not realizing that she'd spoken out loud and not commented on a post. When I looked over at her she shrugged. "I mean, we just have to look at the lineup to see what your subconscious is telling you."

The lineup was the selection of four movies a week that I'd put together for the month of January. Double features that changed on Tuesdays and Fridays. Today, Tuesday, it was a double bill of *The Divorcee* and *The Gay Divorcee* (1934, Fred Astaire and Ginger Rogers.) On Friday we'd switch them out for *The Women* (1939,

Norma Shearer and Joan Crawford) and *Libeled Lady* (1936, William Powell and Myrna Loy).

"That isn't my subconscious you're seeing," I informed them. "It's my marketing genius. I'm leaning in to the publicity about Ted. If I can't fight 'em, I can exploit 'em."

"Uh huh," Callie said, while Brandon began vigorously polishing the espresso machine and Albert found something on the ceiling to claim his attention.

"Just wrap this subplot up and get on with your life," Marty said. "I can't take it anymore." He tossed his papers in the recycling bin. "If there's one thing I can't stand it's drama." With that he flung his scarf around his neck and swept up the stairs to the projection booth.

The text from Ted came during the two-thirty show. I was upstairs in my office when I got it.

Baby. It's nothing. I didn't even know she was going to be there. You know I don't care about her. If you want me to drop out of Sundance I will.

Would he? I doubted it. In fact, I knew exactly how it would play out. He'd claim that he tried, but that the producers insisted. And he didn't want to get a reputation for being difficult, did he? I didn't want him to damage his career, did I? Not over something as silly as a work thing with an ex, right?

Right. Except she'd only been an ex for three months. Before that she'd been the worldwide sex symbol that he'd left me for. So there was that.

I had my finger on the button to turn my phone off when another text pinged in. This one from a lawyer back in Hollywood.

Nora. I know we've been in a holding pattern, but let me know if you want to start the process up again in light of recent developments.

"Recent developments." That was a diplomatic way of describing the possibility of my husband reuniting with his dazzling paramour. And "the process" was a tactful way of referring to divorce proceedings.

I waffled, not knowing which text to respond to. Marty was right about one thing, I was undeniably a waffler. I didn't want to respond to either text. What I wanted was for Ted never to have cheated and left me in the first place. But since no one was offering me passage on a functional time machine, the chances of that happening were slim.

I took a glance at one more text, this one wholly unexpected. It was short and to the point.

Say the word and I will have him killed.

It was from Hector Acosta, a former crime lord and smoldering specimen of South American manhood who had briefly visited San Francisco when his brother was murdered in my theater. He'd stayed in town long enough for me to start having some very interesting thoughts about him, but he'd gone back home to Colombia soon after Ted reappeared. This was the first I'd heard from him since and I assumed he was kidding about having Ted killed. I was sure he was kidding. He had to be kidding, right?

I didn't answer that text either.

Only one thing was very clear to me. I'd fallen in love since moving to San Francisco. Fallen in love with the city and the Palace. Whatever I ultimately decided about Ted, I knew I wouldn't be moving back to LA anytime soon. That was why, before the holidays, I'd marched myself two blocks down Sacramento Street to Howard Realty, introduced myself to June Howard, and started the process of finding someplace of my own to live.

"A house?" I'd suggested when she asked what I was looking for. "Something walking distance to the theater?" I'd been thinking of something like Robbie's house, tall and roomy on a tree-lined street. Lots of windows and character. I didn't need anything as big as Robbie's, but I didn't want something quite as small as the studio-sized guest house in her backyard, where I was temporarily camped out.

June had been cheerful about my prospects. Then she'd told me that the average price of a house on Robbie's tree-lined street was about ten million dollars, and on the rare occasions when one became available it was snapped up in less time than it would take the average banana to ripen.

And I'd thought Beverly Hills was cutthroat.

I honestly didn't know what my budget was, having been in a "holding pattern" on my divorce settlement since Ted had come bounding back into my life. The initial proposal the lawyers sent me had been impressive, but a draft settlement is not a final settlement, and for that matter a separation is not a divorce. On the other hand, an apology is not a reconciliation.

I really had to figure out what I wanted.

Meanwhile, under any scenario, ten million seemed, um, steep. So I'd lowered my expectations and June had gone to work. Two months later I was still looking, and June was due to drop by with an update.

"Knock knock!" She breezed into the office, impeccably and expensively dressed in a winter white suit. She was Chinese-American and had that well-tended-woman-of-a-certain-age thing going on where she could have been anywhere from her forties to her sixties. There was one dramatic streak of white in her otherwise glossy black hair. On anyone else it would have prompted Cruella de Vil comparisons, but on June it looked chic. "You have to promise not to let me have any popcorn on my way out. I can't stop myself—I never could. My teenage years would have been much slimmer if I'd worked at some shoe store instead of the Palace."

I'd heard similar things from any number of locals who'd spent their high school years working at the theater. The fact that June had once worked the concessions stand had made me sure she was the right realtor for me.

"I never get between anyone and fresh popcorn," I told her.

"That's all right. I don't really want you to." She grinned and pulled a tablet out of her large leather satchel. "I come bearing fresh listings!"

Her phone pinged repeatedly as we settled on the ancient leather couch that sagged in front of the office window. The window looked out over the Palace's marquee, which sent a faint pink glow into the room on what had turned into a damp and gray January afternoon.

"Sorry," June said, tapping the tablet screen until it displayed a photo of a dismal kitchen. "I've been gone for fifteen minutes and apparently there's a crisis. Take a look at these while I see what's on fire at the office." She grimaced as she handed me the tablet and donned a pair of rhinestone-encrusted readers to check her texts. The phone was still pinging.

I only had time to swipe through a few disheartening photographs before she made a strangled sound. When I looked over, she was staring wide-eyed at her phone.

"June?"

She turned to me, gripping my arm with one hand while she clung to the phone with the other. "It's Warren."

My mind flashed to Callie that morning, wondering why he'd ghosted her.

"What happened? Is he okay?"

She blinked rapidly, shaking her head.

"June, what's happened?"

Her eyes filled, and I knew.

"They found him this morning," she whispered. "He's dead."

Which is when we heard a scream from the lobby.

CHAPTER 3

What kind of person posts their colleague's death on social media within minutes of hearing the news?

OMG the cops just left. They were here looking for #bossbitch because #officehottie is dead! I can't believe it! He was so cute and flirty and now he's dead! And the cops wouldn't tell us anything! I'm really scared, you guys. And so sad! I just know he was going to ask me out. #gonetoosoon #lifestooshort #goodlookingcorpse #whatmighthavebeen

That was the post from June's receptionist that Callie had seen. That's how she found out he was dead. No wonder she'd screamed.

I'd left June and run down the stairs to find Callie motionless in the lobby. I pried her phone out of her hands and Albert and I hustled her upstairs to the break room. He fussed over her, patting her shoulder and murmuring soothing things while I made her a cup of strong sugary tea. Because I had to do something and that was the only thing I could think of.

June joined us, coming down the hall from the office looking ashen. I made another cup of tea for her while Albert guided her to a chair at the scarred wooden table.

"I just spoke to the office, and the police," she said. "They wanted to know when I saw him last. They'll want to talk to you," she told Callie.

Callie had been disconcertingly silent since her initial scream. She spoke three languages fluently, but she was looking at June with wide uncomprehending eyes, as though she couldn't understand a word that was being said.

"What happened?" I asked June. Then, "Callie, are you up to hearing about it?"

She hesitated, then nodded.

We all looked at June. She had found a napkin on the table and began systematically shredding it into increasingly tinier pieces as she told us what little she knew.

"The police wouldn't say what happened," she began. "I hadn't seen Warren since Friday morning at the office. He was out when he got the news that he'd passed his exam and decided to throw some sort of impromptu party. Half the office was planning to join him at a bar downtown after work. Which was fine," she stressed. "But Warren was supposed to be at an open house on Saturday and he didn't show up. I got so annoyed with him. I have nothing against celebrating, but when it interferes with your work...I sent him texts and called, but he didn't..." She put her hand to her mouth, realizing why he hadn't responded.

June cleared her throat and continued. "The only thing we really know is that his neighbor found him. He subscribed to one of those meal kit delivery services, and the box was sitting outside his door all weekend. Finally this morning the neighbor knocked, and tried the door. It was unlocked, and when she went in, she saw that the place was a wreck, and—" Once again June couldn't continue.

Callie finally spoke, her voice a croak. "Was he...Did they say...?"

June shook her head. "I don't know. They wouldn't say anything else, but it sounds like burglars, doesn't it? Maybe he walked in on them?"

Callie blinked. I glanced at her phone, which I'd silenced. Countless texts and five missed calls. I wondered if any of them were from the police.

Albert pushed the cup of tea toward her. She stared at it, then stood and went to the refrigerator. She opened the freezer, reached in, and pulled out a half-empty bottle of vodka. She unscrewed the cap and took a long swig, shuddering as she swallowed. Then she sat at the table again, still gripping the bottle. "I should have been with him."

"Oh, sweetie—" I began, but she wasn't listening.

"I had to leave. I was working the midnight movie." She looked at me. "If I'd let someone else take my shift I'd have been with Warren. He'd have come to my place, or we'd have stayed out longer, and the burglars would have just taken his stuff and he'd never have...Or maybe if we'd gone to his place, I could have...I should have been with him!" Her speech had increased in both speed and volume as she'd spoken, until she was practically shouting.

"Callie, no," June said, as I shook my head and Albert covered her shaking hands with both of his. "This isn't your fault!"

But she didn't believe us. And I understood. Guilt was natural. It was immediate and it was strong. That didn't mean it was right.

"Callie," I said. "It's nobody's fault except the person who did this. You think it's yours because you left for your shift. You could just as easily say it's mine for putting the schedule together. Or for starting midnight movies in the first place. You couldn't have known. There was no way to know."

"I should have," she whispered.

"That's just crazy." Marty spoke from the doorway. I had no idea how long he'd been standing there. He ignored the rest of us and focused completely on Callie. "This was not your fault. It happened because the world is a terrible place and terrible things happen in it."

"Marty, please!" Albert said.

"My point is," he went on, "There's no blame. There's no 'I should have.' There's just a terrible thing that happened. And now we have to deal with it."

Callie released her hand from Albert's and took another swig from the bottle.

But Marty wasn't finished. "I called your mother," he said. "She's on her way." Callie's eyes opened wide with what looked like alarm. Marty held up a hand. "Don't even start. When terrible things happen you need your mother." He turned on his heel and left.

We all sat in somewhat stunned silence after that. Callie was the first to speak.

"Sooo...you literally can't meet my mom." She was looking at me. "And I need my phone back."

Callie was serious about not letting me meet her mother. When she saw a beige Mercedes pull up to the curb in front of the ticket booth, she practically ran out the lobby doors. It was nearing dusk and still drizzling, so I didn't even get a glimpse of the woman I had never thought about before. Of course, now that I'd been made aware of her existence and banned from meeting her, I was irrationally curious.

The car pulled away and I stood looking out at the soggy evening until a tentative voice interrupted my thoughts.

"Is she okay?"

Brandon flushed a deep red as soon as I looked at him. His pale skin and ginger hair made him susceptible to that sort of thing.

"No," I told him. "But she will be."

I knew he had a massive crush on his coworker. Everyone knew, as he was constitutionally incapable of hiding his emotions. But while a six-year age difference wouldn't be a big deal for someone of my advanced years, it was an insurmountable gap for a high school kid and a grad student. "Poor Brandon" had been a regular theme of conversation over the past few months, as Callie's relationship with Warren had played out like a rom-com montage set to Gershwin tunes right under his tortured gaze.

"What can I do?" he asked.

It was a good question. I'd only been able to make her tea. "Let's take our cue from her, okay? If she wants to talk about it, we talk, but if she doesn't, we don't push."

He nodded, but there was something else, I could tell. Finally he spoke again. "What if I know something?"

"What do you mean?"

He squirmed, his complexion deepening further. "What if I know something about Warren? Something that might make it easier. Should I tell her?"

The lobby was empty, with Marty in the projection room and Albert out in the ticket booth. A dozen or so patrons had settled into one movie and the crowd for the next hadn't yet arrived. Nevertheless, I found myself speaking softly, matching Brandon's low tone. "Something like what?"

He swallowed, looking increasingly uncomfortable. "Like maybe Callie wasn't the only girl he was seeing."

I stared at him, taking in the implications of what he'd just said. All the implications.

First things first. "Brandon, have you been..." I carefully avoided the word *stalking*. "Spying on Callie?"

"Of course not!" He looked appalled. "Never! I totally respect her."

"Sure, sure. But..." I prompted.

He looked at the carpet "But I may have been looking into Warren a little bit. Just to protect Callie."

"Right." I paused. "For her own good."

"Yes!" He looked relieved that I'd understood.

I understood more than he knew.

"Okay," I said. "Two things. One—it is not cool to spy on a friend. Or on the person that friend is dating. Especially if you have feelings for that friend. It's not cool and it's kind of creepy and I know you don't want to be that guy."

"I'm not that guy!" he protested. "I was just—"

"You were just trying to protect a grown woman who was making her own choices," I told him. "A grown woman who would not thank you if you told her."

This seemed to register with him. "I guess not." He took a breath. "You said two things. What's the other?"

"The other is a question." I looked at him. "Is what you know about Warren anything you should tell the police?"

CHAPTER 4

There was nothing in the news about Warren's death. I had no idea if the police were treating it as a break-in gone bad or something else. I'd hoped to get a little information from June, but when I spoke to her the next morning, she told me that they'd asked her a million questions but hadn't given her any more information.

I was worried about Callie. I'd gotten someone to cover her shifts and sent her a text the night before, telling her to take as much time off as she needed. So I wasn't expecting her when she showed up at the lobby doors soon after I put the coffee on.

"How are you? Are you okay?"

She winced, dropping her things to the floor and settling on the stool by the candy counter. "Not to be rude or anything, but can you do me a favor and, like, chill?"

"I'll chill as soon as I know you're okay."

"I mean, I'm not *okay*," she said. "But I'm not a total mess or anything. I just wish I knew what happened."

"Didn't the police tell you anything?"

She made a face. "I haven't talked to them yet. My mom told them she gave me a sleeping pill and that I was in no condition to talk to anyone."

Wow. "Did she?"

"She doesn't believe in sleeping pills," Callie said, taking the cup of coffee I handed her. "She slathered my back with Vicks VapoRub and gave me a couple shots of tequila."

My eyebrows went up.

"You'd have to know my mom," she said, sipping. Then she seemed to realize what that meant. "Not that you ever will. She's, like, a crazy person."

"Everyone thinks their mom's a crazy person when they're your age," I told her. Whereupon I immediately felt ancient. "And who knows? Maybe VapoRub helps." Or maybe just having your mother rub your back while you cried helped. Yep. Probably that.

"When are you talking to the police?" I asked her.

She glanced at the clock above the lobby doors. "Nine." Which was about ten minutes away. "I'm meeting them at the café across the street. It's that detective, the one who was here before?"

"Really? Detective Jackson?"

She nodded. Jackson had investigated the deaths at the Palace back in October, when I'd first come to San Francisco. As far as I knew he was on the homicide squad, so that seemed to say they weren't thinking this was a simple burglary gone wrong after all.

"Sooo..." Callie looked up at the painted stars on the ceiling. "I was kind of wondering...I mean, I know you're busy and everything...but would you come with me? For, like, I don't know, moral support or something?"

It seemed like torture for her to make the request.

"Let me get my jacket."

"Detective Jackson," I greeted the policeman as he rose from the window table at Café Madeleine, a coffee-and-pastry-scented paradise located across the street from the theater. He smiled in recognition, which only slightly countered the imposing presence he projected. A tall, heavyset man with deep brown skin and a hipster goatee, he was made even larger by the quilted parka he wore that chilly morning.

"Ms. Paige," he nodded, then turned his attention to Callie. "Ms. Gee. My condolences on your loss."

I'd forgotten about the detective's voice. Full, deep, and resonant, it was a major component of his overall aura of authority.

Callie asked the server for a triple latte, then turned to the detective. "What happened? Have you caught them yet?"

He had a small notebook, which he opened while looking at Callie. "We're doing everything we can. How long had you been seeing Mr. Williams?"

"Why? What does that have to do with it?"

"It's important to get as complete a picture as possible," he said. "His colleagues say you'd been dating for several months?"

"Since November," I volunteered. Something in the way the detective looked at me implied that I shouldn't volunteer anything else. I let Callie talk.

"Right before Thanksgiving," she said. "We totally clicked."

As she described her whirlwind, made-for-each-other romance I couldn't help thinking about what Brandon had revealed the day before. Had Warren really been seeing someone else while he and Callie were together?

"We were both, like, super busy all the time," she was saying. "I mean, he was interning at the real estate office and finishing up his last coursework before taking his exam. And I work at the Palace while I'm in grad school too. Film school. I'm making a documentary." She ran a hand through her hair, lifting it away from her face in an automatic yes-I-know-I'm-very-cool gesture. "But even with all that, we saw each other literally all the time."

The coffee came, and we paused in the conversation to blow and sip and wait for the server to walk away. The owner of the café, Lisa, was giving me curious glances. We'd become friendly and she was probably wondering what was up with this intense conversation.

"Tell me about the night of the party," Detective Jackson said. "The night you all went to the bar."

Callie nodded, swallowing. "The Irish Bank, downtown."

"Did you go there often?"

She shook her head. "No, it's, like, not my usual kind of place, or Warren's. But he had to go to the Financial District that afternoon to do some mortgage thing or something, so he was downtown when he checked the website and found out he'd passed. He went to the nearest bar—the Irish Bank—and started live streaming to let everybody know. A bunch of his friends started showing up when they all got off work, and it was kind of a scene by the time I got there."

"Which was...?"

She blinked. "I left here around four and took the bus, so probably, like, five? A little before?"

"And who was there when you arrived?"

She thought about it and started counting off attendees. I only recognized a few people from June's firm among many names. Then the detective started getting into the details of who had come later, and who had left when.

"There was sort of a wave of his work friends," Callie said. "They'd all come together, but they all left around the same time, too. They didn't stay long."

"Was anybody from the office still there when you left?"

Callie thought about it. "I think by then it was only, like, Sam. The rest of them were mainly his buddies from school."

"But Sam, he was still there?"

She grimaced. "Um, I usually try to keep it all gender non-binary, but Sam isn't a he. She's a woman. Samantha?"

Jackson flipped back a few pages in his notebook. "Right. Samantha Beach. She was one of the last people known to have been at the bar."

A flicker of surprise crossed Callie's face. "Really? That's random. But she was still there when I left to come back here."

"Which was...?"

"Around ten thirty. Warren called a rideshare for me because I needed to be back by eleven for the pizza party."

The detective gave her a quizzical look.

"It was a theme party for the midnight movie," I supplied. "We've just started having them on Friday nights. Last Friday we showed *Roman Holiday*" (1953, Audrey Hepburn and Gregory Peck.)

"The party started at eleven thirty," Callie said. "We sold pizza and cannoli in the lobby, and if you showed up wearing a tiara you got in for half price."

"If you showed up on a Vespa you got in free," I said. The midnight movies, so far, had been fairly successful. I was hoping they'd turn into real events–the kind that brought in real profits.

A horrible look crossed Callie's face. "Ohmygod. Were we having the party when Warren...?" She turned to the detective with huge eyes.

He gave her a steadying look. "We don't have the official report yet, but it looks like he died early Saturday morning."

That was good. I mean, that was awful, but at least it meant Callie didn't have to have the mental image of her boyfriend being murdered while she was dishing up pizza to the tune of "Mambo Italiano."

But it also meant she didn't have an alibi. Which probably isn't the first thing that would have occurred to me a few months ago, before I'd taken an interest in the murders that had happened at the Palace. Now it was a disturbing thought.

The detective asked his next question. "When did you leave the theater?"

"The movie ended around two," Callie said. "So I think we all cleared out by around two thirty."

"And then you went home?"

"I totally crashed," she nodded.

"I arranged rideshares for the team," I told Jackson. "On my account. They'll have a record of when they took Callie home." And the fact that they took her to her apartment, not Warren's.

"Do you normally do that?" he asked me.

I shrugged. "The midnight movies are a new thing. Callie and Marty usually bike or take the bus, but at that hour only the Owl service would be running, and they'd been great about taking on the extra work, so..."

"Right." Jackson jotted something in his notebook. Then, to Callie, "Do you have a roommate?"

"Two, but they were..." her voice trailed off. I could see her realizing why he might be asking her that particular question. Was she a suspect?

She blinked a few times, reorienting herself. When she answered her voice had a more guarded tone. "I sent Warren a text when I got home. He didn't answer so I went to bed. And no, nobody saw me until I came in for the late shift on Saturday."

"That would have been around four thirty in the afternoon," I supplied, not at all liking where this conversation was going.

"I sent Warren a few texts on Saturday," Callie said. "But after how much he drank at the bar I figured he was sleeping all day. When he still didn't answer by the afternoon, I just got mad. If I'd realized something was wrong..." She turned to the detective. "What happened to him?"

"We'll know more as the investigation goes on," he responded, maddeningly.

"June said his neighbor found him?"

He nodded. He didn't elaborate.

"And that there had been a break-in or something?"

He regarded her. "Where did you hear that?"

She glanced at her phone on the table. "Everybody."

Wait. Was Jackson saying it wasn't a break-in?

A look of weariness settled on his face. "Ms. Gee, I would strongly advise you not to look to social media for news of the investigation. I can tell you that we're checking out every lead we have and doing everything we can to find out what happened to Warren." He cleared his throat. "Did he contact you at all after you left the bar Friday night?"

She nodded. "A couple times, while I was working...what?"

The detective was looking at her intently. "When did he send his last text?"

She slid her phone closer and started tapping the screen. "Here. 1:17." She looked up. "Does that help? Why can't you just look at his phone?"

"It's missing," Jackson replied.

Callie's jaw dropped. "No way. Warren always had his phone. It was, like, surgically implanted in his hand."

"Well, now we know he still had it at 1:17 in the morning," he said. "What did he say in the text?"

Callie's world was still rocked at the thought of a phoneless Warren. She glanced down at her screen and read aloud.

"June's going to lose it when I tell her who I just saw at the bar!"

She looked up. "With five exclamation points and a hand grenade emoji."

The detective's face probably matched mine as he held out his hand for her phone. Intense curiosity. Who had Warren seen? Did it have anything to do with why he'd been killed? Because I didn't believe for a second that Jackson thought this was a routine burglary.

Roman Holiday
1953

Okay. All right. This is the one. This is the movie I want you to watch if you think you don't like old movies. Because this is the one that will turn you around. You will be powerless to resist it. It's that good. Am I not being clear? I LOVE this movie.

The credits begin by INTRODUCING Audrey Hepburn. It's her first movie! And she's absolutely ethereal in it. She plays Princess Ann, and she's on a goodwill royal tour of Europe. (We don't know what country she's princess of, but really, who cares?) Has anyone ever looked more like someone who should be called "her serene highness" as she watches parades and launches ships and waves regally to crowds? This woman was born to wear a tiara.

But late at night back at the Palace, being tucked in with milk and crackers, she looks more like a teenager than a royal. And like a teenager she longs to rebel, even if it's only by wearing pajamas instead of a high-necked nightgown. She has no idea she's about to rebel on a much more cinematic scale.

After the court doctor gives her an injection to help her sleep, she escapes the palace, nestling in between the champagne bottles in the back of a caterer's van. She hops out the back when she gets to downtown Rome. Who wouldn't? It's lovely and moonlit, and she's still stoned on whatever the doctor gave her.

Enter Gregory Peck. You'll be forgiven if you sigh audibly

when you first see him, tie loosened at a late-night poker game with the guys, looking more like a movie star than any man has a right to. Gregory Peck, you guys. Even without the voice he's swoon-inducing. And then when he speaks? I raise a disbelieving eyebrow at any woman who says she wouldn't give up her throne for him. You know you'd at least think about it.

Gregory (Joe) is a reporter with a ticket to see the princess at a press conference in the morning. Eddie Albert is his buddy and a photographer who is likewise on princess duty. When Gregory leaves the game to stroll handsomely through the moonlit streets, he finds Audrey snoozing outside by a fountain. And now we have a movie!

He wakes her and she sleepily quotes a poem. "If I were dead and buried and I heard your voice, beneath the sod my heart of dust would still rejoice." Yes, Audrey. We all feel that way about Gregory Peck's voice. And of course he doesn't just leave her there. He helps her. Because she's lovely and quotes poetry and he's a decent guy. Tall, dark, and decent. And did I mention his voice?

So here's where the whole thing just takes off. He doesn't realize she's the princess (at first) and she doesn't tell him when she wakes up in the morning in his apartment (wearing his pajamas). There's attraction and humor and something called *charm* that you'll notice and say "Huh. Wow. That's so nice and fresh and completely devoid of irony that I don't quite know how to process it." My advice: don't process. Just enjoy.

The runaway princess decides to make a day of it, wandering around a gorgeous sunny Rome. She buys comfortable shoes. She eats gelato on the Spanish Steps. She gets an adorable short haircut that my mother reliably informed me caused a worldwide stampede of woman going to the hairdresser in 1953. I so want that haircut!

When she meets up with Gregory again there are Vespa rides and teasing at The Mouth of Truth statue and dancing by moonlight on a riverboat. Of course, let's not forget that Gregory is a reporter for all of this, and Eddie Albert is a photographer. The story of the madcap princess is worth a lot of money. Plot complications!

Of course I won't tell you how it all works out. You probably think you know. Ha! If it starred Sandra Bullock or Julia Roberts, you might know. But this is a classic film. The rules are different. All I can tell you for sure is that if you don't start reaching for the Kleenex at the end, surely you have a heart of dust.

Roman thoughts:
I mean, Rome. The film proudly announces with the opening credits that it was photographed and recorded in its entirety in Rome. Was it ever. The city is gorgeous and crumbling and crowded and proud. They absolutely could not have made the same movie on a back lot.

That LOOK! If you've seen the movie you know the one I mean. The one at the end. I find it completely overwhelming every single time. You know how I feel about dialogue, but that look is enough to make any self-respecting screenwriter just thrown down their pen and give up. Words are so not necessary.

This is not the first (or last) movie to offer the perspective that when you pretend to be someone else it frees you to be who you really are. Maybe we all just need to take off our tiaras now and then. Have some gelato. Listen to some music. Fall in love with a handsome stranger. Maybe we all need to go to Rome. I know I do.

Movies My Friends Should Watch
Sally Lee

CHAPTER 5

Callie gazed at her phone yearningly as Detective Jackson sealed it in a plastic bag and put it in his pocket. I expected withdrawal symptoms to set in shortly.

I thought the detective would go off to do more detecting after we wrapped up, so I was surprised that he crossed the street with us when we left the café, lingering outside the theater.

The Palace, as its name implies, is an old-fashioned movie palace. Its marquee still juts out proudly over the sidewalk, above a freestanding ticket booth. Movie posters, both of the current lineup and of random classics, line the tiled walkway leading to the lobby doors. The detective seemed oddly interested in the poster of Fred and Ginger, billed as "the King and Queen of Carioca," in *The Gay Divorcee*.

It was a good movie, but I wouldn't have pegged the detective as a fan of vintage musicals.

"Um, is there anything I can do for you?" I asked him.

"No, no, I was just—" His eyes flicked to something behind me. A broad grin crossed his face. "Marty!"

Marty?

I turned around to see the projectionist approaching us from the corner. His brief expression of confusion was almost instantly replaced by a more familiar glare of annoyance.

"David. Why are you here?"

David?

Callie and I both turned from one to the other as Marty joined us, understanding hitting us simultaneously. The vibe between them was unmistakable.

"Sooo..." Callie pointed first at Marty (still glaring) then to Detective Jackson (still grinning). "You two..." Then she flicked her hand. "I can't even." She turned her back and went up the walkway to the lobby.

I should have gone with her. It was abundantly clear that the detective wanted to talk to Marty. It crossed my mind that maybe that was the reason he'd been so accommodating about waiting to speak to Callie, and about having the conversation at the café rather than at the precinct.

"Would you like to come in for some coffee?" I asked him, ignoring Marty. Also ignoring the fact that we'd just left a coffee shop.

"No, he wouldn't," Marty said, still looking at Jackson.

I really enjoyed teasing Marty. And I would tease him, extensively, at some point. How could he have kept what was clearly a personal relationship with Jackson a secret was beyond me. But even I could see that now was not the time.

"Detective." I held out my hand to Jackson. "Thank you. Please let me know if you need anything else. Marty," I turned to him. "I'll see you inside."

Whereupon I went into the theater and—I'm not proud of this—dashed up the stairs to my office to see if I could overhear them from the window above the marquee.

I could not.

"Hiya Nora. Whatcha doing?"

I jumped as Trixie appeared by my side, looking out the window. The way she popped in and out of existence could be a little startling.

"I'm spying on Marty."

"Oh." She leaned closer to the glass. "I can't see him."

I turned away from the window and sank onto the couch. "I didn't say I was good at it."

She grinned. "Catch me up. What have I missed? How long

have I been gone?"

It wasn't clear where Trixie went when she disappeared. She just called it "away," and never had any memories of it when she came back. She also had no sense of time when she was away. Before she had me to help her keep her bearings, she'd oriented herself by checking the marquee to see what was playing and matching it to the blackboard in the office that showed a three-month schedule of films.

"Just since yesterday," I told her. "Remember how Callie hadn't heard from her boyfriend all weekend?"

"The stinker." Trixie wrinkled her pert nose and perched on the desk.

"The stinker was murdered," I said.

Her mouth formed a lipsticked O. "Oh, Nora. That's awful! Poor Callie! Is she okay?"

"As well as can be."

"What happened?"

I shrugged. "The police are trying to figure it out."

She shivered, then nodded, as if she'd made up her mind. "He was a good guy. I'm sure someone good came for him."

The way Trixie understood things, someone in your family comes to take you along when you die. It was only because Trixie had refused to go when her ancestor came for her that she still haunted the Palace.

"I'm sure they did," I agreed, pushing any doubts about Warren's character firmly out of my mind.

"Aw, the poor kid," Trixie said. "She was really in love with him."

"She was."

She rested her chin in her hands. "Isn't love the most terrible awful thing in the world?"

I blew out a breath. "It is."

"And isn't it the best?"

I smiled at her. "It really is."

Callie and Warren. Marty and Detective (David!) Jackson.

Even Audrey Hepburn and Gregory Peck. The sparkly days of a new relationship. It made you think. It made me think, at least. And what I thought about was Ted. About Ted in the sparkly days, when he'd been this amazing, funny, sweet guy who wanted to be an actor. Who'd told me he wouldn't be able to do it—do anything—without me. Who'd made me feel brilliant and invincible when I was around him. That was before he'd turned into Ted Bishop, International Action Hero. Back then he'd quoted Shakespeare and cracked me up with improv and completely captivated me until I was drunk on him. Dizzy with love. Giddy and happy and so, so sure that it would always stay that way.

"Whatcha thinking, honey?" Trixie brought me back to the present.

I sighed. "Love."

"I thought so. You had that kinda dreamy look on your face."

Had I? How embarrassing.

"Can I ask you something?" she said. "Do you regret it? Falling in love with your husband, I mean? Because, even with how everything turned out, I'm still glad I fell for Eddie."

Eddie was the reason Trixie was sitting there with me instead of enjoying whatever more attractive options an afterlife might have to offer. He'd been the guy she'd had a crush on back in 1937, when she was a twenty-year-old usherette. Because of a brawl he'd gotten into in the balcony one night, Trixie had met her death at the Palace. It was also because of Eddie that she'd given up her chance to move along when her grandfather had come for her.

"Are you?" I asked. Eddie had never seemed like much of a catch to me. Case in point: on the night in question he'd been out with another girl.

"Sure," she said. "There's nothing else like it. Why else would they make so many pictures about it?"

I had to agree with that.

She brought her perfectly plucked eyebrows together. "But it also kinda makes you crazy, doesn't it? Stupid, even. Take the pictures. Look at any of those women. Joan Crawford, Bette Davis,

Garbo—don't even get me started on Garbo—perfectly rational people until they fall in love, and then it's everything else they've ever worked for right out the window. And we don't even blame them, because he's Spencer Tracy or Clark Gable or somebody, and we'd do the same if we were in their shoes, don't you think?"

"I think you've captured the essence of a successful screenplay," I told her.

She went on as if I hadn't spoken. "But it's strange, isn't it, how most pictures end? I mean when they end. It's with the big kiss, mostly, or with the wedding sometimes. But not the part where she finds herself alone every night when he starts working too late at the office, if you know what I mean."

She was looking at me intently. I think I knew what she meant.

"And they hardly ever show what this woman—Joan or Bette, you know—what she does when that happens. How she picks herself up. How she tells him to scram, maybe, or how she might start *working too late at the office* herself." She gave me a knowing look. "I suppose I got to thinking about it because of the picture that's on now, with Norma Shearer?"

"*The Divorcee*," I said.

"Right." She nodded. "There's someone who tells her husband what she thinks of him, and then goes out and, well, you know."

I knew. The movie had been made before the moral strictures of the Hayes Code were enforced, so when Norma finds out about her husband's philandering, she makes it quite clear that she's entitled to even the score. Which she does. Gleefully. All over Europe. And without anything horrible happening to punish her.

"Trixie," I said carefully. "Are you suggesting that I should even the score with Ted?"

"Oh, honey, I would never tell a girl what she should do." Her eyes grew disingenuously large.

"Right."

"All I'm saying," she glanced nonchalantly out the window. "Is that maybe a girl should realize it when the first reel is over. And decide how she wants the second reel to go. I mean, at some point she has to ask herself, is she Bette Davis or is she Norma Shearer?"

I told myself that Trixie probably wasn't suggesting that I follow Norma's lead and sleep my way across Europe. On the other hand, the first image of Bette Davis that came to my mind was her standing with a smoking gun over the body of her dead lover in *The Letter* (1940, Davis and Herbert Marshall). But Trixie probably wasn't suggesting I should shoot Ted, either.

Probably.

CHAPTER 6

"I'd make a terrible detective."

I greeted Marty with this a while later in the break room. He was pouring milk into a bowl of cereal.

"You're the last person in this room to realize that."

We were alone in the room.

"I had no idea," I told him. "I mean, I knew you were crushing on Detective Jackson back in October, but—"

He whirled around, holding up a spoon. "I was not *crushing* on him. I have not *crushed* on anyone since Chris Katsoros in the eighth grade." He sniffed. "That did not end well."

"And this?" I leaned against the counter. "Is this going well?"

"It's going none of your business."

"Says the man who has no problem telling me what I should do about my marriage."

"That's different." He took his bowl to the table. "The state of your marriage is broadcast to the entire planet on a daily basis." He shoved an overflowing spoonful of brightly colored fruity somethings into his mouth, which didn't stop him from talking. "Of course, it wouldn't be if you moved on from that spotlight-seeking pretty boy, but who am I to judge?"

"Says the most judgmental man on the planet."

"I'm not judgmental. I'm opinionated."

I grinned. "You're opinionated with a boyfriend."

He ratcheted his default glare up a few notches. "I'm past forty, and so is David. I may be seeing him, but he is not anyone's *boyfriend*. Nor am I."

"Noted." I sat at the table. "I just don't know how you find the time. You're always here."

"Of course I am. I'm indispensable."

Which was and wasn't true. Yes, Marty was the only one who knew how to keep a lot of the Palace's ancient projectors and equipment running. But I'd learned a lot about the theater business in the last few months. Like the fact that we didn't actually have to use most of the old equipment most of the time. The majority of classic movies we showed were available digitally, and any old idiot—myself included—could run that equipment.

Marty clung to the old technology, and I understood that up to a point. The soft hum of a digital projector is no match for the clackety-clack excitement of a vintage reel. Even the smell of the old prints...but I digress. I understood there were a lot of reasons for Marty to want to hide up in the projection booth, tinkering with cogs and splicers all day. I also understood that he was hiding.

I looked at him as he tilted the bowl to his mouth to finish the last of the milk. "I'm happy for you," I said.

He shot me a look, waiting for the punch line.

I laughed. "No, really."

He nodded, looking supremely uncomfortable. "Thank you. And I'll be happy for you once you get off your ass and do something about your whole..." he waved the spoon in my general direction, "situation."

I sighed. "Noted."

After Marty left the breakroom, I got off my ass and did something about my whole situation. I sent my husband a text.

Don't cancel Sundance. It makes sense for you to go. You need to support the film. Besides, Sundance is fun and we could use a little fun. Which is why I'm going with you.

The whoosh sound of the message flying off to him had a certain air of commitment to it. And I was glad. It made the most sense, if we were really getting back together. And if we were really getting back together, I was going to have to face the old crowd at some point. All those people who had suddenly remembered urgent commitments when he'd left me. The ones who broke coffee dates and canceled on dinners and said we really had to catch up while they backed out of rooms. Getting back together with Ted didn't have to mean returning to my LA life. I wasn't going to let it mean that. But it did mean I'd have to see a few people who had written me off the minute his arm was around some other woman's waist. And I figured I might as well see them in the snowy backdrop of a mountain film festival.

I should have felt triumphant. I'd made a decision. A sensible one. I should have felt relief. Happiness, even. Lots of people were happy when they gave their marriages another try. But I had a vague memory of what happiness felt like, and this wasn't it. In fact, if I had to identify the main thing I was feeling, I'd have to go with queasy.

I did want to go to Sundance with Ted. The problem was, I wanted to go with the Ted I'd been thinking about earlier. The Ted of late-night walks home when we couldn't afford a cab. Of running lines before an audition, him telling me he couldn't do it without me. I was still madly in love with the Ted who had piled everything we owned into a beat-up Subaru and held my hand across the gearshift all the way to Hollywood, assuring me that we were both destined for greatness. I just had to make sure he was still there, buried somewhere in the guy who had parked a Tesla in Robbie's garage after leaving me for someone else. Who assumed a Tesla would fix it.

Norma Shearer made another movie about divorce. *The Women.* And she took her husband back in that one, too, beating the scheming other-woman Joan Crawford at her own game. At least I hadn't had to go to those lengths. I'd just sent an email. I was just going to a film festival.

Ted didn't send a reply.

*   *   *

I wandered down to the lobby after the five-fifteen started. As I expected, Brandon was alone at the concessions stand.

"Hey, Nora. People really like the new espresso machine."

"I'm so glad." Mainly because it had been the biggest capital expenditure of my reign. But at the rate we were selling expensive caffeine it should pay for itself in a couple of months.

"Brandon," I perched on the stool behind the counter. "Did you speak to Detective Jackson yet?"

A guilty look spasmed across his face, which immediately flushed bright pink.

"Don't worry," I told him. "I haven't told Callie. I just wondered what he had to say when you told him."

"Um..." The flush deepened.

"Brandon?"

He looked at me, wincing. "I just don't want Callie to know I was...you know."

"Spying on her boyfriend?" I asked. Maybe a little too harshly.

"It's not like it matters now, right? I mean, it can't have anything to do with somebody breaking in to his place." The teenager clearly wanted me to agree with him.

I didn't. "We don't actually know that's what happened," I reminded him. "The police need to know everything so they can sort through it all and figure out what really matters."

He flinched.

"Look," I told him. "You've already told me you think Warren was seeing someone besides Callie. I'll make you a deal. Tell me what else you know. If I think it makes a difference, I'll go to Detective Jackson with it."

He glanced around the empty lobby. Callie had gone home a while ago, but he didn't want to be overheard by anyone else.

"Okay. You know how Warren was always on his phone?"

I nodded. Compulsive phone checking was one of the things he and Callie had in common. /

Brandon raised his eyebrows and have me a Highly Significant Look. "That wasn't his only phone."

I tilted my head. "What?"

"I found a phone on the floor of the break room a few weeks ago. I didn't know whose it was, so I woke it up to see. You know how new messages can appear just for a second before the screen asks you for your password?"

"Sure."

Another look, loaded with meaning. "These were from a girl. And, I mean, they were, um..." The flush returned with a vengeance.

"Sexy?" I guessed.

He nodded, and then recited from memory, not meeting my eye. "'Hey dub-man. I can still smell you on my sheets.'"

Ugh. "Okay, that sounds pretty incriminating."

"And there was a picture," he said.

"Did you recognize her?"

He looked down and mumbled something.

"Brandon?"

"It wasn't of her face," he repeated.

"Right." And, again, ugh.

"So you're thinking 'dub-man' was Warren."

He nodded. "Dub as in W. Like everyone uses when they talk about the Warriors."

I didn't follow sports, but I was aware of the wildly popular Bay Area basketball team. "Dub Nation," I said. "I've seen the bumper stickers. Still, how do you know it was Warren's phone and not some random Warrior fan's? For that matter, if it was Warren's phone, how do you know the message wasn't from Callie?"

He looked profoundly distressed at that thought.

"I know it was Warren's phone because I put it back on the floor and waited," he said. "He came looking for it. His jacket was on the coat rack and it must have fallen out of the pocket or something. But he also had his normal phone, the expensive one he's always carrying. This was a different one."

"Did he explain anything when he picked it up?" I asked.

"Well, ah, he probably didn't see me."

The break room was not that big. "How—"

"I was, ah, in the broom closet." Brandon's voice trailed off into nothingness.

I gave him a look.

"I'm not proud, okay, but the point is he was cheating on Callie. And before you even ask me, I know the texts weren't from her." He took a huge breath. "Because I saw him with the other girl when I followed him home."

I held up my finger. I needed a minute.

Okay, so my fresh-faced young employee was a stalker. Right. I'm sure other managers of other theaters had similar personnel issues to deal with. My primary concern now was how to tell Detective Jackson what Brandon had found out without getting the teenager into trouble. Or giving him a plausible motive for the police to consider—Jealousy.

Which, I realized, would be the same motive they could assign to Callie.

Sure, managers of other theaters probably had to deal with things like this all the time.

CHAPTER 7

I left Brandon with some stern words about personal privacy as well as some unasked-for words about getting over his crush on Callie. I had little expectation of his heeding any of it. High School seniors aren't exactly noted for taking advice.

After leaving him I grabbed my jacket and bag and went out for a walk. I've always thought best while walking, and I needed to think this through.

The early January evening was damp and chilly, the streetlights coming on to show the lightest of all possible drizzles, which would have been very atmospheric if I were making a film noir, but as I wasn't it was just annoying. I pulled my hood up.

Did the police suspect Callie in Warren's death? If so, I didn't want to hand them what looked like a gilt-edged motive. But if the other woman Brandon had found out about did have anything to do with the crime, I didn't want to withhold that from Detective Jackson.

It would be a lot easier if Brandon had actually seen the woman's face. If he'd be able to identify her. But, although he'd admitted to following Warren fairly frequently, and seeing him meet her more than once, he hadn't ever gotten a good look. He said she was taller than Callie, with short blonde hair, but that was about all.

I'd stopped digging for details when he'd said, "It was hard to get a good look at her face with Warren's tongue down her throat." That had pretty much eliminated any "maybe there's a simple explanation" argument.

The explanation was simple. Warren was a cheating fink.

But did that matter to the investigation?

My rational brain shouted "Hell, yes!" But my protective brain cautioned "What are the consequences?" And I wasn't at all sure.

So I kept walking.

I wandered around the city for over an hour. I'd gotten to know the area around the Palace pretty well in the last few months. I went uphill along streets lined with houses that were definitely out of my price range, then turned to follow the perimeter of the Presidio, a former military base that was now largely public greenspace, and back down through blocks of more houses until I found myself on the sidewalk in front of the place I had probably meant to go all along. June's office.

The Howard Realty sign was still lit. I knew June and her staff kept whatever hours their clients demanded, so even though it was after seven and there was nobody at the receptionist's desk, I knocked on the glass door.

A moment later June herself appeared in the lobby. She waved when she saw it was me.

"Nora, I'm so glad to see you," she greeted me as she unlocked the door and let me into the blessedly warm waiting room. "I wanted to touch base."

"Why? Have you heard something?"

She looked momentarily confused. "Oh, about Warren? No. Have you spoken to the police yet?"

"I was with Callie when she did."

This conversation took place as she led me from the windowed lobby down a hallway to her office in the back of the building, overlooking a tiny garden. The office was small but decorated in the same faultless style that June showed in her wardrobe. Neutral tones, understated and expensive. The kind of place where Grace Kelly would feel right at home. I hadn't noticed anyone else working late in the rooms we passed, but June closed the door once I'd taken a seat.

"How is Callie?" she asked. She opened a cupboard to reveal a small bar. "I was just going to have a glass of wine. Can I tempt you?"

"Without even trying," I said. "She's okay. I mean, as okay as you could expect."

June uncorked a bottle of something white. "The poor kid," she said. "Did they tell her anything?"

"It was more of an asking situation." I accepted the glass she handed me. Instead of taking the guest chair opposite mine, she moved around to sit behind her desk, which made things feel more businesslike. "Have the police told you anything more?"

She shrugged. "What else is there to say, until they catch the burglar."

If it had been a burglar. "How is everyone here doing?" I asked.

It couldn't have been easy to lose a colleague to violent death. Even if he'd only been there a short time.

June shrugged. "As well as can be expected. A few tears in the breakroom. A lot of gossip and speculation about what happened." She took a healthy swallow. On anyone less chic it might have been a gulp.

"What's the prevailing speculation?" I didn't come out and ask if it involved a mysterious blonde.

She shrugged. "Oh, all the kinds of stuff they'd see in movies. Was he involved with drug dealers? Did he owe someone money? Had he pissed off someone's husband?"

That last one sounded promising. "Is there any basis in reality for any of it?"

"Who knows?" She took another swig of wine. "But it's all more dramatic than what probably really happened, which was that it was just his dumb luck to be home when somebody broke in. And lord knows everyone wants drama." There was a bitterness to her voice that she probably hadn't intended.

"How about you?" I asked. "How are you holding up?"

She gave her wine a contemplative look. "I'm sad, of course.

And shocked that something like this happened. You read about things in the papers, but when it's someone you know..." She made a face. "I called my security company to get a check on my home system. You can't be too careful if this is turning into the kind of city that has this kind of crime."

I was on the point of commenting that all kinds of cities have all kinds of crime, as do all kinds of small towns. But everyone reacts to this sort of thing in their own way. Instead I just said something like "Hmm."

"Not that I would ever say anything like that to a client," June said conspiratorially. Forgetting, apparently, that I was a client.

"Have you heard anything more from your team?" I asked her. "Callie mentioned a couple people were there at the bar on Friday night."

"We were all so pleased for Warren." This came out a tiny bit robotic. I got the impression that she'd said it a lot recently.

"Right. So I wondered if anyone had mentioned when he left the bar, or what condition he was in?" June gave me a curious look, so I hastily elaborated. "Callie just said it seemed like he was drinking fairly heavily."

She pursed her lips. "I *was* happy to hear he didn't drive home."

So she had heard something. Had she heard about the last text Warren had sent to Callie? The one that said June would freak out about someone he'd seen at the bar? Had he texted June?

"That's what I was worried about on Saturday," she said. "When he didn't show up at the open house he was supposed to be working, I thought he might have..." she shuddered. "But Sam told me he got a rideshare, so then I just went from being worried to being pissed." She finished her wine and poured another glass. "If I only knew."

I made a soothing noise. Then, "Sam stayed until the party broke up?"

June shrugged. "I suppose so. I didn't interrogate her."

"But she's spoken to the police," I said. Then, at the look of surprise on June's face, I amended that statement with, "I would assume."

"We all did," she said. "Not that we had much to say. It's not as though Warren's work life had anything to do with his death."

"Of course." Unless it did. I was just about to ask her whether she'd been told about the text when she changed the subject.

"Nora." Her tone became a little brisk. "I'm glad you came by. We should talk about Monday."

Monday? Monday! I'd completely forgotten about the event June and I had planned for the next week. It was a corporate off-site. An all-day series of meetings, networking, and informative talks for her employees, as well as the staff of two other independent real-estate firms, roughly a hundred people in all. When she'd mentioned she was putting it together, I'd suggested that she cancel her reservations at a boring downtown hotel ballroom and hold it at the Palace instead. She'd instantly loved the idea of using the local landmark for her event. I'd loved the idea of opening up a new source of income for the theater.

"Of course," I said. "Do you want to postpone?" Even as I asked her, my heart sank at the idea. I'd arranged for catering and the rental of furniture and equipment for the day's speakers. I'd lined up a film crew to record the talks so June could post them on her website—okay, the crew was just some of Callie's friends from film school, but still. I'd put a lot of work into the planning, hoping that renting the theater out for special events like this one might turn into a lucrative revenue stream. I hadn't even thought about it since Warren's death, but of course it would be in poor taste to hold what amounted to a corporate pep rally the week after a colleague was killed.

"No," she said, surprising me. "I've thought about it, and as much as we all cared for Warren here, the event isn't just for my company. A lot of very busy people have cleared their calendars for this, so I think we should go on with it."

As the person who wanted to make the Palace financially viable, I was relieved. But as a *person* person, I felt more than a little squicky about it.

"I think we should start with a moment of silence," June said. "For Warren. And then carry on."

"And maybe shift the order of events?" I suggested. I knew the day was scheduled to begin, after coffee and pastries, with a rousing motivational speech entitled "Get Pumped and Stay Pumped." It didn't seem like the sort of thing that could easily follow a moment of silence for a murdered colleague.

June frowned. "You're probably right. I'll have Sam take a look at it all and call you in the morning."

"Okay." I finished my wine. "I'll let the gang know we're still on. Callie was going to help out, but I'll find someone else." I couldn't imagine she'd still want to direct the filming.

"Good." June looked relieved.

She stood, which gave me the feeling I was being very professionally kicked out. I hesitated when we got to the lobby door, but at the last minute I decided not to ask her about the text.

I'd ask someone else instead.

As I walked down the street toward the Palace, I took my phone out of my pocket, noted that my maybe-ex-husband still hadn't responded to my text about Sundance, and dialed Detective Jackson.

CHAPTER 8

"Your not-a-boyfriend isn't answering his phone."

I informed Marty of this when I got back to the Palace. He was up in the dimly lit projection booth, fiddling with some piece of machinery and half watching through a tiny window as Fred and Ginger drifted elegantly around a gloriously art deco set in *The Gay Divorcee*. Fred was graceful and sophisticated. Ginger was too, but backwards, and in heels.

"He's not my—" Marty began. Then he shot me a hostile look. "I'm not his keeper."

"But it occurred to me that you might know if he has plans this evening." I came into the booth and closed the door behind me. This was Marty's lair, and I always felt a little nervous in the cluttered, confined space. One false move and I could break the last thingamajig on earth that made the ancient projectors work. And with carefully arranged mechanical junk balanced everywhere, it wouldn't be hard to make one false move.

"Why do you care?" Marty regarded me narrowly. "What are you up to?"

"I have to tell him something," I said. Leaving out that I also wanted to ask him something. "So I was thinking. If you were planning to meet for an after-work drink or late dinner, maybe I can tag along for a few minutes."

I gave him my friendliest smile. He looked like I'd suggested something obscene.

"You one hundred percent cannot tag along," he said. "And besides, David doesn't drink."

"Really?" Several dozen cop clichés sprang to mind. That's

what happens when you're a recovering TV writer. I'd already mentally spun out a plot involving the tragic death of his partner and a shaky hold on recovery before I caught my next breath.

"Really," Marty said. Then he gave me a long-suffering look. "He does, however, eat ramen."

My eyebrows went up. "So you're meeting him? I can go with you?"

"Don't be insane. But if you were to go to Marufuku in Japantown right about now you'd probably find him ordering the deluxe pork belly special. Extra spicy."

"Thanks, Marty." I reached for the doorknob.

"Don't mention it," he said. "Also don't mention the fact that I'll close everything out and lock up around here with only the help of one mopey teenager. Really, don't worry about it. It's no bother."

Oh. Right. I guess I had been making an assumption that I was free to traipse off again after already leaving the theater once that night. "Thank—"

"Do *not* thank me again," he said swiftly. "If you want to thank me, just be gone by the time I get there." He sniffed. "I'm meeting David at the Kabuki to see an after-hours animation festival, which is his idea of entertainment, not mine. And before you even think to ask, *no*, you may not tag along."

"I wouldn't dream of it."

I knew Fred and Ginger would wrap things up in twenty minutes or so, and Marty would probably be able to lock up fifteen minutes after that. So I didn't have time for the thirty-minute walk to Japantown. I called a rideshare instead, wanting to make sure I was finished with Detective Jackson by the time Marty arrived for their date.

Marty and Detective Jackson. I still couldn't quite wrap my head around that. Marty and anyone, really.

The restaurant was inside the confusing warren of shops and restaurants that made up the Japan Center mall. I'd only been to the center once before, when checking out the huge and modern Kabuki movie theater that anchored one end of it. That time I'd gotten hopelessly turned around in the mall, but luckily Marufuku was on the street level and the driver let me out at the entrance closest to it.

It was due to close in less than half an hour but was still filled to capacity. Once I stepped in and inhaled the heavenly scent of rich spicy broth, I realized the Kabuki-adjacent location probably wasn't the only reason Jackson was there. I also realized I hadn't eaten all day.

I saw him seated at a table for two against the wall and told the hostess I was expected. Which wasn't a lie. Jackson looked up as I approached, and the lack of surprise on his face told me Marty must have sent him a warning.

He half-rose from his seat. There was an awkward little dance because the server chose that moment to bring him a huge bowl of steaming yumminess and she seemed a bit thrown by my late arrival.

"Please eat," I told Jackson. "I promise I won't stay long."

Then I caught a good look at his ramen and turned to the server. "I'll have what he's having," I said. Then, hastily, "To go."

Detective Jackson poured a cup of tea from a small iron pot and pushed it toward me as I sat down. "Ms. Paige. What can I do for you?"

"You can eat your noodles and call me Nora," I told him. "I really do apologize for hunting you down like this, but there's something I think you should know. Something about Warren."

"What's that?" He'd unwrapped his chopsticks and began stirring chunks of pork and hard-boiled egg into the noodles and broth of his soup.

I hesitated. "I know you said Warren's phone was missing. Have you been able to find it?"

"Do you know something about it?"

I noticed he didn't answer the question. "I just thought I should tell you that he had more than one phone."

He glanced up from his noodles. "How do you know that?"

"Did you already know?" I asked.

"Ms....Nora," he said. "We have something of a history, so I'm cutting you some slack. But the way this works is *you* tell *me* things. I'm the one who gets to ask the questions. I'm the one with the gun and the badge."

"Right," I said. "Got it." Apparently, I wouldn't be finding out what he knew about Warren's last text to Callie. I cleared my throat. "The thing is, one of my employees found a phone in the staff break room a while ago, and it turned out to be Warren's. Not his everyday phone, but another one."

At this Jackson looked interested.

"And this person saw some texts on that phone," I blundered on. "From a girl. A woman. Not Callie." I grimaced. "I thought I should tell you that you should be looking for two phones, and for this other woman. She's tall with short blonde hair."

"And your employee could tell that from her texts?"

"Um, well, as it happens, he saw Warren with her a couple of times."

Jackson sat back, regarding me. "That seems coincidental."

I shrugged, all innocence on Brandon's behalf. "Nevertheless. I just thought that this woman might be worth looking into. If she found out that Warren was serious about Callie, that he had a girlfriend and this blonde was just a...a fling or something..."

I was full-on babbling by that point, worried that any suspicion I might throw on Blondie was also something that could be said about Callie. Also that I was painting Brandon as a stalker with jealousy issues. Why hadn't I minded my own business? And for that matter, why hadn't Brandon minded his?

"I'm going to have to speak with this employee of yours," the detective said.

Of course he was. What had I been thinking? I couldn't tell the police something like that second-hand and expect to leave it at that.

"Tomorrow," he said, picking up his spoon. "First thing. I'm assuming it isn't Albert?"

I probably winced in response. "Brandon," I said. "He really doesn't want Callie to know that he'd been…"

"Understood," he said. Which wasn't a promise of discretion. "As for Ms. Gee…" Jackson slurped an enormous spoonful of noodles, making me wait for the rest of his words. "You can tell her she can have her phone back."

I let out a breath. I'd been bracing for something entirely different. "Really? She'll be so happy." Happy like a junkie about to get a fix.

"We cloned her data," he said. "We don't need to keep the actual phone."

"That's great," I said. "Should she drop by the precinct, or…"

He sighed heavily and pulled Callie's phone, no longer in its plastic evidence bag, from an inside pocket. "I was going to give it to Marty, but will you be seeing her?"

"In the morning," I said. I hadn't planned on it, but it was the least I could do. Particularly since I might have just given the police her motive for Warren's murder.

"I don't suppose you could tell me anything," I said. "I mean, if it really was just a break-in gone wrong, then none of this really…"

I trailed off as his eyebrows came down in a meaningful way. He handed Callie's phone over. "Thank you, Nora."

I may not be a great detective, but I deduced that was the end to our conversation.

I picked up my to-go order on the way out and stood on the sidewalk outside the shopping center after summoning another car to take me home.

I'd failed spectacularly in finding out whether the police had figured out what Warren was talking about in his last text to Callie. Who had he seen at the bar that night? In fact, I'd failed spectacularly in finding out anything new, except perhaps where to get good ramen.

I waited for the car down the block from the Kabuki. I was mad at myself for bungling the conversation with the detective, and that anger somehow turned into hostility toward the bustling theater. Bustling at this late hour, when Marty and Brandon would have already closed up the Palace for the night. Hostility—and, yes, jealousy—bloomed at the number of people streaming in and out of the Kabuki's large glass atrium. What would it be like to draw those kinds of crowds? To have reserved seating and computerized ticket kiosks? To have a full bar in the balcony?

Then I saw what was playing and consoled myself. Things with robots and superheroes. Things with helicopter chases instead of witty banter. I'd take my small crowds and silver screen classics any day.

The car came and I went home with my soup.

Tomorrow, Scarlett, would be another day.

CHAPTER 9

The day dawned chilly and clear. I knew that because I was awake for it. I'd been far too occupied with obsessing over everything to sleep in.

I knew that Callie's mother had insisted she stay home for a while, and that "home" meant her parent's house, not the tiny flat near Ocean Beach that she shared with two other grad students.

I got her mother's phone number from the emergency contact info on Callie's employee file, and from there it only took a minor amount of internet sleuthing until I had her address. Which was, I found, in the eye-wateringly expensive neighborhood of Pacific Heights.

It was still early, too early for an unexpected visit, so I puttered around at home for a while, drinking coffee and asking myself a lot of questions I couldn't answer. It took all of five minutes to tidy up the perfectly appointed little kitchen of Robbie's guesthouse, throw a load of laundry into the compact stacked washing machine, check my messages and emails (still no acknowledgement from Ted about Sundance, and I *refused* to send him a follow-up text) and take a concerning number of empty wine bottles to the recycle bin.

Then, having waited until the eminently reasonable hour of eight o'clock (reasonable to me, although possibly less so to a grad student) I locked up and headed to Callie's. She might not be thrilled to see me (on her mother's doorstep, especially) but I knew she'd be thrilled to see her phone.

It was about a forty-five-minute walk to the Gee home, up to

Washington, over to Lyon, and then uphill some more. As the hills grew steeper the houses grew larger, until they gave way to actual mansions worthy of having suspects gathered in their drawing rooms on dark and stormy nights.

At the corner where Lyon met Broadway the street ended. It was at the crest of the hill and the downhill drop was too steep for cars, so there were just stairs for two blocks down. Gorgeous, greenery-filled, garden-lined steps, with what looked like a fountain in a square at the midpoint.

If I ever write a musical set in San Francisco, you can bet there will be a dance number set on those steps. I stood at the top and took in the view. The bay was sparkling in the near distance, the woodsy Presidio to the left, and I would have bet anything that right down the street was the house they had used for the exteriors in Fred Astaire's *The Pleasure of His Company* (1961, Late-career Astaire, early-career Debbie Reynolds, and the timeless Lili Palmer).

I've seen my share of mansions. I've even lived in them. Beverly Hills estates with pools like football fields and balconies for days. Villas in Tuscany, Châteaux in the south of France, manor houses in the English countryside. I was—am—after all, married to one of the biggest movie stars on the planet. We got around. That being said, the Gee house was impressive.

It looked directly onto the garden-filled Lyon street. Looked down, I should say, since it was accessed via semi-circular staircases on either side of a fountain featuring a lion's head spitting water into a round flower-bedecked pool. More flowering bushes ran the length of the house, which rose three stories in pristine white stone to a classic California red-tiled roof.

Callie had once told me that her father was a doctor. A second-generation Chinese American who had worked his way through Stanford medical school. She'd also told me that he loudly and frequently despaired of his filmmaking daughter's career prospects. If this was the kind of place you could buy on a doctor's income, I kind of saw his point.

It didn't look like the household was awake. But with a house that big it was hard to tell. There was a balcony inset on the third floor, discreetly hidden behind three arched openings. As I stood looking up, wishing I knew which window was Callie's so I could throw some pebbles at it or something, she saved me the trouble by stepping out onto the balcony.

"What are you doing here?" she hissed down.

"I was just in the neighborhood," I said. Because I'm hilarious.

"Wait right there!" She vanished inside.

I had no intention of waiting right there. I was more curious than ever about her mysterious mother. I jogged up the stairs and was standing on the doorstep when Callie opened it. She popped out and pulled the door shut behind her.

"How did you find me?"

"Were you in hiding?" I asked. "And yes, it's nice to see you too." I smiled broadly.

"This is literally not happening," she said. Probably more to herself than to me.

"Don't worry," I relented. "I won't say anything to destroy your starving student street cred."

She gave me a wary look. "Just because my parents are, like, loaded doesn't mean I am."

"Of course not," I agreed. "And thank you, I'd love a cup of coffee."

"You are so not coming in." She placed herself between me and the door. "Why are you here, anyway?"

I was about to say something else hilarious, perhaps about craving caviar for breakfast, but then I took a closer look at her. The shadows under her eyes and drawn look to her face reminded me that she was staying at her parents' house because she needed a place of refuge. She was grieving.

She was also barefoot, and her feet must have been freezing.

"How are you, Callie?"

Something in my voice must have told her that the teasing had stopped. She brushed the hair off her face. "I mean, my mom is driving me crazy and that detective literally won't tell me anything."

I nodded. "I spoke to him last night. He sent you this." I pulled the phone out of my messenger bag.

I had expected wild glee at the sight of it. Instead she just took it, turning it over and looking at it with an expression I couldn't read.

"Thanks," she said. "But I got another one yesterday." She reached into the back pocket of her jeans and produced a shiny new phone. "I didn't know how long they'd keep that one."

"Sure," I said. "Well, you can always keep the old one as backup."

I had to bite my tongue to keep from asking her if Warren had kept a second phone as backup. That would inevitably lead to her asking why I'd asked, which was a road that could only lead to Brandon's revelations about Warren, and last thing I wanted to do was cause her any more pain.

She sniffed. "How's everything at the Palace?"

She'd only been away for a day. "Pretty much the same," I said. "Marty and Albert send their best." Which they would have, I was sure, if I'd told them I was going to see her.

She shivered, and I realized again how cold she must be. "Okay, you get inside before you catch cold," I said. "And stay in touch, okay? Come back whenever you feel like it, but take as much time as you need."

She nodded. "Thanks, Nora."

And then, much to my surprise, she threw her arms around me in a fierce hug. I hugged her back, feeling her shaking through the fabric of her sweater. When she pulled away, she wiped at her eyes. "I mean, you're still not going to meet my mother."

"Not today," I agreed.

She went back inside, and I retraced my way up the steps. I had a lot to think about.

I'd had no idea Callie came from wealth. Not that it mattered, but it showed me how much I didn't know about the people around me. I'd had no idea that Marty was dating anyone, much less David the homicide cop. On top of that, I'd learned that the cherub-faced Brandon was something of a stalker. Who knew what I'd find if I started looking into Albert's private life. Or anyone's.

We all had secrets. I certainly had mine. Case in point: I used a pen name to blog about classic films and nobody at the Palace knew about it. Marty's head would explode if he ever found out, because he actually liked my blog—Sally's blog. It would kill him to know he'd actually complimented me.

Warren, too, had kept secrets. At least one, anyway, involving a blonde and a second phone. Were there more?

Had one of his secrets gotten him killed?

CHAPTER 10

It was still before ten when I got to the theater. Our first showing of *The Divorcee* wouldn't start until twelve fifteen and I knew the others would meander in sometime around eleven. The early shift today would consist only of myself, Albert, and Marty, as Brandon and the other two employees who were regulars—Claire and Mike—had pressing commitments in high school. I wondered if Detective Jackson had interrogated Brandon before first period.

"Hiya, Nora!"

Trixie waved from the top of the balcony stairs as soon as I was in the lobby door.

"Morning, Trixie." Knowing we were alone I called up to her, unafraid of being overheard and subsequently locked up in a tasteful sanitorium somewhere. I punched in the code to turn the building's alarm system off and started up the stairs.

"What did I miss?" she asked. "Have they figured out what happened to that stinker Warren yet? Did you tell your husband he can go peddle his papers at that film festival?"

"No, and no." On the balcony landing I opened the semi-hidden door to the back offices and headed for the break room. I needed coffee.

"Oh." She seemed perplexed. And a little disappointed. By which answer I wasn't sure.

"The police are still investigating, and I told Ted I'd go to the film festival with him," I elaborated.

Her eyes flashed. "Why, Nora. That's brilliant! That way you'll get to see him with Miss Homewrecker and see for yourself if it's over between them!"

I stopped, my hand on the coffee scoop. In my mind, I'd seen myself going to Sundance with Ted. With just Ted. I knew I'd see a bunch of old acquaintances and industry people as well, but it hadn't actually occurred to me that I'd be seeing Ted with her. The internationally breathtaking Priya Sharma. But of course I would. They'd be doing press and speaking on panels and going to all the events to promote the movie. That's why they were going in the first place.

"I think you're so smart," Trixie was chirping on, oblivious to the fact that she'd just made me realize what an idiot I was. "Why, you'll know in a minute if there's still any hanky-panky going on between them. He may be an actor but he's still a man. He won't be able to fool you."

My stomach did a flip. I'd impulsively told Ted I'd go with him in a moment of nostalgia, not really thinking it through. Would I even be able to handle the sight of the two of them together? It was hard enough not to slap Ted every time I saw him by himself. What would it do to me when I saw him with her?

"Nora?" Trixie asked. "Are you okay?"

"I really don't think so," I told her. "I really think I'm...*angry*."

Her eyes grew wide. "Well, of course you are, honey."

She saw it. Saw my anger right there on top of everything. Why hadn't I? All this time I'd been telling myself that I was hurt. That I was rejected. That I was miserable. All true, of course, but what I hadn't faced about myself—not until just now when I'd imagined seeing Ted and Priya smiling together in the snowy streets of Park City—was that I was furious.

The thought of them together made me want to kill them both.

Which is when my phone pinged with an incoming text.

Babe. I'd love you to come to Sundance but a bunch of stuff is happening. Don't make any plans yet. Stay tuned. I'm back in LA and I'll sort everything out. Miss you already.

I stared at the screen, then at Trixie, who was giving me the kind of look usually reserved for unexploded bombs.

"He's *waffling*," I told her.

She blinked a few times, then asked hesitantly, "Is that good or bad?"

"It's infuriating."

She pursed her cupid's bow lips. "What do you want to do now?"

And I knew. Everything else just sort of fell away, and I saw, stark and clear, what I wanted to do. It had been there all along.

"I want to divorce him."

Saying it out loud gave me the sensation that a tornado had just swept through the break room.

Trixie put her hands on her hips. "Well, I didn't want to say anything, you know, until you made your mind up..." She nodded once, her shiny curls bouncing. "But it's about darn time."

I needed something stronger than coffee.

I needed a stiff drink or a punching bag or a nice, shiny gun.

No, not a gun. If I had a gun and a quick way to get to LA, things would end badly.

And if I had a stiff drink I might not stop, which would not bode well for setting up for the twelve-fifteen. Or for the rest of my life.

I knew the maze of rooms in the theater's basement contained a lot of junk, but I didn't remember seeing a punching bag. Lots of knickknacks that might be very satisfying to smash, but then I'd just have to clean them up, so that sort of took the thrill out of it.

Coffee. And stronger than I could make in the break room. That's the best I could do at the moment.

Which is how I found myself across the street at Café Madeline, ordering the maximum amount of caffeine possible in a hot beverage and furiously—*furiously*—texting my lawyers.

"Are you okay?"

From the look on her face this was probably not the first time

Lisa had said something to me, but it was the first time she got through. I looked up, dazed. "I'm furious."

She grimaced. "There's a lot of that going around."

Lisa owned the café. She'd named it after her daughter, who was currently a freshman at Yale. It was a busy and comforting hub to the neighborhood, with plenty of tables, free Wi-Fi, and a sinful selection of pastries. I'd developed a casual friendship with her over the past few months. She was a few years older than me and letting her hair go gray, which made her comforting to be around, somehow. Or maybe it was because she always smelled faintly of cupcakes.

Today she looked as angry as I felt.

"Why? What's going on?" I pocketed my phone. I'd sent the texts. There was nothing more I could do now.

She nodded her head toward a less crowded area of the shop. I followed her and listened as she leaned across the counter, her voice lowered. "McMillan," she said darkly. "Has he been after the Palace, too?"

Alarm bells went off. "What do you mean?"

"Stan McMillan," she said. "The real-estate developer? He's trying to take over this whole block. Is he coming after your side of the street too?"

"I haven't heard anything," I said. "What do you mean 'take over?'"

"He's trying to buy every business on the block," she said. "He wants to tear it all down and put up one of those big mixed-use developments."

"No!" I said, probably louder than I should. People glanced over at the two of us. "No," I said more quietly. "Has anybody sold yet?"

"The yarn shop and the kitchenware place on the corner," she said. "He got to them before anyone found out his big plans. Marla at the nail salon thinks her landlord will be next and she'll be out. Now that everybody knows what he's up to the prices are going up. But I don't want to sell."

"Of course not!" I knew Lisa poured her heart and soul into her café. You only had to bite into one of her chocolate-filled croissants to realize that.

"But I don't know if I can take the pressure of being the last holdout. He has a reputation for getting nasty."

I hadn't ever heard that. Of course, I hadn't heard a lot of things. I was still new to the neighborhood. What I did know is that McMillan Real Estate was one of the three firms that would be participating in the event June and I had set up at the Palace for Monday.

"He hasn't come after your side of the street?" Lisa now asked.

"Not as far as I know," I told her. "But he wouldn't have to talk to me." I wasn't the owner of the Palace. My best friend Robbie had a one-quarter share, as did Monica Chen, who owned a cannabis shop a few blocks away on Divisadero. There were two other partners I didn't interact with much, one about an hour south in Silicon Valley, and another in LA. This McMillan might have gone to any of them and I wouldn't know anything about it.

"But Robbie or Monica would have told me," I said. As much to myself as to Lisa.

"Well, be careful," she said. "That man's a snake. And when it comes to real estate, there's no such thing as a friend."

Great. Something else to worry about.

I took my coffee and left, dialing Robbie as I crossed the street.

The call went straight to voicemail.

CHAPTER 11

Running an entire theater with a crew of only three people can be great for taking your mind off everything else. For the next few hours I was too busy to worry about what Lisa had told me. Or for that matter, to think about Ted. Or Warren's death. There's nothing like a broken cash register with a crowd (okay, a handful) of impatient filmgoers to focus the mind.

Once Marty started the film, he came down to the ticket booth, bringing a small bundle of tools that I hoped would mean an easy repair rather than an expensive replacement of the register.

I took over the concessions stand from Albert, encouraging him to go upstairs and take a break until the next rush. Sometimes, when he was slinging popcorn and making change, I forgot that he was over ninety years old. But then he'd sit down with a sigh and I could see every year in the droop of his shoulders.

"You know, I think I'll take you up on that offer," he said, adjusting his round glasses. "I could use a rest. I was up late last night working on my project."

He seemed to want me to ask, so I did. "What project?"

He tapped the side of his nose, channeling Paul Newman in *The Sting* (1973, Newman, Robert Redford, and an amazing ragtime score.) "I don't want to say anything yet," he said. "But I think you'll like it."

Cool. More secrets.

I poured myself a cup of coffee from the old drip pot, not having fully mastered the complexities of the new espresso maker yet. I'd just pulled out my phone to check for messages when a windblown woman came in from the street.

I glanced at the big round clock over the lobby doors. "You've missed the first few minutes," I told her. "But I can tell you what happened. Norma Shearer's husband is a fink." He'd probably already told her that the other woman didn't mean a thing.

"That's okay," she said. "I'm not here for the movie. June sent me."

"Oh! You must be Sam." Samantha Beach. The realtor who had been among the last to leave the bar the night of Warren's celebration. "June told me you'd call."

She set a large leather tote bag on the glass countertop. "I was going to, but then I thought I'd drop by instead. I haven't been here in years." She looked around the lobby appraisingly, which ordinarily wouldn't have given me a second thought. Most people gawked a little when they first came in. Gilded accents and spectacular chandeliers aren't exactly common in movie theaters anymore, nor are grand (if threadbare) staircases leading to full balconies. That's why the Palace was a palace.

So, no, normally I wouldn't have even noticed someone taking it all in. But after what Lisa had said about that realtor gobbling up all the businesses across the street, I found Sam's assessing gaze more than a little disconcerting.

"You've updated the agenda for Monday?" I asked her. Maybe a little more sharply than the question called for.

"Yeah." She rustled around in her bag and pulled out a folder, which she handed to me. "We're going to have a moment of silence for Warren. June will handle that, and then we'll go into the state-of-the-market presentation instead of the lets-get-pumped session. We decided to push that to after lunch, when people are starting to lose momentum anyway. Everything will be in the right order on the PowerPoint deck. Will we be projecting that onto the big screen?"

"Yes," I told her. "The podium will be in front of it, off to the side. Then when you have your panel sessions, we'll raise the screen so you can have full use of the stage."

The Palace had been built when vaudeville was still clinging to life, so we had a full-sized stage, complete with backdrop rigging and boarded-up trapdoors hidden behind the movie screen. Not that it got much use anymore.

"Perfect," she said. "Can you think of anything else?"

"Not right now." My eye was drawn to one of the topics. "Crushing the Market with Mixed Use." Was that on the agenda because Stan McMillan planned to put up a mixed-use development in the neighborhood? Was he already prepping the brokers to sell it? Was he already planning to tear down the Palace?

Sam cleared her throat meaningfully. I glanced up at her. "Sorry," I said. "I do have a question. I'm going to have a film crew here to record the sessions so June can post them on her website. Do you think she'll want to film the moment of silence?"

She looked startled. "Oh, I don't know. Do you think so?"

I didn't, because I couldn't imagine June wanting to post it. Nevertheless. "I'll ask her," I said. Then I asked my real question, "It was so terrible about Warren. Did you know him well?"

She put on a brave face, which struck me as being rehearsed. "We were very close."

Interesting. "He seemed like such a nice guy," I said. "He was dating someone who works here, so he came around fairly frequently."

She blinked a few times. "I heard about her." She glanced up the stairs. "Is she around?"

"Not today," I said. "She mentioned that a lot of people from Warren's office were at the bar that night. Were you there?"

I knew she was. I also knew she'd been among the last to leave.

She nodded, her face assuming the silent-film version of a tragic heroine. "Who could have imagined that would be the last time we'd all see Warren?"

I shook my head. "It's terrible."

"So terrible," she agreed. And something about the way she seemed to enjoy saying it made me wonder if she'd been behind some of the wild speculations making the rounds at June's office.

"You probably had to talk to the police," I said, with the tiniest suggestion that this made her special.

She preened. "A couple of times."

"Oh, that must have been so hard for you." I was being shameless now.

Another brave face. Or maybe she was going for noble. In any case, nothing about her behavior struck me as genuine.

"But I'm sure they want to know about absolutely everyone who was there." I leaned across the candy counter, as if we were just a couple of girlfriends dishing about any old Friday night. "I gather Warren was surprised by some of the people who showed up." Particularly the person he'd referred to in his text. Had she seen them too? It might not be important, but I still wanted to know who it was.

"Yeah..." She seemed about to say something more, then stopped herself. Another look crossed her face. This one speculative. "Um, I'd better be going." She reached for her tote bag.

If she did know who the mysterious person had been, she wasn't going to share it with me.

"I'll see you on Monday," I said, unable to come up with any line of conversation that would keep her here, spilling her secrets.

She nodded, looking preoccupied, and was out the lobby doors with a purposeful stride before I could think of anything else.

I watched her leave. She was an attractive woman. Probably a few years older than Callie or Warren. And tall. A tall woman with short blonde hair.

And she was hiding something.

"Do you think she was Warren's other girl?" Trixie asked breathlessly.

"I don't know," I admitted. "There are probably a bunch of tall women with short blonde hair running around the city."

We were in my office, me sitting at the desk and Trixie perched on the arm of the sofa, her petite feet on the seat cushion.

"But this one worked with him. And she said they were close."

A perfectly plucked eyebrow was raised.

"Let's just say she was," I picked up a pencil and twirled it, thinking. "And let's say she wasn't just the last person at the party, but she actually went home with him..."

"Then why isn't she dead, too?" Trixie asked.

"She might have been, if it really were a case of a burglary gone wrong," I said. "But if it wasn't..."

"Oh, Nora!" Trixie sat up straight, her eyes wide. "Do you think she killed him?"

"Who knows?" I said. "But if she did go home with him, she might have seen his phone or something—his main phone—and seen Callie's texts. I mean, it seemed like she knew about Callie but maybe she didn't think they were serious? Maybe Warren had said Callie didn't mean anything? And then she found out...?"

"And killed him in a fit of jealous rage!" Trixie proclaimed. "Like Joan Crawford in *Mildred Pierce*! Wait, was that jealous rage? Was that even Joan, or was it her daughter?" Her brow wrinkled.

"Her daughter," I said. Although Joan in *Mildred* (1945, Crawford and Ann Blyth) had much more to be upset about, in my opinion, than Sam did in the real world.

"Then like Bette Davis in *The Letter*!" Trixie declared. She sighed. "Gee, I loved that movie." She placed the back of her hand to her forehead in a dramatic pose and deepened her voice to quote Davis's famous line 'With all my heart, I still love the man I killed!'"

"Right." I'd just been thinking about *The Letter* the other day. "We'll have to show that one soon."

"Show what one?"

Marty stood at the office door, suspicion on his face. Trixie looked from me to him and back again, then mouthed "I'm sorry"—although it wasn't as if he could hear her—and vanished.

"What are you up to?" Marty came in and loomed over the desk. "Why are you talking to yourself? Have you finally lost your mind? And when they come to take you away, do I get your job?"

"I haven't lost my mind," I informed him. Although some

might beg to differ. "I was just thinking out loud."

He made a harrumph sort of noise and collapsed onto the couch. "I fixed the register."

"Yay. Thank you." There were still a thousand other things in need of repair, but I'd take whatever wins I could get. "How was the animation festival last night?"

He gave me a dark look. "David went back to work. I blame you."

"Blame the murderer," I said. "I just told him something that he apparently felt was worth looking into." Which meant he probably thought Blondie was involved somehow. Had she killed Warren? And had I just had a nice chat with her downstairs in the lobby?

"What did you tell him?" Marty asked.

"I can't tell you."

"Oh, come on. You're dying to," he said. "Look at you, you're bursting."

"I'm doing no such thing." But I automatically sucked in my tummy anyway.

"Fine. You don't tell me what you know about Warren's murder and I won't tell you what I know about Sally Lee's blog."

"*What?*" Sally Lee is the name I blog under. But the smug way Marty was looking at me didn't make me think he'd found me out. If he'd found me out, he wouldn't be smug. He'd be apoplectic.

"I think she's local," he said smugly. "I bet she is, and I bet she comes to the Palace."

I blinked a few times, catching up. "Hang on, I thought your theory was that Sally was a man."

He waved a hand. "That was just an idea. And it may still be true, but more importantly, look at what she's written up in the past few weeks. *Summertime*? *His Girl Friday*?" He paused for dramatic effect, then announced "*Roman Holiday!*" as if he were Perry Mason summing up a particularly compelling case.

"All excellent movies," I said. *Summertime* (1955, Katharine Hepburn and Rossano Brazzi) had been one of my predecessor's favorites. We'd shown it recently in a lineup that had paid homage to her taste. *His Girl Friday* (1940, Cary Grant and Rosalind Russell) was a fast-talking masterpiece that we'd run before the holidays. And of course *Roman Holiday* had been our midnight movie just last...oh. I saw where Marty was going.

"That could be a coincidence," I told him.

"*Or,*" he said, "she could be in this theater right now!"

Well, she was, but I didn't think that was what he meant.

"I've been paying attention to the regulars, and I have some ideas," he said.

"Please don't start accosting the few paying customers we actually have."

"I'm not going to *accost* anybody. I'm simply going to figure out which one she is, and then worship her."

I had a feeling he really, really wouldn't.

"Great," I told him. "Sounds like a plan. Just don't get arrested or anything."

He shrugged that possibility off. "David would get me out." His gaze sharpened. "So are you going to tell me what you told him last night?"

"Nope." I shuffled some papers on the desk.

"Come on. I told you mine."

"Yours is a ridiculous theory. Mine could be evidence in a murder."

He sniffed. "Since when did you get all ethical?"

Since what I knew had the potential to hurt Callie even more. But I didn't tell him that.

The Letter
1940

We begin with a moonlit night on a rubber plantation in Singapore. A shot rings out. A man staggers from a doorway across a veranda. Bette Davis follows, wearing a diaphanous gown and firing a gun until she empties it.

Fix yourself a gin sling, my friends, and settle in for some DRAMA. Because what we have here is *The Letter*.

This is high Bette Davis. She gets to be bad, and she gets to be calculating, she gets to play the innocent, and she gets to suffer for love. She is glorious.

But back to the plot: Yes, she killed him. She sends one of the workers for the police. "Tell them there's been an accident and Mr. Hammond is dead." An accident, Bette? She sends for her husband and the family lawyer. Everybody knows the victim. He was part of their expat social circle. So what happened? "He tried to make love to me and I shot him."

The men's reactions demonstrate how swell the patriarchy can be when it's on your side: "May I say that I think you behaved magnificently... It's obvious the man only got what he deserved." Sure. Then she dons a frilly apron and makes them all breakfast. Seriously. Of course, she'll have to be arrested, but she's not to fret about it. "The attorney general is a decent chap."

We might relax at this point, but the next shot of her shows the light through the louvered windows creating the effect of bars. Visual cues, people. Notice them.

Herbert Marshall, as her husband, comes off as noble, stalwart, and not terribly bright. "You've been the best wife a man could possibly have," he tells her. Has she, Herbert? We'll see.

Flash forward. Bette's been in jail for a while as the investigation takes place. They've found that the victim, Hammond, was married. But more than that, he was married to a "Eurasian woman," described as "all covered with gold chains and bracelets and spangles," which sounds pretty fabulous to me, but it's totally turned public opinion against the victim. Now Bette has racism as well as the patriarchy on her side.

Until! Late at night an Asian clerk (wearing glasses, because this is 1940 and all Asian clerks wear glasses) comes to see the lawyer. There is in existence a letter. Written by Bette on the night of the murder. The original is in possession of the Eurasian wife. Uh oh.

Our noble lawyer goes to see Bette. He's got a copy of the letter. In it, she invites Hammond to come see her while her husband is away. Oops. "Howard, I swear to you I did not write this letter," she says. Two minutes later: "I did write that letter." Ultimately, she faints. I mean, what other choice does she have?

Sadly, the lawyer has principles. Even though the Widow Hammond is willing to sell it to them, that would be wrong. Bette does not understand how he could be so cruel (pronounced with two syllables). Surprise: she talks him into negotiating for the letter. Turns out the widow has only one condition: Bette has to bring her the money in person. It's on!

Another moonlight night. Bette, released into the lawyer's custody, will go to the Chinese Quarter to see the widow. The Chinese Quarter is clearly where the fun is. And I bet the best food. But I digress. The car moves slowly down crowded streets. Bette looks ridiculous wrapped in an enormous lace scarf.

As they wait for the widow in an antiques shop, Bette is drawn to a set of matching engraved daggers. Yup. Noted. They're led through the back door to an opium den. Because let's not leave any Asian stereotypes unturned.

And THEN—Through a sparkling beaded doorway appears...Gale Sondergaard! Because if you're making a movie in the forties on the Warner Brother's lot, and you need a sinister female, you go with Gale every time. You may gather from her name that she's a white lady, but she's all done up in bejeweled Asian drag and lit to personify Exotic Evil. Okay, but let's not forget who killed whose husband here.

The first thing she does is have Bette remove the preposterous lace shawl. Thank you, Gale. And now we have a Diva-off. Looks are exchanged. Eyebrows are incredible. Gale throws the letter to the floor. Bette has to kneel before her, after which she primly says, "Thank you" and leaves Gale to glower in rage and fabulous accessories.

And we come to the trial. "If ever there was a simple, uncomplicated case, it's this one," the lawyer says. Sure, once you've bought the evidence. But if you think the trial is where this story will end, you have not seen nearly enough Bette Davis movies. She needs her big moment, her Movie Star scene, and oh, yes, people, she will have it. And you will love it.

Racism, oh, racism:

What's so shocking about the racism here is that it's so casual. It's just assumed that the audience will understand that the community of white planters is the only community that matters. The people who actually lived here before them, live here with them, and will be here long after they're gone, are either servants, mild irritants, or inherently evil. I mean, all they have to say about Hammond's wife is "Eurasian" and he's condemned. What would it have been like if he'd married a full-blooded Asian? Or was that just too unthinkable at the time?

You should still watch this movie. And then you should go out and support any recent movie that was written by, directed by, or stars an Asian cast. Because Bette is eternal, but Hollywood still needs to hear a few things.

Movies My Friends Should Watch
Sally Lee

CHAPTER 12

I still hadn't heard back from Robbie by the time the seven thirty started. Which didn't mean a thing, I told myself. She was one of the busiest women in Hollywood. Plus she was the single mom of a teenaged daughter. Plus there might be nothing to the rumors about Stan McMillan taking over the neighborhood. There might be no reason to worry.

I really wished she'd call.

Meanwhile, I sent a text to Monica. She was both proprietress of a cannabis shop a few blocks away and one-quarter owner of the Palace. We'd met when I'd investigated some shady goings-on at the theater soon after I'd arrived in San Francisco, and had formed a friendship after that.

Hey Monica. Haven't seen you in a while. Let's catch up. I've heard some rumors about the neighborhood. Has someone offered to buy the Palace?

There. She'd get back to me and tell me everything was fine.

I really hoped she would.

While I waited, I looked up Stan McMillan. The first thing I noticed is that the real-estate developer wasn't afraid of publicity. One simple search showed him everywhere. He had the expensively cut graying hair and overly white smile of generic wealth. If Hollywood were to put out a casting call for a "white male executive type" they'd see a hundred of him. In his many online photos he was breaking ground here and shaking hands there, and he appeared to be fond of quotes that sounded like they'd been culled from TED talks on the entrepreneurial spirit of America.

I hated him instantly.

When Monica texted back it wasn't the greatest of news.

Haven't heard anything, but I've been up to my eyeballs lately. I'll ask around. Let's catch up over the weekend.

It wasn't great, but it wasn't a confirmation of my worst fears. Yet.

Brandon had relieved Albert for the evening shift, but I hadn't had a chance to speak to him alone. Which was partly because he was trying to avoid me—*nobody* volunteered to clean the downstairs bathrooms if it wasn't their turn—and partly because we were pretty busy.

Thursday nights are like that. On the other hand, Mondays had always been slow. The decision to save on expenses by leaving the theater dark had been made before my time and it made sense. It also left Mondays free for events like the one we'd be having with June and the rest of the realtors in a few days. With a little luck it would go well enough to build on. With that in mind, I took position at the candy counter, going through the "Goings On" section of a local website on my phone, trolling for potential business and envisioning nice fat corporate checks. And waiting for Brandon to come back up to the lobby. He could only clean those bathrooms for so long.

I pounced when he opened the stairway door. And by "pounced," I mean I gave him a friendly grin and waved him over.

"So," I said chummily, "did you hear from anyone interesting this morning?"

He flushed, which was always his first response. "Last night," he said. "That detective came over at ten thirty. It totally freaked my mom out."

I made a sympathetic noise. "What did he say?"

He glanced around the lobby guiltily. "That he couldn't promise Callie wouldn't find out that I was following Warren."

Of course that was the teenager's main concern. And of course Jackson wouldn't be able to make that promise.

"It'll be fine," I tried to reassure him. "Especially if what you told the police helps find Warren's killer. Callie will forgive you for a lot in that case."

He looked marginally hopeful at that. "Then I really hope that blonde lady did it," he said.

"Did Jackson tell you anything? Does he think she's important?"

Brandon thought about it, then shrugged. "He doesn't really say much, you know?"

I nodded. I knew.

I was thinking about Callie as I went upstairs to the office. Which is why I checked myself when I got to the doorway and saw her sitting at my desk, focusing intently on my computer screen. For a moment I thought I was hallucinating, the way I'd thought Trixie was a hallucination when she first started appearing to me. Then she glanced up.

"I'm totally not looking at your stuff," she said.

"Uh huh." I came in and closed the door. "What are you doing? And how did you get in without me seeing you?"

"Marty let me in the alley door. I came up the back stairs." She grimaced in frustration. "I had to come in. My mom, like, banned me from the Internet. She took my phone and locked away literally every computer in the house."

"Uh huh," I said again. "Why?"

Another grimace. "She thinks I'm obsessing."

Yep, that sounded right. "Are you?"

"Of course I am! Somebody killed my boyfriend! How can she not expect me to see what everyone is saying?"

I sat in a chair opposite the desk. "Well, not to side with your mom or anything, but maybe you shouldn't be seeing all of that. There are a lot of rumors flying around and you could make yourself crazy if you—"

"Crazier than I already am, not knowing what's going on?" she demanded. "And besides, I already know what everyone's saying. My mom didn't know you gave me my old phone back, so I've been seeing everything anyway and I know what everyone's posting. I just need to see it all on a bigger screen."

She swiveled the laptop so I could see what she was looking at. Photos. Most of them blurry and chaotic. Someone's social media feed.

"Just about everything's already gone from Insta," she said. "But a bunch of people posted on other sites and they're all still up."

The look on my face must have been blank, so she elaborated.

"Pictures from that night at the bar," she explained. "Everybody was taking selfies, and, like, video and everything. Once Warren died everyone started posting literally everything. So they've got to be here."

"Who's got to be there? The killer?"

"Maybe. That whole story about the burglary is sketch. Everyone's saying all his stuff was still in his apartment. What kind of burglar doesn't take anything?"

"The kind that gets interrupted by someone coming home?" Never mind that "everyone saying" something didn't mean it was true.

She shook her head. "I don't believe it. I looked it up, and statistically, most burglaries take place between ten in the morning and three in the afternoon. While people are out. Do you know how rare a middle-of-the-night break-in is?"

"No, but—"

"Whoever killed him wasn't after his stuff. They were after him. Tell me honestly, do you really think it was random?"

"No," I admitted. But not because of social media. It was because Detective Jackson seemed to think there was more to it than that.

I looked at Callie. "Okay, let's assume someone wanted to kill Warren. What makes you think they were at the bar that night?"

"I keep thinking about that last text he sent."

I'd been thinking about it, too. Great minds.

"Warren saw someone there that night," Callie went on. "Someone he thought June would 'lose it' if she knew about. What if that person didn't want to be seen? What if it was an escaped criminal or something?"

"Why would an escaped criminal interest June?"

"I said 'or something!' Maybe it was someone from work who had called in sick, or someone who was cheating on his wife or something. Anything!"

"Right," I said in a way that I hoped was calming. "Someone with something to hide. Someone with so much to hide that he'd kill Warren to keep him from mentioning it to anyone?"

She took a deep breath and ran a hand through the tangles of her hair. "It's, like, all I can think about."

I understood. "You're looking for this person in all the photos," I said.

"But I can only blow things up so much on my phone," she explained. "I needed a bigger screen, and I didn't want to ask any of my friends because they'd think I'm, like, crazy or something. I thought maybe I could get in and out of here without you even knowing." She gave me a haunted look. "Don't tell me you think I'm crazy."

What I thought was that she'd come here because she wanted my help. Whether she'd admit it to herself or not. But that's not what I said.

"I think," I said slowly, "that we can do better than a laptop screen."

Ten minutes later I'd hooked the laptop up to the powerful projector that we'd be using for Monday's event. On Monday we'd plug June's laptop in and be able to project her PowerPoint slides onto the movie screen. But now instead of that I plugged my laptop in and projected the social media posts of Warren's friends onto the freshly-scrubbed whiteboard in the break room.

"We don't care about anybody in the foreground of the pictures, right?" I asked Callie.

"I don't think so. I think whoever Warren saw wasn't there for his party. If there is a picture of them, I bet it's someone in the background."

"How will we recognize them if we don't know what we're looking for?"

"I have literally no idea," she said. "I just kind of hope that Warren sent me that text about them because I might know them too."

"Let's hope so."

Half an hour later I felt I'd gotten to know the interior of the Irish Bank intimately. The after-work crowd was pretty much what you'd expect for an established bar in the Financial District. Lots of thirtyish guys with their ties loosened, lots of thirtyish women with aspirational handbags. The crowd thinned out as the evening went on, and more and more of the patrons seemed to be there for Warren's party.

Warren himself was all over the place. With his arm around Callie in a lot of the early-evening shots, and then by himself or surrounded by friends later on. I glanced over at Callie to see how she was doing.

"Are you okay?" I asked.

She sniffed. "I'm fine."

I doubted that. "We can probably skip the ones from earlier in the evening," I suggested. "He didn't send that text to you until after one, right?"

She nodded. We kept looking. Callie and Warren's friends posted *a lot*.

"Hang on," I said eventually. "There, in the corner." I got up and moved closer to the image on the whiteboard. "The guy with the grey hair."

"I don't know him. Do you?"

"No, but he's older than the rest of them. And we're looking for someone June would lose it over, right? So maybe we should be looking for someone more her age?"

It was at least a way of focusing our search. We looked for anyone who seemed like they'd be too old for Warren's gathering, scrolling through the feeds more quickly now. Samantha Beach was there in all her tall blonde splendor, but it didn't look to me like she and Warren were up to anything. She was in a fair number of pictures, but mainly on the outskirts. If she was the other woman he'd been seeing, they were very good at being discreet.

And then I saw him.

"Wait!" I stopped Callie from moving on. "There!" I pointed at a man's profile in the upper right corner of an image. "That guy." It was a well-groomed man in his fifties who seemed to be talking to someone just out of the frame. All I could see of that person was an arm with an oversized watch dangling from an undersized wrist. But the main guy I knew.

"Hang on," Callie said, and clicked on next photo. In this image the man had moved. He was looking toward the camera, but not at it. It seemed to me like he was looking directly at Warren.

"Who is it?" Callie asked.

"Stan McMillan," I told her. I'd just been looking at dozens of pictures of him online. "Real estate developer and known snake."

Was he also a murderer?

CHAPTER 13

Friday morning my phone woke me. I reached for it, seeing but not quite believing that someone was calling me at five fifteen. I hit the Answer button.

Robbie spoke in a rush. "Nora, are you okay? I just saw. I can't believe it. I'm so, so sorry. That bastard! How are you?"

For one half-sleeping moment I thought she was apologizing for selling the Palace to the snake and possible murderer Stan McMillan. Then I woke up.

"What happened?"

A brief silence. "You haven't seen it."

"It's five o'clock in the morning. I haven't seen anything. What is it?"

"Ted."

I had a quick mental image of him lying dramatically dead somewhere, the victim of my murderous thoughts yesterday. But that couldn't be true. If I could think him dead, I'd have done it months ago.

"What?" I demanded.

"Oh, Nora." Her voice broke. "It's all over the gossip sites. He's back with Priya. He gave her an engagement ring."

All of the air left the room and I got a sort of floaty feeling, as if gravity had finally given up. "I'll call you back."

I had to check online. I had to see this for myself. I had to check my messages to see if he'd at least had the decency to text me. I had to get a grip.

But first I ran to the bathroom. I had to throw up.

*   *   *

"*Canoodling*," I said to Robbie. I'd called her back after pulling myself together. Not that I was together. But I'd called her back. "Have you ever actually heard the word canoodling? I mean, out loud? Spoken by a human being?"

It was the word emblazoned in hot pink text above the photo of Ted and Priya in a shadowy booth of a swanky restaurant. A booth designed for canoodling.

"They invented it for the tabloids," she said. "They must have."

"The only thing I want to know," I said. "The only thing I really don't understand, is how I can have been such a total and complete idiot."

She said all the right best-friend things, but I didn't hear them. I was looking at another photo, this one of Priya's movie star smile next to her left hand, the third finger of which was sporting a diamond bigger than the first apartment Ted and I had shared.

"It's not so much the diamond," I told Robbie. "It's the lying sniveling weaseling cheating lying that I mind."

"Damn right," my best friend said.

"I mean, I'm *furious*," I told her. "With him, of course—"

"Of course."

"But even more with me. How can I still feel this horrible when I'd already made the decision to divorce him? It's over. *I* decided it was over. *I* decided not to take *him* back. So why do I still feel like the trash he pays someone else to take out?"

"Probably because you're a human woman," she said. "He, in stark contrast, is a low-down dirty dog."

"I could kill him," I said. "If he walked in here this minute, I could kill him. This is how murders happen, isn't it? And I don't even love him anymore. Imagine how hard I could kill him if I still loved him."

"You need to use all that and write a dark, twisty screenplay," she advised.

"I would, except I'm not you." Robbie's first hit TV series had been set in a cutthroat firm of divorce attorneys. Following her divorce. From a divorce attorney.

"No you're not. You're a better writer." Which wasn't true. But it was nice of her to say so.

"Robbie, I just feel so *stupid*," I wailed.

"Okay, I'll give you today for that, but tomorrow you get on with things. You're the one who's always telling me about strong female leads. How many times did Bette Davis get divorced?"

"Four."

"Right, and Joan Crawford?"

"Four," I said. "No, three. The last one died."

"Well there you go. Strong women go on. And you're a strong woman if I've ever met one."

"Thanks, but film stars of the forties are not exactly role models for happiness."

"You'll be happy when you get past this. Which you will, in less time than you can imagine right now."

I sniffed. "I know you're right."

"Do you want to come down for the weekend? Or for me to come up?"

There was no way I'd willingly go into the den of slavering paparazzi known as Beverly Hills right now. "I'd love it if you came up," I said. "But I know you can't." She was too busy to catch her breath most days. "I love you for offering."

"And I love you for being you. Take a shower. Call your lawyers. And go watch a movie. What's playing?"

The lineup would be changing today. "*The Women*," I told her. "And *Libeled Lady*."

"Okay. Not the best choices for right this minute." True. One concerned a group of women largely failing in their high-society marriages, and the other was about scheming journalists inventing scandal. "Maybe just go for a long walk."

I took a deep breath. "I will," I said. "And then I'll divorce that lying liar and I'll buy a place up here and I'll build a whole new life for myself."

"A whole new happy life," she said.

"Damn right," I agreed. "Damn happy."

Then I hung up the phone and cried. But only for half an hour.

At which point I remembered why I'd thought Robbie was calling. She still hadn't told me if Stan McMillian was trying to buy the Palace.

"He's a shit and you're better off without him. Do we have to discuss it further?"

This is how Marty greeted me on the sidewalk outside the theater. He'd just come down the ladder from changing the lineup on the marquee.

"Please let's not," I replied.

I knew Albert would say something sweet and comforting, so I avoided him and went straight up to the office. I didn't want to start crying again.

Callie sent me a text, as did Monica. Both were supportive. Neither made me feel better. Hector also sent a message.

You should have taken me up on my offer.

Presumably he meant his offer to have Ted killed. Which I still chose to believe had been a joke. Because I still chose to believe that Hector was retired from a life of crime. I liked to think of him as a scrupulously legitimate businessman enjoying the economic boom back home in Colombia. Sometimes with his shirt off.

I answered his text.

Make me another.

Then I did the only thing I could. I got through the day.

Callie and I had called Detective Jackson the night before with our theory about Stan McMillan. We'd sent him the incriminating photo from the bar, but we hadn't heard anything back from him yet. So there was nothing new to distract me on the who-killed-Warren front. I busied myself with tickets and popcorn and schedules and bills, all while obsessively checking my phone for messages from my lawyers. They streamed in throughout the day, calming and terrifying by turns, and ultimately saying nothing in very expensive, lawyerly words.

The seven-thirty was just about over, and I was dreading the thought of heading home for an evening of solitary wallowing when there was a knock at the office door.

"Nora?" The door opened.

Callie hadn't come back to work yet, so I was surprised to see her. I was doubly surprised to see her wearing much-too-big pink striped pajamas, rolled up at the cuffs and sleeves.

"Sooo...are we doing this?" She came in. Her mass of thick curls was piled into a messy bun and she looked cute and girly and very unlike her normal ultracool self.

"If I say 'doing what?' am I a bad person?" I asked.

She came into the room and I realized she was holding another set of pj's. These sporting enormous purple polka dots. "*Pajama Game*," she said. "The midnight movie?"

The look on my face must have shown two things. One, that I'd totally forgotten it was Friday night and that we were having a special showing of *The Pajama Game* (1957, Doris Day and John Raitt). And two, that I'd rather do just about anything than put on a pair of polka-dot pj's and serve "1950's company picnic" food to a light-hearted crowd humming along to the score.

"No," I told her.

"That's what I thought," she said. "But then I thought, like, if I can you can. And I decided I can. So you totally have to." She plopped the pajamas down on the desk in front of me.

"How about neither of us do, and instead we head for the nearest bar? My treat."

"I would literally love to do that," she said. "But it would mean leaving Marty in charge of something that's supposed to be, like, fun. And we kind of want the Palace to still be here in the morning, right?" She pushed the polka-dots toward me.

"Oh, my God. I have to do this," I realized.

"OMG you do," Callie agreed.

Trixie materialized just behind her, clapping her hands and beaming. "Oh, how fun!" she said. "A pajama party!"

Right. Fun.

CHAPTER 14

The Pajama Game was made back when America had a middle class and workers belonged to unions and went to company picnics and sang songs about not being in love as they danced all over the factory floor. Okay, maybe that last bit was only in the movies.

In any case, the Friday night midnight movie event I'd planned—I had only myself to blame—was a pajama party. Anyone who showed up in pj's would get half off their ticket. Which was only fair, as we'd doubled the normal price of tickets because this was a party and because I'm a financial genius. We were also selling hot dogs, potato salad, and ice cream sundaes in the lobby before the show while playing the movie's score over the sound system. But it wasn't only about the profit we might make that night. It was about seducing people into loving classic movies.

"That was such a good picture!" Trixie enthused. "Oh! I have an idea! You could turn the balcony into Hernando's Hideaway and serve drinks!"

"I could if we had a liquor license," I said, at which she made a dismissive gesture.

The movie had been made twenty years after Trixie's death, but she must have seen it dozens of times over the years at the Palace. She was keeping me company in the office as I changed into the polka-dot pajamas. Callie had gone downstairs to start setting up.

"It's not like the coppers will raid the joint," she said, her phrasing reminding me that her tough-guy lingo dated mainly from the time of James Cagney movies. "Not with all the murders going on."

"Just one murder," I said. "Just Warren. Unless there's something you're not telling me."

She gave me wide-eyed innocence. "Never."

"I wouldn't be surprised if one copper in particular did show up," I told her, rolling up the sleeves of the enormous pj's. I'd pulled my less-blonde-every-day hair into a ponytail. My LA highlights were growing out and my natural color included more gray than I'd realized. I'd have to find a new hairdresser, which shouldn't be too difficult. There were a ton of salons in the neighborhood. They couldn't all be about to close because of some evil real estate developer.

"That detective fella," Trixie agreed. "The one who's been canoodling with Marty."

I turned from the mirror to stare at her. First because she'd said the word 'canoodling,' and second because she knew about Marty and Jackson.

She grinned, enjoying my reaction. "Oh, I see things, Nora. And I may be a hundred years old, but don't you dare think I'm old-fashioned."

I held up my hands in surrender. "Never."

"Not one word." Marty put up a warning hand as I met him at the bottom of the balcony stairs.

He was wearing the most ridiculous pajamas I'd ever seen in my life. How they could be oversized on someone as towering as Marty was beyond me. But that was nothing compared to the pattern: giraffes in top hats and monocles.

"Callie?" I guessed.

"It's a good thing I'm being such a supportive friend in her time of need, because if someone hadn't murdered her boyfriend, I'd never have agreed to this."

"You're a prince," I told him, at which he glowered more darkly than usual.

Brandon was there too, his pj's patterned with teddy bears,

which probably said a lot about how Callie thought of him. Also in for the shift were Mike and Claire, siblings and high schoolers who worked nights and weekends as their schedules (and parents) permitted. Claire was wearing puppies and Mike was sporting kittens. Albert, sensible man, had wished us well and gone home hours ago.

My phone rang and I saw it was June, so I popped into the empty auditorium away from all the activity in the lobby.

"Nora, I'm glad I caught you." June's voice was breathless, as if she'd been on the run. "I know you spoke with Sam yesterday, but there's been another change in the agenda for Monday and I wanted to let you know."

"Okay, no problem," I said, taking the aisle seat on the back row. "What do you need?"

"Well, you know we'd been planning on a moment of silence for Warren, but now we're not going to do that after all."

I was surprised. "Really? Why not?"

She sighed, and I thought I heard impatience in it. "Stan—you know Stan McMillan, don't you?"

I sat up straighter. "Only by reputation." Reputation as a real estate developer, snake, and possible murderer.

"Well, you know McMillan's is one of the firms we're having the event with, and Stan feels—he feels quite strongly—that it would be a poor use of our time to have a moment of silence for Warren when so few people who will be attending actually knew him."

"Oh. Right." So he was heartless, too. Was he dangerous? Is that why June had given in to him about this?

She was still speaking. "He made the point that it would just raise more questions among people who didn't know Warren and hadn't heard about his death. Stan thinks—and he's probably right—that people who didn't know Warren will get sidetracked, asking who he was and how he died and so forth."

And so forth. Like who killed him. Like maybe Stan McMillan had something to hide.

"So the PowerPoint deck is being reshuffled again," June concluded. "I'll have the right version on my laptop come Monday."

I had a million questions for her, but there was something about her rush of words and defensive attitude that held me back. She didn't seem defensive on her own behalf so much as on McMillan's. Why? I'd intended to ask her what she knew about McMillan's rumored mixed-use development plans for the neighborhood, but now I hesitated. Suddenly I felt like I shouldn't let June know that I'd heard about it.

She was waiting for some sort of response. I swallowed my questions. I'd think about why later. "Thanks for letting me know," I said.

She let out a breath. "Of course. And, Nora, another thing..."

Something in the tone of her voice reminded me of a studio executive I knew who would spend an entire meeting talking about nothing and then oh-so-casually bring up the one thing that mattered just as he had one foot out the door. I braced myself. "What is it?"

"I don't mean to be a busybody," she hedged, "but I couldn't help but see the news about Ted and that, um..."

"Actress?" I said drily. "It's been hard to miss."

"I'm so sorry. I know you two were trying to work things out. But when I put on my realtor hat, I have to think that maybe it's for the best. I mean, not for the best, but at least this way you'll have some clarity about what you can be looking for now."

Oh. I got it. She was thinking about the *money*.

She cleared her throat delicately. "At least when you negotiate whatever settlement...well, you've been a little hazy about your budget, and maybe this will end up helping your house hunting. It will define your parameters." She concluded with a little relief in her voice, having successfully navigated through a tricky subject to get to her point.

"That it will," I agreed.

"Good. As soon as you're ready I can't wait to help you find the home of your dreams."

By *ready* I assumed she meant *flush with Hollywood divorce cash.* "Thanks, June."

I hung up feeling that my parameters were still pretty undefined. June apparently thought I'd be getting a whopping sum from Ted, a sum that would open up whole new vistas of real estate possibilities. And she might be right. When the lawyers had sent me a preliminary figure back in the fall it had been a lot more than I'd expected. But, of course, it had been preliminary. There was a long way to go and a lot to do before it would be final. June probably shouldn't start spending her commission just yet.

Nor should I start thinking about houses in Pacific Heights. First things first. I had a pajama party to throw.

The Palace didn't have a commercial kitchen, so I'd arranged for a guy with a hot dog cart to come in for the evening. Between getting him set up in the lobby and putting up the tables for the other food and hanging banners and a giant sign that said "Sleeptite Company Picnic" we were all pretty busy. The good news is that it was worth it. The crowd started showing up around eleven, and for once I didn't have to use air quotes when I said "crowd."

I made sure everyone was at their appointed posts and things were going smoothly before taking up my position at the cash register next to the sundae station. Marty was on ice cream duty.

"All the regulars are here." He gestured with a dripping scoop at the assembled throng.

"Not just the regulars," I said. "Although hopefully after tonight they'll all become regulars. Musicals are the gateway drug of classic film." I handed a happy customer his change.

"I think *she's* here," Marty said. Then he muttered out of the side of his mouth. "You know. *Sally Lee.*"

"Marty, please don't make a thing out of this." I knew I'd tell him the truth at some point or another, but this was not that point.

"It's not a *thing*," he said. "It's an insanely clever deduction, based on a close reading of her blog. I've deduced that she lives in

San Francisco and comes to the Palace all the time. But she didn't always. Her writing has only started to trail what we're showing in the past few months. So she's new in town. Ergo, I'm looking for a new regular."

Ergo? But I had to hand it to him. He was right.

"My leading suspects are that one on the landing—" he nodded toward top of the stairs, "in the heart-patterned pajama top and blonde wig—"

"It's a Doris Day costume," I pointed out. "From the finale."

"I'm aware," he said. "Or it's the woman in the wheelchair over by the hot dog guy. She's been coming in at least once a week for the past few months. But Doris up there is…"

He kept talking but I tuned him out. I was looking at the woman in the wheelchair. And now that he'd pointed her out, I did remember seeing her a few times before. She was memorable not just because of the chair, but also for her striking, almost dramatic looks. She was probably in her thirties, had long wavy black hair, and wore thick black-framed glasses that would have made most women look like the "before" picture in a not-so-sexy librarian contest. But on her they just emphasized her amazing cheekbones.

"Who is she?" I asked Marty. "And don't say Sally Lee."

He was scooping ice cream for another customer, but glanced over to the woman when he saw I was looking at her. "In my mind she's Dolores del Rio," he said, naming one of the few (okay, maybe the only) Latina actresses from 1930s Hollywood. "But if she pays with a credit card tonight, what do you want to bet we find out that her name is really Sally Lee?"

"It isn't," I assured him. This was one thing I could say with certainty.

I was still looking at the woman. There was something about her that seemed familiar to me. I was embarrassed to be caught staring at her when she turned and suddenly met my eyes. I smiled and she wheeled her way over to us.

"Would you like a sundae?" Marty asked. "We take credit cards. It's no problem."

I gave him a quick elbow to the ribs before introducing myself. "Hi, I'm Nora. I manage the joint," I said. "I'm so glad you came tonight."

She grinned. "I had to. Where else could I have worn this outfit?"

The outfit in question was an elaborately embroidered dressing gown worn over crimson silk pajamas that made me want to say the word "opulent" out loud.

"It's gorgeous," I told her. "You could wear it to the opera."

She shrugged. "But musicals are so much more fun."

"Then you'll love what we've got coming up," I said. "We're doing a whole month of musicals in the spring—'Musical May.'" I'd just thought if it.

"We are?" Marty asked.

"Your scoop is dripping," I told him. There was nobody waiting to pay, so I turned back to the woman. "Are you new to the neighborhood?" Why was she so familiar to me?

"Oh, no," she said. "I don't live around here. But once my cousin told me about your theater, I haven't been able to keep away."

"Really? Who's your cousin?"

She grinned again. "I think you know him. Hector Acosta."

CHAPTER 15

Monica's jaw dropped. "Cousin Gabriela came to your pajama party?"

It was Saturday morning and we were having breakfast at Café Madeline before Monica's cannabis shop opened and way before anyone would think of showing up at the Palace.

I nodded. "Hector's cousin."

Monica was in her forties, Chinese-American, and only ever wore workout clothes. I'd never known her to work out. Now she rolled the sleeves of her fleece jacket up in preparation for attacking an extremely flaky spinach-and-cheese croissant. "And Raul's cousin," she said.

Raul Acosta, Hector's brother, had been murdered at the Palace. I'd found his body on my first day there. I'd never known him, but Monica had. They'd worked on something having to do with her running a completely legal pot shop and him coming from a family of notorious crime lords. Reformed crime lords, as Hector was often at pains to stress.

"Gabriela's some sort of computer type, isn't she?" Monica asked.

"A programmer," I nodded. "She's working on something with robotics. She told me a little bit about it last night."

A glint appeared in Monica's eye. "I wonder if she's reporting back to Hector about you."

I was spared answering this by the arrival of Lisa at our table. "Everything okay with you two?"

"This is so good," Monica answered, her mouth full of croissant. She made a waving motion, inviting the café owner to join us.

"Can you sit for a minute?" I asked her.

She glanced around and apparently found the bustling shop under control. "Are you two talking about McMillan?" she asked as she pulled out a chair, speaking the developer's name in a whisper.

"We were just about to." I turned to Monica. "Have you found anything out?"

She took a gulp of coffee before answering. "I asked around other shop owners I know in the area, and it seems like a lot of people have been getting interest from a lot of different realtors lately. I mean, that happens all the time in this market, but when you put it all together this seems different. It's more...strategic." She seemed pleased with her choice of word.

The cranberry scone I'd wolfed down suddenly turned into a rock in my stomach.

"A lot of different realtors?" I asked. "Not just McMillan?"

"No, but I figure if he's trying to buy up whole blocks, he might use proxies, you know? So people don't realize what's happening and hold out for more money."

"That sounds like something a conniving snake would do," I nodded.

"Please," Lisa said. "McMillan gives conniving snakes a bad name." The look on her face was grim. "I heard the owner of the nail salon is definitely selling. That makes me the only holdout on this side of the street."

"That probably means you can name your price," Monica offered hesitantly.

"There is no price." Lisa's eyes flashed in anger. "I put every cent I had into a mortgage on this place because I was sick of being at the mercy of landlords raising my rent. I own this building, and I'll be damned if I'm going to let myself be ousted—" She cut herself off, shaking her head. "Sorry. I'm just sick of being pushed around."

I put my hand over hers. "Don't apologize. You have every right to be angry. And nobody should be able to force you out."

"Damn right!" Monica raised her coffee cup in a toast.

I turned to her. "What about the Palace? Is McMillan trying to buy our side of the street, too?"

She shook her head. "Nobody's made me any offers. I was going to shoot an email to the other owners, asking them, but then I held back." She scrunched her forehead. "I thought, if they don't already know McMillan is making offers, I don't want to tell them, you know? Just in case one of them might want to sell if the price was right. I don't want to start the thing we want to stop."

I nodded. "I'll check again with Robbie. Although I'm sure she would have told me if she'd heard anything about it."

"You haven't talked to her?" Monica seemed surprised.

"I talked to her yesterday, but there was a lot of other stuff going on." Other stuff like my husband proposing to another woman all over the tabloids.

"Ugh. I heard," Lisa said. "I couldn't believe it. Ted seemed so nice whenever he came in here. He really seemed like he wanted you back."

"He's good at that," I said. "Seeming."

"How are you?" Monica asked.

"I'll be fine," I said automatically. Then I saw the way they were looking at me. "Okay, I'm a mess. Ted still hasn't had the guts to even send me a text and my lawyers are getting cagey all of a sudden and I think I got all of three minutes of sleep last night. But I *will* be fine."

"Of course you will," Lisa said. "But let me get you a slice of my chocolate peanut butter tart anyway. Chocolate and peanut butter make everything better." She squeezed my shoulder before leaving the table.

"No offense to Lisa's tart," Monica said. "But I've got something that will actually help you sleep." She started rummaging around in her bag.

"Oh, that's okay. You know I'm not a huge fan."

What I meant was that I'm not a huge fan of cannabis products. I'd tried enough to know that I generally preferred a glass of wine. Or maybe a bottle. Which, okay, maybe wasn't the healthiest way to cope, but I was going through something, all right?

Monica ignored my protest and pulled something out of her purse, sliding it to me across the table. I looked at it warily.

"A meditation CD?"

She gave me a very Monica look. It managed to combine a sort of accepting tranquility with a grounded been-there understanding. She had a deep streak of empathy that had brought me to messy tears with just such a look before. But not in a crowded café.

Monica had gone through much worse than being left by a philandering husband. Hers had been abusive, and when she'd fled him it hadn't been to the warm embrace of new friends and enjoyable work doing something she loved. She hadn't been nearly as lucky as me.

"What are you smiling about?" she asked me.

"I just have to tell Robbie something," I said. "I don't need to look back to the movie stars of the forties for my strong leading lady role models. I've got them right here."

"That's nice," she said. "But you should still take the CD. And the tart."

Oddly, I wasn't thinking about the snake McMillan, my rat of a husband, or the murder of Callie's boyfriend as I crossed the street to the Palace. I was thinking about Gabriela. Before she'd gone into the auditorium to see the movie, I'd told her to say "hi" to Hector for me. Now I found myself wondering why I'd done that. If I wanted to say "hi" to Hector I just had to send him a text. Or call. In fact, given that he'd once bugged my office (for my own protection) I might only have to say it out loud from my desk.

So why was I making a big deal of it in my mind? Why was I wondering if he'd tell her to say "hi" back, and send us all into a ridiculously eighth-grade level of social interaction? I had enough to think about without Hector and his perfect hair and his deep dark eyes working his way into my head.

I had Ted to think about. And the inevitability of a messier divorce than I'd imagined. And I had the Palace to think about, finding ways to protect it from real estate pirates and make it profitable. I had June's event to think about. And Warren's murder. There was no room for Hector in there.

But damn if he wasn't there anyway.

Late that afternoon I once again opened my office door to find Callie in residence. This time she wasn't using my computer. She was lying on the couch looking at her phone. On her back with her hair in a great cloud around her she looked a little like a high-tech Ophelia, or one of Esther Williams' waterlogged chorus girls.

"Escaping from your mother again?" I asked her.

She didn't answer until I'd sat at the desk. Then she turned to me. "Are people just basically, like, awful?"

"I'm guessing you're still on social media."

She sat up. "The police aren't telling me anything, and I just keep looking at what everyone else is saying. But nobody actually knows anything, you know? Because the police aren't telling anyone anything. So what they're all saying could literally all be just...nothing, right?"

"Have you watched *The Women* yet?" I asked her.

She blinked. "I mean, I've seen it before."

"Remember how everybody gossips all the time? How Rosalind Russell hasn't got a nice thing to say about anyone, and they all pass rumors and scandal around through the manicurist?" I said.

"Jungle Red," Callie replied. "If you ask to get your nails painted Jungle Red you get the good scoop."

I looked at her. "The Internet is today's manicurist. Everybody's just passing their story around. Everybody's trying to outdo each other's scandal. And none of it is any more true now than it was back then."

She nodded, then took a deep breath. "I get that. And you're probably right. But I'm pretty sure Warren was seeing someone else. People have been sending their condolences to this girl named Ingrid. They're all treating her like she was his girlfriend."

Ingrid. Brandon hadn't gotten the other woman's name, but someone named Ingrid sounded like someone who would be tall and blonde.

"Do you know her?"

"No. I only saw her profile because some of my friends are friends with some of Warren's friends who are friends with some of her friends."

I assumed she used the term "friend" loosely. "How are you feeling?"

She gave me a look. "Can you possibly know what it's like to find out your man's been cheating by reading it online?"

"I have a vague idea."

"It sucks."

"Amen, sister."

The Women
1939

If you're familiar with this film, the first thing you think of is probably the cast. All women. Not one man. But the tagline on the original lobby poster says it all. Under the glamorous images of Norma Shearer, Joan Crawford, and Rosalind Russell are the words "It's all about men."

It really is. Every scene, whether in an Upper East Side spa, the dressing rooms of a posh boutique, or the ladies' lounge in a swank nightclub, is overflowing with gossip about who's marrying whom, and whose husband is stepping out.

So don't go looking for anything that will pass the Bechdel test here, my friends. But do go looking for whip smart dialogue, glittering performances, and a window into the lives of the wealthy housewives of 1939. Or at least the lives as Clare Boothe Luce, who wrote the play this film is based on, saw them. (But keep in mind that Mrs. Luce famously had no use for society women.)

From the first time we meet Mary Haynes (Norma Shearer) with her daughter Little Mary (a blessedly un-cutesy Virginia Weidler) their entire conversation revolves around Daddy. Even the consult with the family cook is all about what Mr. Stephen Haynes should be eating to stay trim and how often he's staying late at the office these days. Hmm.

We meet Mary's friends, all of whom have something to say about marriage and infidelity. Peggy (Joan Fontaine) a newlywed with stars in her eyes, Edith (Phyllis Povah) a self-absorbed mother of seven girls, Nancy (Florence Nash) a sharp-eyed "old maid" writer and Sylvia (Rosalind Russell) a society wife who dips her every word in gleeful poison.

The term "frenemy" should have been invented in 1939 and applied to Sylvia. Everything with her is "I'm devoted to her, but" or "She's my very dearest friend in all the world, but..." The "but" is that Sylvia is awful. Hilarious, but awful. Mary finds out about her husband's affair from the manicurist Sylvia deliberately sends her to.

Okay. Now Mary knows. Stephen has fallen prey to a shop girl named Crystal (Joan Crawford!). Mary's mother counsels her to turn a blind eye, as she did when Mary's father strayed. "It's about the only sacrifice spoiled women like us have to make." Okay. Mary tries, and it works for a while, until...until...the fashion show.

Fashion alert! The fashion show is in color! The gowns, the gloves, the hats! Costume designer Adrian really outdid himself here. It's all fun, but it also tells us what the idealized day of an idealized wife would be. Frolicking at the beach. Feeding animals at the zoo. Attending a bizarrely formal garden picnic, and a yet more formal evening of theater and cocktails. All frills and no substance. But such pretty frills. And did I mention the gloves?

It's in the dressing room after the fashion show that wife and mistress finally meet. They both want the same nightgown. (It costs $225, roughly four grand in today's dollars, and Crystal boldly says she could use a few more like it.) She's opened an account in Stephen's name.

This is happening, people! Dressing Room Wars! Mary, in an elegant evening gown, is on the moral high ground, telling Crystal she isn't worried. "You're even more typical than I'd dared hope." (In 1939 that was how you called someone a basic bitch.) Crystal, in shiny lingerie, knows sex will win over high morals any day. When Mary condescendingly tells her Stephen wouldn't like anything as obvious as what she's wearing, she shoots back with "If anything I wear doesn't please Stephen, I just take it off." Crystal drops the mic.

Inevitably Mary winds up on the train to Reno for a quickie divorce, where she meets a Countess (Mary Boland) and a chorus girl (Paulette Goddard). The countess, whose first husband left her rich and whose next three husbands tried to kill her, is a fool for love, and a lovable one. Miriam the chorus girl is sharper and more cynical. She's been seeing a married man. They all wind up at the same divorcee dude ranch, run by Marjorie Main, playing Marjorie Main like nobody else can.

It's all terribly sad and wistful until Sylvia shows up at the ranch. Her husband has been seeing someone, and it turns out that someone was Miriam. Which leads to a brawl that lets Rosalind Russell prove herself a queen of physical comedy. It strikes me that if she had married a Cuban band leader, instead of Lucille Ball, history might have turned out entirely differently. And now I need to go watch *Stage Door*, which features both Lucy and Roz expertly cracking wise while Katherine Hepburn learns to act. Oh! And Russell and Ball both played Mame! But I digress.

Cut to eighteen months later. Crystal has managed to

land Stephen in marriage. We find out that she's in the penthouse now, and the shop girl's dreary life has become nothing but one long bubble bath. We also find out she's cheating on Stephen. Oh, Stephen. You're so stupid.

How will it end? In gorgeous evening gowns, of course, and with nails painted jungle red.

The men:
For everything this script has to say about women, it totally objectifies men. Stephen isn't a person. He's just the prize they fight over. And he doesn't seem to have much agency. He's manipulated by all of them (poor thing.) Crystal's phone call, convincing him to ditch his wife and come over for her fake birthday, is a master class in twisting a lover around your little finger. None of which means I'm on his side. Team Mary!

The blame:
Somehow it ends up being Mary's fault that her marriage breaks up. In fact, Miriam makes quite a speech about how Stephen's infatuation was like a fever, and Mary shouldn't have gone off and left him alone, staggering helpless as a lamb around New York with no protection from the she-wolf who was after him. Um. Okay. But Mary buys into it, telling her mother "I had the only one I ever wanted. If it hadn't been for my pride..." Really? So he gets a pass on his infidelity? The only problem is that you didn't keep looking the other way? Really?

Mommy dearest:
Mary's mother always has something to say. "You mustn't kid Mother, dear. I was a married woman before you were born." And even offers comfort of a sort after the divorce. "Living alone has it's compensations, heaven knows it's

marvelous to be able to spread out in bed like a swastika."
Like a what? A *what*?

Movies My Friends Should Watch
Sally Lee

CHAPTER 16

Callie and I were interrupted by the chime of an incoming text. She glanced down at her phone then jumped to her feet, panic all over her face.

"What is it? Have they found something?" From her reaction I assumed the text must be from the police.

She was already on her way to the door. She paused only long enough to shoot me a look filled with dread and say, "Don't come downstairs."

Of course I followed her downstairs.

The five fifteen was well underway, so there weren't any customers loitering in the lobby. There was just Brandon, Albert, and a woman I'd never seen before who seemed to be playing some weird of game of tag with Trixie.

With Trixie.

"Yoo hoo!" Trixie stood in front of the woman, waving. "I'm here! I'm right here!"

The woman, middle-aged with thick dark hair and a stylish red raincoat, had her eyes closed and her hands raised.

"I feel a presence," she intoned.

"Of course you do, honey," Trixie said helpfully. "I'm right in front of you." She reached up to touch one of the woman's hands.

"I feel you," she said. "So cold...so cold..."

"Mom!" Callie yelled.

The woman opened her eyes and beamed at her daughter. "Calandria, she's here!"

Trixie looked up at me. I was still on the balcony stairs, taking it all in. "Nora, I think she can feel me!"

"Mom, go out to the car!"

The woman (Callie's mom!) waved her hands dismissively. "Don't be silly, dear. There's a Presence here that's trying to communicate." She started to raise her arms again, but before she could get going Callie grabbed both hands and pushed them down.

"Mom!"

Callie may have been an incredibly laid-back, screamingly cool young woman. A grad student and filmmaker. But in that instant, she was every kid that's ever been embarrassed by their mother at a school drop-off.

"Mrs. Gee!" I said, practically floating down the last few stairs. *This* was why Callie didn't want me to meet her mother. "What an absolute pleasure to meet you, finally."

Callie glared, Brandon and Albert backed away, and Trixie practically scampered with excitement.

"Nora, tell her to try again. I really think she might see me!"

"You must be Nora!" Mrs. Gee shook Callie's grip off and extended both her hands to me. "Callie's told me so much about you."

"*Mother*," Callie said, a valiant attempt at sternness totally undercut by her desperation. "Let's *go!*"

"Don't go," Trixie wailed. "Nora, don't let—"

"Don't be silly," I said. "Please, Mrs. Gee, let me get you a cup of coffee. An espresso maybe?"

Brandon snapped to attention and rushed to his coffee machine's side.

"She can't stay!" Callie insisted, at the same time her mother said, "How lovely, thank you."

"Nora," Trixie turned to me.

"We're going!" Callie grabbed for her mother's hand again.

"I can do a mocha," Brandon called from behind the counter.

"Nora," Trixie said again, more insistently.

"We're staying, Calandria," Mrs. Gee said, disentangling

herself from her daughter's grasp.

"Mom!" Callie shouted.

"Nora!" Trixie yelled.

"What!?" I yelled back.

Everybody—that is, everybody with a pulse—froze and stared at me.

I swallowed, then put on my most gracious face. "What...would you like to drink?" I asked Mrs. Gee.

She tightened the belt of her raincoat and gave Callie a look which said something along the lines of "that will be all from you, young lady." Then she turned to me, her expression changing to long-suffering maternal forbearance. "An espresso would be wonderful."

Brandon leapt into action.

"Nora," Trixie whispered. "Do you think she could see me if she tried really hard?"

"Pardon me for asking, Mrs. Gee—" I began.

"Lillian, please," she said.

"Lillian," I nodded. "May I ask what you were...what, um..." I raised my hands tentatively, the way she'd been doing.

"Of course!" she trilled. Clearly, she was dying to talk spirits.

Callie slumped onto the bottom stair with the air of someone who's given up.

"I have a very small talent," Lillian confided. "For perceiving things beyond the veil."

Callie groaned.

"Which my daughter does not appreciate," she finished.

"Is that me?" Trixie asked. "Am I beyond the veil?" She waved a hand in front of Lillian's face.

Albert cleared his throat. "Do you mean ghosts, Lillian?"

She turned to him. "I do, Albert."

I assumed they'd introduced themselves to each other before Callie and I had arrived on the scene.

"She means me!" Trixie told me.

"Well, now, that's very interesting." Albert adjusted his

glasses. "Because I happen to have seen a ghost here myself once or twice. Just a glimpse, mind you."

At that point Callie hid her face with her hands.

"Was it the usherette?" Lillian asked breathlessly.

"Still here!" Trixie said, waving.

"Yes it was," Albert said. "I knew her in life, you know, when I was a very young boy."

"Oh, my. You must tell me everything!"

Albert began to tell Lillian the story he'd once told me. That he'd been there on the fateful night in 1937 when Trixie had fallen from the balcony to her death. That since then, over the years, he'd caught a glimpse of her now and then. Just a few times. But enough to make him believe.

While he was holding Lillian in rapt attention, I caught Trixie's eye. She came over, shining with excitement.

"Touch her again," I said very softly, covering my mouth.

Trixie looked bewildered.

"Lillian," I said. "I think she felt you."

I'd felt Trixie once, when I'd forgotten she was a ghost and tried to hug her. Mrs. Gee was right. It was a very cold sensation.

"Oh!" Trixie exclaimed. "Oh, that's so smart!"

She went back to Lillian, and just as Albert was wrapping up his tale, she put her arms around her and placed her head on the woman's shoulder. Her jaunty little cap would have tickled Lillian's ear, if it hadn't been ghostly.

Lillian froze. She looked startled, amazed, and just a little freaked out.

"She's here!" she said, breathlessly. "I can feel her!"

I held my breath, looking at the expression of utter joy on Trixie's face. Then Brandon, who had been about to hand Mrs. Gee her coffee, tripped and sent it splashing all over her. Trixie yelped in surprise and vanished. Brandon blushed a furious red, stammering apologies, and Callie leapt to her feet.

"That's it!" she announced. She grabbed her mother's hand again and half-dragged her to the door. When they got there she turned around, held up one finger, and made a general announcement. "We will never speak of this again!"

Oh, yes, we would.

Trixie didn't show up again that night. That happened sometimes. She just went *poof* when she was startled. It wasn't something she could control, she didn't remember where she'd been, and she didn't come back until she'd recovered.

Trusting that I'd see her again sometime soon, I locked up after the last show and practically froze on the walk home to Robbie's guest house. I turned up the heat as soon as I got there, and had just opened a bottle of her wine, thinking *Bless you, Robbie, for your excellent taste in pinot* when the phone rang.

"Robbie, I was just thinking of you."

"I'm psychic," she said. "Or I'm a terrible person for just having realized that I never answered your question about that real estate guy."

"Stan McMillan," I said, taking a seat on the couch and wrapping myself in one of her cashmere throws. "And you're not a terrible person, you just respond to my emergencies in order of priority. I'm a terrible person for having so many emergencies."

"Let's blame Ted, shall we?"

"Always. What did you find out?"

"McMillan hasn't tried to get in touch with me, and I asked Mitch, and he hasn't had any offers either."

Mitch was Mitchell Black, a sitcom director that Robbie worked with occasionally. He owned a quarter of the Palace, and he'd been the one who'd offered Robbie the chance to buy her share of it a few years ago.

"Oh, thank goodness." I sank into the cushions and took a massive sip. "And nobody's contacted Monica, so unless McMillan's gone after Tommy, we're in the clear." Tommy May was the fourth co-owner of the Palace. Theoretically I should have met him by now, since he lived only about an hour away, in Palo Alto, where he'd made a fortune with some app.

"Right. Um, about that..."

I sat up. "Tommy's had an offer."

"Just a couple calls," Robbie said quickly. "Which he hasn't even returned. I didn't talk to him, but he told Mitch somebody's been trying to get a meeting with him."

"McMillan," I said, certain of it. "Or one of his proxies."

"It doesn't matter who," Robbie reassured me. "Because even if it is your snake developer and even if he did go after Tommy and even if Tommy wanted to sell, that would still only be one quarter of the owners."

All good points, which did nothing to loosen the many knots in my stomach.

"You know, Nora, if Tommy is open to selling, he doesn't have to sell to some developer," Robbie said. "You could buy him out."

I'd be lying if I said this hadn't crossed my mind. Not buying out Tommy specifically, but having some ownership of the Palace. I'd feel so much better knowing I had some control over its long-term fate.

"How much do you think McMillan is offering?" I asked.

"Probably less than the gigantic divorce settlement I hope you have coming."

"Right. But I don't have it yet."

"You will. I mean, this is box-office-king Ted Bishop you're divorcing. You know better than anyone how much he's made."

I knew because I'd put my own career as a screenwriter on hold so I could act as Ted's manager and agent. His unpaid, unacknowledged manager and agent.

"Think big," Robbie said. "Manifest an abundant universe."

"You've been listening to those self-help books again."

"I'll send one to you," she promised.

"Great. I've already got a guided meditation that's supposed to help me sleep."

"Then get off the phone and sleep, girl. Everything's fine. And everything's going to get better."

I could only hope she was right. I could hope, and I could push the lawyers to do their lawyering quickly. Because suddenly I needed that settlement. Forget buying a house—I needed to buy into the Palace. It was the only way I could be sure of protecting it. Because tearing it down was unthinkable. And not just because it was a landmark and a bastion of all the films I loved. It was something more than that.

If the Palace was ever torn down, what would happen to Trixie?

CHAPTER 17

The next morning I staggered into Café Madeline for caffeine, wishing there was some way they could legally serve it intravenously.

Ted still hadn't made contact, I was still no closer to figuring out who had killed Warren, Lisa's café was still on the chopping block, the Palace was officially under attack, and—this should probably go without saying—the meditation CD had not worked.

I didn't see Lisa as I waited in line for my life-giving elixir, and it occurred to me that if McMillan had murdered Warren all Lisa's troubles would go away. Likewise the threat to the Palace. Which was kind of a terrible thought. But then, Warren had already been murdered. It wasn't like I was wishing him ill. Simply wanting the police to catch his killer wasn't wrong. And if catching his killer coincided with getting the evil developer who had designs on my theater off the streets, so much the better.

I took my coffee to go. I had to make the final preparations for hosting the evil developer, along with June's Howard Realty and another firm of realtors from the neighborhood. The big event would be the next day, and there was a lot to do.

If this were an episode in one of Robbie's TV shows, I'd be able to come up with some insanely clever way to get McMillan to publicly confess to Warren's murder in front of the crowd of realtors tomorrow. Could I tamper with the PowerPoint deck, showing incriminating evidence? That would be easier if I had incriminating evidence. What I had was a picture of a man in a bar. Try as I might, I couldn't see how that would get McMillan to crack.

*   *   *

Once inside the Palace I called out to Trixie but got no response. The scene with Callie's mother must have really taken it out of her. Still, I'd been hoping she'd be there. It made me nervous when she stayed away too long.

I went straight to the auditorium. The latest electric bill had been staggering, so I didn't turn all the house lights on in the big space. Every little bit helps. I made my way to the stage by the glow of the exit lights. There had once been an orchestra pit—home to a massive Wurlitzer organ—but those glory days were gone. The pit had been covered over and in its place were steps leading up from the auditorium to the stage.

I found the control panel on the wall and turned on the stage working lights, then flipped the switch that raised the screen. Thank goodness that equipment was fairly new, and it went up without a hitch to reveal the stage as a large empty space, but a filthy one. I went down the back stairs to the supply room and hauled up a broom, a bucket, and a mop, for what would no doubt be a less-than-glamorous day in show business.

When I was just finishing up with the mop, I heard the blare of the 20th Century Fox overture and knew Marty had arrived. A few minutes later he called down from the window of the projection booth.

"I've set up that projector for tomorrow, but I hope you don't think I'm going to sit around all day pushing the 'Next' button for a bunch of slides about real estate. I have a life, you know."

"Good morning to you too," I yelled up to him.

"You don't have to yell. The acoustics in this theater are fabulous. Did you hear what I said?"

"You won't be here tomorrow," I confirmed. "I know. Enjoy your day off. One of June's people will be on slide duty."

There was silence from the booth. High above the balcony seats I saw Marty's head and shoulders silhouetted at the small window. "Someone I don't know?"

"Yes."

"Someone I don't know will be in my booth?"

"I'll make sure to tell them not to touch anything."

More silence.

"I mean, he's absolutely going to be here tomorrow."

I jumped when I heard this, not realizing that Callie had entered the auditorium. I shielded my eyes, the glare from the lights on the stage making it hard to see the seats below.

"What are you doing here?"

"I'm directing the filming tomorrow. I need to mark the camera positions and figure out the lighting." She started up the steps.

"I thought you were going to have someone else do it." We'd talked about it soon after Warren's death, when she'd been at her most distraught.

"Yeah, that was before I found out Warren had another girlfriend." She gave me a meaningful look. "I'm in a different head space now."

"Sure," I said slowly. I understood better than most the effect that finding out you'd been cheated on could have on a person. "But I'm still not sure it's a good idea. You may be angry at Warren, and hurt, but you're still grieving."

"Maybe I am," she acknowledged. "But I'm also a professional." She gave me a defiant look. "This is a paid directing job that I'll be able to put on my résumé, and I'm not going to let my stupid feelings about stupid Warren get in the way of that. I can handle it."

I looked at her closely. She seemed okay. In fact, she seemed more assured than I'd ever seen her. It occurred to me, not for the first time, that she might actually be a good filmmaker. "I know you can handle the work," I said. "Just be sure you can handle being around all of Warren's colleagues."

Because being around everyone probably meant hearing gossip from everyone, and Callie didn't need to put herself through that.

"I'll be fine," Callie insisted. "Where's the podium going to be?" She gave me a steely-eyed look I didn't know she had in her.

Okay, then. "Right over here." I stood where the podium would go the next day and she whipped a piece of chalk out of her pocket and marked my clean stage floor.

We couldn't position the actual furniture, the podium and chairs that June had requested, until after the last show that night. But we marked where everything would go, so Callie could figure out how to direct the lights and where to place her camera crew to get maximum coverage.

At only one point did I attempt to bring up the subject of what had happened in the lobby the day before.

"How's your mom?"

Her chin went up. "Don't you dare make fun of her."

"Callie, trust me, I'm the last person on earth who would ever make fun of someone who believes in ghosts."

She inspected me for visible signs of mockery but seemed satisfied that I was serious. "Good."

"I would, however, totally make fun of someone for being embarrassed by their perfectly charming mother."

She rolled her eyes and went back to her measurements.

I still couldn't believe Lillian was sensitive to Trixie's presence. In my long night of not sleeping I'd thought about what it would be like to tell her. To tell her everything about Trixie appearing to me after I got conked on the head by a light last fall. To tell her how we chatted, and what a delight Trixie was. To tell her how she'd saved my life.

It would be such a relief to be able to tell someone. But I knew I couldn't do it. Because even if Lillian believed—especially if Lillian believed—it wouldn't end there. She'd want to tell the whole world. And that story had only one ending: a friendly attendant telling me to swallow the nice pills in a cozy little psych ward somewhere in wine country.

My fears about this were very specific.

"Is the microphone stand adjustable for height?" Callie

interrupted my thoughts. "Stan McMillan is probably taller than June."

"Yes," I said, irritated simply at the sound of McMillan's name. "I can't believe Detective Jackson hasn't gotten back to us about him." Although there was nothing new in Jackson not telling me anything. But the picture we'd sent him proved the shady developer was at the bar that night. I'd at least expected an acknowledgement.

"I wonder if he's even, like, talked to him yet," Callie said. She glanced over at me. "You probably shouldn't put that there."

I'd just rolled a simple freestanding backdrop into place behind the spot we'd marked for the chairs.

"You've got that on a trapdoor." She came over and moved the backdrop. "It's tilting a bit, see? One side is lower than the other."

I could see the outline of the door clearly. I'd noticed it and its twin on the other side of the stage when I'd been mopping. I'd also seen them from below many times, boarded-over high in the ceiling of the basement prop room. Back when the Palace still had live shows, magician's assistants and vaudeville villains had disappeared through them to the delight and amazement of the crowds.

I let her reposition the backdrop, trying to figure something out that was just on the tip of my brain. I really wanted McMillan to be the killer, because I really wanted him locked up and in no position to threaten the Palace. But me wanting him to be the killer didn't make him the killer. There was still the scenario of the tall blonde girlfriend who might have killed Warren in a fit of jealous rage.

But I kept coming back to the text Warren had sent that night. He'd said June would "lose it" if she knew who was at the bar. McMillan had been there. And then I realized what had been bothering me. McMillan had been there, sure, but he hadn't been alone. He'd been sitting across from someone.

Which left me wondering: Whose wrist was just visible across the table from McMillan in the photo I'd seen? Who was with him at the bar that night? And what did they know?

CHAPTER 18

I was taking the back stairs up to my office when my phone rang. A number I didn't know with a 213 area code. Los Angeles.

I answered it warily, assuming some enterprising tabloid blogger had gotten my number.

It wasn't a blogger.

It was a law firm.

It was my law firm.

They were calling from a conference room at their office on Wilshire Boulevard. All of them were on the phone. The entire firm.

To tell me some very bad news.

"Everything?" Robbie's voice carried the same stunned disbelief I'd felt. I'd called her as soon as I got off the phone with the lawyers. "You're saying everything's gone? All the money? All the real estate? All the—"

"Everything," I said. "Ted sold the house in Beverly Hills, the flat in London, the beach house in Maui. He sold all the investments. He liquidated all the accounts. He spent every single penny." I still couldn't believe my husband—my *husband*—had done what the lawyers had described.

"Spent it?! We're talking about millions! Tens of millions! How could he—What could he possibly have spent it on?"

"A movie." I didn't recognize my own voice. "He invested everything in a movie."

"Like hell he did!" she fumed. "Nobody's that stupid."

"He isn't stupid," I heard myself say. "I had no idea he was this smart. This deceitful and underhanded and calculating and smart. I had no idea he was stalling for time all the while he was up here begging me to take him back. I knew he was a good actor, but I had no idea he was that good. I had no idea." I looked around my office and didn't recognize anything I saw.

"How could he do that? I mean, not even how could he be so awful as to do that, but practically speaking, how could he sell the houses without you knowing? Weren't you on the deeds?"

"Not since he incorporated a year ago," I told her. "We did it for tax reasons. Our accountant pushed for it, but I wonder if Ted was thinking of this even back then. If he was already planning to leave me. And to take everything."

He'd gazed longingly at me while his lawyers and accountants had siphoned everything away. He'd made promises. He'd sworn oaths.

He'd lied, and lied, and lied.

"Once he incorporated, all our holdings became assets of the corporation," I told Robbie. "And now it's all gone. I didn't have to sign a thing. I didn't know a thing."

"But it can't be *gone!*" she protested. "Even if he did invest it all in some movie—"

"I know," I said, wondering why I sounded so calm when I was so very not calm. "My lawyers have been trying to track it all since I told them to start up again on Friday." Was that only two days ago? "Ted has a complete paper trail that says he sank everything into a movie production that's gone bankrupt. On paper it looks like he's lost everything."

"Like hell he has!" Robbie fumed. "He's hidden it all somewhere."

"Of course he has. He must have." Because that's who he was. The man I'd been married to for a decade. "The lawyers say they'll get accountants and court orders and..." I stopped. I couldn't go on. I heard the lawyers' voices echoing in my head, but none of it meant anything. The only thing that was real was that Ted had betrayed me. Again. In a way I never even saw coming.

"It's going to be awful," I told Robbie. "And it's going to take a long time and it's going to cost a fortune in legal fees and there's no guarantee about anything at the end of it."

"Oh, Nora." What else could she say?

"It isn't the money," I said. "I mean, yes, it's the money. But it's the lying, you know? The cold-heartedness of it. He knew what he was doing to me all the time he was up here swearing how much he'd changed. He knew what he was doing to me a year ago before I even heard the name Priya Sharma."

"I could kill him," Robbie said.

"Don't," I sniffed. "That would just make the paperwork harder."

The only reason I was able to make it through the day is because I didn't tell anyone else what had happened. Somehow, I did whatever it was I did until the audiences for four showings had come and gone from the Palace.

Suddenly it was after ten at night. I was alone in the office, thinking everyone had left, until I heard familiar clomping footsteps in the hallway. Marty appeared at the door. "What's the matter with you? You've been weird all day. Are you getting sick or something? Because I will *not* deal with a hundred realtors on my own tomorrow."

"I didn't even think you were coming in tomorrow."

He narrowed his eyes. "Sure. I'll just let god-knows-who hang out in my booth all day unsupervised. That sounds like me."

I waved a hand. "Do what you want."

He glared. "You are sick. What's the matter with you?"

"My husband stole all my money." Quick, like a Band-Aid. I just said it.

"He—" For once Marty seemed to be at a loss for words. He stood in the doorway for a moment, then came into the room and almost sat in the chair opposite my desk, then apparently decided not to. So he just hovered awkwardly, he *loomed,* over the desk.

"I don't know why I told you." I looked up at him.

"Do you need me to...*hug* you or something?" Nothing in his body language said he was up for that, but I appreciated the offer.

"I'm good," I told him.

His relief was palpable. Then, "Do you need me to beat the shit out of him?"

"That's sweet," I said. "Or something. But no. He's left town anyway."

"For that I'd travel."

I laughed, which I think freaked Marty out even more.

"Never mind," I told him. "It's with the lawyers now." I stood up. Too quickly, as it turned out. I got a little lightheaded.

"I'll walk you home," Marty said. He was looking at me like I had one blue wire and one red wire and he didn't know which one to cut.

"Don't worry about me. I'm going to hang out here for a while. I'll finish getting the stage set up for tomorrow."

"I can help," he said.

I looked at him. "Marty, you should leave. Because you're being really nice. It's weirding me out. And if you aren't careful, I might decide to take you up on that offer of a hug."

His eyes widened.

"Go home, Marty. Or go see your not-a-boyfriend. And if you do see him, and he's arrested Stan McMillan, let me know, okay? I could use some good news."

"Why would—" Marty started to ask, then he saw the look on my face. "Sure. I'll go see David. I'll let you know." He still looked indecisive. "And you just..." Here's where most people would say "take care" or something equally considerate. Marty said, "You just don't lose your shit until after the realtors thing, all right?"

"All right."

A furniture rental truck had delivered the podium and six red chairs to the back-alley entrance earlier that day. We'd left them wrapped up in plastic and bulky moving blankets at the back of the stage. Now I raised the screen and began unwrapping everything, placing the furniture in the spaces Callie had marked with chalk that morning.

It didn't take long. And then I looked around. The auditorium was dark, and the stage was lit only with working lights. And a ghost light, a bare-bulb floor lamp that was always supposed to stay lit on a theater's stage, either to keep the ghosts away or to comfort them, depending on who you believe. I'd seen this old one in the basement a while ago and I brought it up tonight. With the screen up and the stage in use it seemed appropriate. Plus I liked the idea of keeping it lit for Trixie. I hadn't seen her since the incident with Callie's mom. It had only been one day, but it had been quite a day. I missed her.

"Trixie?" I called out.

"What?"

I yelped a little, because it wasn't Trixie who answered me.

"Sorry!" Callie came into view at the bottom of the steps to the stage. "I didn't mean to startle you. What were you saying?"

I'd been calling the name of my friend. The one who'd died over eighty years ago.

"I was saying 'Testing,'" I told Callie.

She gave me an odd look. "People usually wait for the microphones to do a sound check. I'll have a sound guy for that tomorrow."

"Why are you here?"

"Marty called me." She crossed the stage and slung her bag onto one of the carefully placed chairs before flinging herself into another one.

"I take it he told you." I sank into the chair next to her.

"I mean, he told me that the shittiness of Warren having another girlfriend paled in comparison to the epic shittiness of your shitty husband," she said.

"It's not a contest. At least, it's not a good contest."

She shrugged.

"You didn't have to come," I told her. "I'll be fine."

"I literally knew you were going to say that." She reached over to her bag and pulled out a bottle of wine. "Sooo...I brought this with me."

I looked from the bottle to her.

"Okay. You can stay."

CHAPTER 19

"Joan Crawford in *Mannequin*!" Callie announced proudly.

"Oh, good one." We were still on the Palace's stage, listing every movie ever made where a strong, smart, brave, and true woman got mixed up with a low-down rotten skunk of a man. *Mannequin* (1937, Joan Crawford and Spencer Tracy—as the good guy, not the skunk) was pretty obscure but met the criteria.

"Go, Joan," Callie said. "Leave that sleazy what's-his-name—"

"Alan Curtis," I said. He'd played the skunk.

"Leave that sleazy Alan Curtis in your badass dust, Joan!"

We'd already listed many movies. Also, we'd finished the wine.

"Ohmygod!" I slapped my forehead. "What's wrong with me? *Born Yesterday*!" (1950, Judy Holliday and William Holden).

"Yeeessss," Callie exhaled. "Don't you just love Judy Holliday? I mean, isn't she the greatest comic actress of literally *ever*?"

"Of literally ever," I agreed.

"Let's have a Judy Holliday film festival," she proposed.

"Done," I promised.

"To badass women!" Callie raised her paper cup in a toast, attempted to drink, and then held the empty cup upside down. "All gone."

"How sad," I said. "Mine too. Did you only bring one bottle?"

She nodded. She'd sunk further into the red chair on the stage.

"Then it's a good thing I'm here," a voice called from the shadows.

I held my hand up to shield my eyes. "Who's there?"

Monica loped up the stairs to the stage. "I heard you were holding a wake."

I raised a hand languidly "Not wounded, sire, but dead," I quoted Katharine Hepburn from *The Philadelphia Story* (1940, Hepburn and not-a-skunk-at-all Cary Grant).

"One bottle of wine did this to you?" Monica took in our reclining forms.

"One bottle of wine, no food, and the treachery of men," I told her.

"Uh huh." She joined us in the semicircle of chairs. Tomorrow there would be a no-doubt rousing panel discussion on mortgage rates on this stage. Tonight there was sisterhood.

"How did you get in?" I asked Monica. "And why are you here?"

"I have a key," she said. "I'm an owner, remember? And yes, I locked the door behind me." She settled in and gave me a look. "Callie called me. She told me what that...*actor* did."

I really thought she was going to say something other than *actor*.

"We're not talking about him," Callie informed her. "We're not wasting our breath on him. He's nothing but a minor character. Nora's the star."

"Aw, thanks Calandria."

She gave me an evil look for using her full name. I'd have to remember to do it more often.

"Very sensible," Monica said. "Waste no more time on men. I've only met a handful in my life that were worth putting on lipstick for." She grinned. "But were they worth it." She turned to Callie. "I brought you what you asked for," she rummaged in her bag. "Nora, I know you don't normally—"

"Chocolate!" I said. "That's what this party's been missing."

"It's *very* strong chocolate," Monica warned, holding up a purple-wrapped bar. "And I don't mean in terms of cocoa powder."

I held out a hand. "I'll proceed with caution."

"And I'll order pizza," Callie whipped out her phone.

Sisterhood.

*   *   *

"I mean, I know there's no comparison between some guy I've been dating for a few weeks having another girlfriend and your husband of ten years publicly humiliating you," Callie leaned forward in her chair, elbows on her knees. The three of us had decided to stay in our little pool of light on the stage until the pizza came.

"Thanks," I said. "And let's not forget his thievery."

"And thieving from you," she agreed. "But at least you can yell at your man. I can't even do that. All I see all day long is what a great guy Warren was." She held up her phone, then dropped it into the chair in disgust. "You literally can't speak evil, right?"

"You can with us," Monica assured her.

"Ugh." She collapsed back into the chair again, staring up at the rafters. "And, I mean, I may not even be in the right. What if *I'm* the other woman? What if Warren was seeing this Ingrid person first? She might have every reason to hate me, or be just as hurt as I am or something."

"Do you think she knows about you?" Monica asked.

I'd been only half listening since Callie had mentioned the possibility of my yelling at Ted. Maybe it was the wine and the pot-laced chocolate talking, but yelling at Ted sounded like a really good idea.

"I mean, if she didn't before Warren died, she must know now," Callie said. "She must be looking at the same posts about Warren that I am."

I sat up. I could yell at Ted later. And I undoubtedly would. But right now something else was tickling my brain. "What do you know about Ingrid? Is she a realtor? Does she work for June?"

Callie shook her head. "She works at a bank. She does, like, mortgage loans."

"That's realtor-adjacent," I said, more to myself than to her. "What else do you know about her?"

"I mean, more than I want to. She's twenty-seven, and she went to Stanford and majored in economics. So she's definitely smarter than me."

"Stop that," I told her. "What else?"

"She bakes." Callie made a face. "She posts pictures of cupcakes and things. Do you think she seduced Warren with cupcakes?"

"Oooh, I'd kill for a cupcake," Monica said.

Cupcakes sounded amazing, but I was trying to focus, and Callie was now on a roll. "She has a tiny little dog that she carries around in a Chanel bag," she went on. "Fake Chanel, I think."

"I would hope," I said.

"His name is Picante—the dog's. And she has two nieces and a nephew who are obsessed with Harry Potter."

"You got all of this from her social media?" Monica asked.

"And tons more. I know she'd be a Hufflepuff from one quiz and that she's Carrie Bradshaw on another. She's lived in her place for a year and just painted her bathroom a super dark shade of blue."

"This is getting scary," Monica said. "You don't even know a person and you can know all this."

"She's had her job at the bank for about two years. She volunteered with AmeriCorps for a few years after she graduated. So she's literally a perfect person. Did I mention that she bakes? And she's a Carrie?"

"Again, stop it," I told her. "Is this bank in the Financial District?"

"Yeah, it's—wait." Callie stared at me. "Why? Do you think she was there that night?"

I thought about it. "At the rate Warren and his friends were posting selfies and live streaming, anyone would have been able to find him at that bar. And if it was near where Ingrid works..."

Callie was already on her phone. "She works at Chase," she said. "It's just a couple blocks from the bar." She looked up at me. "What if she was there?"

It was possible, but..."We didn't see another woman in the pictures from that night," I reminded her. I'd been looking for something incriminating in Warren's interactions with tall blonde Sam when we'd looked, so I was pretty sure I'd have noticed anything incriminating with this tall blonde Ingrid. "I don't think Warren was getting cozy with anyone after you left. At least not on camera."

Monica didn't let that detail get in the way of a good theory. She jumped up. "But Ingrid might have been there! She might have seen Warren with you! What if that's how she found out he was seeing someone else?" She turned to me. "What if she saw him with Callie and hung back, watching? What if she stayed out of sight until everyone taking pictures left, then went home with Warren? What if they argued and she killed him!" She seemed a little breathless.

"In a fit of jealous rage." I couldn't help myself from saying it.

"I mean, that would make it my fault, wouldn't it?" Callie said, looking stricken. "That would mean Ingrid killed Warren over me."

"Warren's still a two-timing dog," Monica reminded her. "He has only himself to blame."

"Sure, but he didn't deserve to get *killed* over that. I mean, I wouldn't have killed him over Ingrid. I'd have wanted to, for a minute, but...oh." Her eyes widened.

"Right," I said. "A minute is all it would take in the right circumstances."

"Like being wasted and furious and having a blunt object close at hand?" Monica said.

We all sat with that for a moment. Then Callie spoke again. "But she seems so nice. Online, I mean."

"Bakers have killed before," I said. I couldn't think of any offhand, but they must have.

Monica held up a finger. "If Ingrid did it, what does that real estate guy have to do with anything?"

"That's a different theory," I said. "That's the Warren-saw-McMillan-up-to-no-good-and-had-to-be-silenced theory." That was still my favorite.

"I mean, I hope it's that one," Callie said. "Just because I'm not in it anywhere."

"And who knows?" Monica offered. "It could be something we haven't even thought about yet."

"True," I said. But I didn't think it was. I thought either Other Girlfriend Ingrid had something to do with Warren's death or Evil Snake McMillan did.

And the evil snake would be in the theater tomorrow.

Born Yesterday
1950

If you learn nothing else from this movie, learn these two things. One: Judy Holliday was a comic genius who should be worshiped on a regular basis just for what she could do while she was humming. And Two: if William Holden gave us all personal civic lessons, voter participation in this country would soar.

This is a movie about America and politics and corruption and toxic masculinity and entitlement and bullying, and also about overcoming all of the bad stuff because you realize you deserve the good stuff. Like information and education and the god-given right to wear glasses if you need them. This is a movie about redemption.

Judy Holliday plays Billie Dawn, a former chorus girl who is now employed as the long-suffering girlfriend of the horrible Harry Brock (Broderick Crawford), a guy who made a fortune in junk and now wants to buy a few politicians so he can get even more of whatever he wants.

Brock, Billie, and their entourage are first seen checking into a plush Washington D.C. hotel. Billie casually throws a pile of furs at the bellboy. She has more. These are vulgar people, with Brock an obnoxious blowhard who constantly tells anyone who'll listen how much everything costs.

Once they're in their hotel suite Brock's lawyer shows up (played by Howard St. John, who communicates in every gesture that he knows he's sold his soul.) He warns Brock that a journalist is coming up to interview him. An intellectual. Someone who could be trouble. The lawyer's advice? "Take him in, then he doesn't go poking." Because Brock has a lot of shady things to hide, and of course the journalist, like everyone, will have a price.

Not so! Because the journalist in question, Paul Verrall, is played by the eternally stalwart William Holden, looking bookish and sexy in a tweed sports coat and glasses. (Why William Holden isn't on every advertisement for glasses in existence is a mystery to me.) Paul is smart and he's dreamy, and the instant he meets Billie we see that he is also kind.

About that meeting. Brock bellows for Billie to join the men and she enters wearing a floaty dressing gown with a shy smile and does a little almost-curtsy thing that tells you that this dumb blonde is also sweet and a bit self-conscious and just plain endearing. And then she opens her mouth. All of Brooklyn is in her voice, and the loud raspy grating of it in contrast to her wide-eyed bombshell looks is *everything*.

It's here that Brock reveals himself. He yells at Billie in front of everyone. "Do what I'm tellin' ya!" (This is something he yells a lot.) Humiliated, Billie leaves with exaggerated dignity. The lawyer says something, and Brock literally pushes him around. Paul the journalist observes it all. He's seen bullies before.

Because all movies need a plot, Brock hires Paul to give Billie a little educational polish. He's afraid she'll embarrass him in his meetings with crooked politicians and their judgy wives. Ever look in a mirror, Brock? No? Okay, moving on.

Now we have a chance for Paul to teach Billie (and us) everything that's wonderful and unique and problematic and inspiring about America. Not that she's really up for it, at first. She's happy being dumb. She has everything she wants. "As long as I know how to get what I want, I'm happy." Sure, Paul agrees. "As long as you know what you want." Got it. She's not going to be happy with mink coats much longer.

Paul takes her to monuments, he answers her questions, they talk and talk and talk and eventually her questions aren't that dumb anymore. He gives her books, and more importantly, he gives her glasses. And when she starts to see what's going on things gets really, really good.

Speaking of really, really, good, I can't say enough about what Holliday does with this role. She goes from dumb blonde punching bag to righteously defiant heroine without missing one single beat along the way. There is so much detail in her performance, from the way she hums to herself while playing solitaire to the actual sparks we see lighting in her as she realizes, to her own amazement, that she's got the smarts and the power and the right to see Brock for what he is and take him down.

"Hey, you think we can find somebody to make her dumb again?" Brock eventually asks. But no. That's the thing about a little learning. Once you understand the world you're actually living in there's no going back.

There's No Describing Comedy:
If you've never seen what Judy Holliday could do with physical comedy, I can't explain it to you. It's just brilliant, but you have to see it yourself. For a master

class, I encourage you to search online for the gin rummy scene from *Born Yesterday*. I could tell you how she puts out her cigarette, adjusts her jewelry, arranges and re-arranges her cards, and does a dozen other little things, but you really owe it to yourself to see it. Please!

Judy, Judy, Judy:

Judy was also a singer. If you haven't seen *Bells Are Ringing,* you have such a treat in store. Why am I even talking about *Born Yesterday* when *Bells Are Ringing* is out there? In any case, she sings—both with and without Dean Martin. She even released an album of torch songs, titled *Trouble is a Man.* The next time you're up at three in the morning killing a bottle of wine and wondering how you can have been such a fool for some guy (or is that just me?) just throw on "I Got Lost in His Arms" and know you're not alone.

Movies My Friends Should Watch
Sally Lee

CHAPTER 20

"What about *Fried Green Tomatoes*?" Monica offered.

She'd been right about a little of her chocolate going a long way. We were now back to listing movies with badass women and skunk men, and Monica was trying her best. "Or, what's the one where Angela Basset sets her husband's stuff on fire?"

"*Waiting to Exhale*," Callie and I answered in unison.

"I mean, I see where you're going," Callie told her. "It's just that they're so...new."

"1991 and 1995, respectively," I said. I blamed the chocolate for the fact that I couldn't remember who had starred in *Fried Green Tomatoes*.

"Right. I forgot you guys don't like anything made within living memory," Monica said.

"Kathy Bates!" I called triumphantly.

They both looked at me.

"From the movie," I explained. "*Fried*...hey, didn't we order a pizza?"

Which for some reason they thought was hilarious.

"Maybe we should start selling pizza at the concessions stand," I mused.

"No." Callie shook her head. "I don't want the Palace to smell like pepperoni."

"Good point. I don't either." But I had to figure out some way to generate more income. Without the promise of a settlement in the foreseeable future I didn't have hope of being able to perk up the Palace finances, let alone buy Tommy's share and keep it out of McMillan's evil clutches. "Maybe I should get a job."

Monica glanced around the empty theater. "Don't you have one?"

"Sure, but right now I'm costing the Palace." I wasn't costing it much, but that hadn't been an issue so far. "If I got a real job, I might make the kind of money I could put to use around here."

"That's crazy," Callie said. "You shouldn't put your own money into it."

"Not unless you're an owner." Monica gave me a thoughtful look.

"Besides, what could you do?" Callie asked. "For a job, I mean."

"Ouch," I said. "What does anyone do?"

We thought about it.

"Joan Blondell would get a job on Broadway as a chorus girl," Callie suggested.

"That's helpful. But we're nowhere near Broadway. Lana Turner would flip burgers at a hash house."

"What language are you guys speaking?" Monica asked.

"You don't want to flip burgers," Callie said. "Think of your complexion. Greer Garson would become a secretary."

I shuddered. "Too many paper cuts. How about—"

But whatever brainstorm I was about to have was cut off by the sound of a loud banging coming from the lobby.

"The pizza!" Callie said. "That must be the delivery guy."

"I'll go," I stood quickly. Which perhaps wasn't the best of all possible ideas. "I can still afford to pay for a pizza."

I left them on the stage and went up the aisle of the darkened auditorium. When I opened the lobby door, I saw a figure silhouetted at the glass double doors to the street.

I paused. When Ted had come roaring back into my life he'd shown up silhouetted at those doors. Why had I ever let him in? Oh, right, because I'm an idiot.

I crossed the lobby, realizing that I couldn't actually pay for the pizza after all. I'd left my purse in my office. I'd have to run up and get it after I let the pizza guy in.

"I'm so sorry, but—" I opened the door and stared. There was a guy holding a pizza, but he wasn't the pizza guy. He was an unbelievably attractive guy, with dark eyes and thick lashes. Also, his hair was perfect.

I don't know how long we would have stood there staring at each other. My excuse was the wine and Monica's chocolate. I don't know what his was.

In any case, the spell was broken by a delighted squeal from behind me. Trixie's unmistakable voice. "Nora, it's the dishy Latin Lover!"

Yes it was.

"Hi, Hector."

"Let him in, Nora!" Trixie looked from Hector to me in confusion. "What's the matter? I thought we liked him."

I held up a "one minute" finger to Hector and closed the door in his face. Then I turned my back to him.

"Trixie, I'm really glad to see you, but can you do me a favor and let me talk to Hector by myself?" I didn't know much, but I knew enough to know I was in no condition to keep up a conversation with a very observant man and a very chatty ghost at the same time.

Trixie dimpled. "Sure, honey," she said. "I get it. You want to be alone with Ramone Navarro here."

"Something like that."

"Good luck, honey. I always did like this one better than that phony husband of yours." She vanished.

Great. Even Trixie had seen Ted was a phony.

There was a tapping from behind me, and I turned to see Hector, pizza still in hand, giving me raised eyebrows. I opened the door.

"You should know that I'm not in the habit of waiting patiently for a woman after she's closed the door in my face," he informed me. "Particularly when I've just tipped a delivery boy rather extravagantly to let me deliver her pizza."

I looked at him. "You should know that I have a bad history of letting the wrong man into this lobby in the middle of the night."

"I am not the wrong man."

"Time will tell."

He handed me the pizza. "May I come in?"

I'd forgotten that his words weren't so much accented as spiced with South American inflections. I looked up at him. He looked good. His hair was very slightly longer but still fell just right. His skin was a little darker, no doubt from all that South American sunshine. Which for some reason made me wonder about tan lines.

I looked away as a flash of something behind him caught my eye. The tiled walkway leading from the lobby doors to the sidewalk was lit dimly by streetlights. But something brighter flared briefly across the street. The glass door of Café Madeline had just closed.

That was weird. I blinked, straining to see. There was another light, coming from inside the café. A dull orange glow.

I looked back to Hector, who was gazing at me with an amused expression. "I don't usually have this effect—"

"Call 911." I shoved the pizza back into his arms and moved past him to the sidewalk.

"Nora?"

"Call 911!" I yelled again. Because I could see it clearly now. The café was on fire.

I ran across the street and wrenched at the door handle. It was locked.

"Nora!" Hector yelled. I looked around for something to break the glass. The fire was still small, in the open kitchen area behind the counter. If I could get to it quickly...

"Move!" Hector shoved me out of his way. He'd taken off his leather jacket and wrapped it around his right hand. Now he punched at the glass door, shielding his eyes with his other arm.

The glass broke and he reached in to unlock the door. I hoped our breaking and entering would set off an alarm and summon help.

The fire was growing, smoke filling the room, billowing along the ceiling. Hector ran straight to the fire and began beating at it with his jacket.

"Hector, no!" I yelled.

"Get out!" He thrashed at the growing fire. I couldn't tell if he was making any progress. I ran to the other side of the counter, to the hallway leading back to the restrooms. Mounted on the wall was a fire extinguisher. I hadn't spent every morning at the café for the past three months without noticing something. I unlatched it from its mount and pulled the pin as I raced back around the counter.

Hector was backing away from the growing flames, still beating at them with his now-singed jacket.

"Hector, move!" I pointed the extinguisher at the heart of the fire. I pulled the handle and was knocked back a step by the force of the foam shooting out the nozzle. But it did it. It put the fire out.

I kept shooting foam until the extinguisher was empty. Then I kept shooting air until Hector took the thing out of my shaking hands. He dropped it to the floor and put his arm around my shoulders, leading me back through the café to the street.

We were both coughing, covered in soot and splattered with foam. Hector still held his smoldering jacket. I knocked it out of his hand and stomped on it until the embers were out. We both turned to the sound of approaching sirens.

"I will say this for you, Nora." He slung his arm around my shoulders again. I glanced up at him. His hair was still perfect. "It's never dull with you."

CHAPTER 21

The police had been summoned by the alarm we'd set off, then they called the fire department and the EMTs, who bandaged a cut on my hand from the fire extinguisher that I hadn't noticed. We both got oxygen and were draped in thermal blankets and told to wait in the open back of the EMT truck.

I glanced up at the theater to see Trixie's anxious face at the office window above the marquee. I smiled as best I could behind the oxygen mask and gave her a thumbs up, shielding my hand from Hector's view with the blanket. She waved back, mouthing something I couldn't make out but looking relieved.

Then the doors to the theater burst open and Callie and Monica spilled out into the street.

"Nora!" Callie yelled. "What's—"

"Are you all right?" Monica called as they crossed the street to us. "What happened?"

I lifted the mask from my face. "I'm fine. There was a fire at the café."

"And you went in there?" Monica stared at my bedraggled state. "What's the matter with you? Are you crazy?"

"You tell her, lady," a passing fireman said. He looked over at Hector and me. "You guys are idiots. You should never have gone in there. Nothing is worth getting killed over."

He was right. Of course he was right. But my instinct hadn't stopped to check with my common sense when I'd seen Lisa's café on fire. My instinct could have gotten me killed. And Hector. I shivered.

Callie was still staring at all the flashing lights and activity in confusion. Monica was fussing with my blanket. "You guys should go home," I told them.

This seemed to call Callie back to her senses. She looked at me. "I'll put some coffee on. Tell everyone the lobby's open if they need to come in and get warm." She turned on her heel and left. She hadn't even noticed Hector.

"I'll bring some CBD salve over in the morning," Monica said. "It'll help with—" She stopped. She'd just noticed the man sitting next to me.

He removed his oxygen mask. "Hello, Monica."

"Hector?" She looked from him to me.

"He came with the pizza," I explained.

"You...why are you here?" she asked him.

"Yes." I turned toward him. "Why are you here?"

He looked at me. "Gabriela told me you said 'hi.'"

Served me right.

The police asked me a hundred questions, but I really couldn't tell them anything. I'd seen a glint of light. I hadn't seen the person leaving. It had been dark. The door had been locked. I had been an idiot.

Hector had his turn with the authorities as well. He hadn't seen anyone leave the café. He'd broken the window and unlocked the door.

"Were the deadbolts thrown?" a policewoman asked. "There are three deadbolts on the door. One at ground level."

Hector shook his head. "Just the lock in the knob."

The policewoman had written that down.

Eventually Lisa arrived, wild with panic at first, then ridiculously grateful when she was told what Hector and I had done, and finally grimly stoic as she assessed her ruined kitchen.

"They say I'm lucky," she told me. We were standing in the street after hugs and tears, staring numbly at the storefront. She was wearing pajamas with a raincoat over them. "We'll have to close for repairs, but they don't think it looks structural."

"Who could have done this?" I asked. There was no doubt in my mind that someone had deliberately set the fire. Someone I'd not managed to see skulking away.

"Who do you think?" she said bitterly. "McMillan. I told him I wouldn't sell, and he thinks he can burn me out." She looked at me, hatred lighting her eyes. "I'll see him in hell first."

It was close to three in the morning before I made it back to the lobby, where Callie was cleaning up as the last of the first responders cleared out.

I slumped at the stool behind the candy counter. "You should go home now," I told her. "I'll call for a ride." I reached for my phone.

"Thanks," Callie said. "But you don't need to. One of the guys said he'd give me a lift." She glanced out the door, where an extremely fit young EMT was hovering.

"That makes sense." I gave her a vague wave. "Thanks for everything. I'll see you tomorrow."

"OMG tomorrow," she said, eyes widening. "I need to get some sleep."

OMG tomorrow was right. "Are you still up for it?" I asked.

"Of course. Are you?"

"I don't think I have a choice."

Callie went off with her EMT, leaving me alone in the lobby. At least for a moment.

"What's happening tomorrow?" I hadn't even noticed Hector had gone anywhere, but now he was coming down the balcony stairs, carrying my jacket and bag.

"We're hosting a corporate event," I told him. "It's part of my ingenious strategy to keep the Palace from financial ruin." Although at the moment I was having trouble keeping my head from falling to the counter.

"I always suspected you of genius." He draped the jacket over my shoulders.

"We'll be playing host to a hundred or so realtors," I said. "Including the one who may have murdered Warren, and probably set that fire tonight. Oh, and also he wants to tear down the Palace."

"Now you have my undivided interest," he said. "I suggest we find someplace that's open at this late hour where we can get a strong drink and you can tell me everything that's been going on."

Speaking of the late hour...I looked at the clock above the lobby doors and groaned before I could stop myself. "I'd love to," I told Hector. "But I really do have an early morning tomorrow. How long are you going to be in town?"

He leaned one elbow on the candy counter in a casual sort of way. "That depends. San Francisco has become very appealing to me. I'm thinking of buying a place."

"Oh." Okay. Lots of implications. Most of which I wasn't prepared to deal with. But there was one intriguing possibility. I looked up at him again. "I can introduce you to a realtor."

His glance sharpened. "The murderer?"

"The possible murderer," I hedged. As much as I loathed him, MacMillan was only one possibility. We still had Other Girlfriend Ingrid to think about.

"That sounds delightful. Meanwhile, since you have such an early morning tomorrow, and since it is so very late tonight, perhaps I should take you home."

He held out a hand and I took it.

"Yes, perhaps you should."

CHAPTER 22

I woke up reeking of smoke and panicking about the day ahead. After Hector had left me at my door I'd fallen into bed and crashed for all of three hours. Now I had to shower and get to the theater, where shortly a hundred realtors would arrive expecting coffee and pastries. Which would have been no problem if Café Madeline, where I'd placed an order a week ago, hadn't been set on fire last night.

I called for a rideshare and went to a different bakery, a place off Clement that specializes in croissants, where I bought everything they'd let me, which surely wouldn't be enough. The driver helped me carry it all up the walkway to the lobby doors.

"What happened across the street?" he asked, taking in the café's boarded-up door and blackened interior.

"Arson," I told him.

I set all the boxes out on the candy counter and started a pot of coffee. Even with the new espresso maker there was no way I'd be able to keep up with the demand. I was just about to dash out again when I heard keys jangling at the lobby door.

Albert and Marty came in with a blast of cold morning air, carrying just a hint of last night's smoke. Marty had six pink bakery boxes stacked in his arms, and Albert was pulling a cart filled with bottled juices.

"I have never loved anyone more than I love you two right now," I told them.

Marty scowled.

"Callie called us," Albert said. "She told us what happened to the café. We've got this and she's sending one of her film crew to

Peet's to bring in gallons of extra coffee."

"You guys are amazing," I told them.

Marty set his boxes on the counter next to mine. "The Palace has a reputation to uphold," he said. "No fire is going to make us look bad."

"Go, team Palace!" I held up my hand for a high-five.

He looked at my raised palm as if it carried the Ebola virus. "Don't."

Go, team Palace.

Sam Beach was the first to arrive. June had asked her to come early and make sure everything was on schedule. The last time I'd seen her I'd wondered if she'd been Warren's other girlfriend. Now I knew about Ingrid, but Sam was still interesting to me. After all, she was one of the last people who'd seen Warren that night.

She was smartly dressed and professionally groomed in a way I'd never have been able to pull off at seven in the morning. Her hair was smoothed back, and she wore a tailored gray pantsuit and chunky heels. She had a laptop bag over her shoulder and carried a file box filled with nametags and stuffed folders for all the attendees. "Careful!" she yelped as I took the box from her. "I've got all the nametags arranged alphabetically so I can just spread them out on the registration table." She took in the near-empty lobby. "Where's the registration table?"

Albert and I had just finished setting up two long folding tables at the bottom of the stairs. He was smoothing tablecloths over them. "Here you go." He patted the table. "All ready."

The morning went on like that, with us keeping just inches ahead of whatever was needed. Sam handed her laptop off to Marty, who took it up to the projection booth to do a dry run, then she arranged her materials while Albert and I laid out what the agenda called a "Continental Breakfast."

"What are we going to do about lunch?" Albert asked quietly.

"That's under control," I told him. "We weren't using the café for that. The party rental people should show up at ten, when everyone's gone into the auditorium. They'll set up tables and chairs in the lobby and on the balcony landing. We've got three food trucks who'll park on the street outside so everyone can order whatever they want and—Oh! Let's get the cones out to keep the parking spaces open." I'd gotten the city permits and traffic cones the week before. "Once we get through the arrivals and breakfast, everything should go smoothly."

Looking back on things, I really should have knocked wood.

Callie and her film crew arrived about an hour before the guests were scheduled to start showing up. Three guys with cameras, one young woman for sound, and a production assistant who pushed a wheeled black trunk full of equipment into the lobby. With five gallon-sized insulated boxes of hot coffee on top.

"You're my hero," I told her.

Callie told me their names, but as they were all dressed in black and moved swiftly and unquestioningly at Callie's commands, I just mentally referred to them as the film ninjas.

"Who's going to be in my booth?" Marty called down from the balcony landing.

Sam, seated at the registration table, looked up from her phone. "I will. What do you need?"

He stared down at her. "I hooked your laptop up to the projector, and it's all working. The only thing in the room you're allowed to touch is your keyboard. Got it?"

Her eyebrows went up and I went over to her. "Don't worry, Marty. Sam won't break anything in the booth."

He gave me a "you better hope not" sort of look, then went back to his lair.

"Sorry," I said to Sam. Then I told her what several people had told me when I'd first come to the Palace. "Marty isn't really that bad."

She waved a hand. "Trust me, I'll have him eating out of my

hand by the lunch break."

I could only wish her well. As I was turning to go my gaze fell on the nametags she'd arranged in neat alphabetical lines on the tabletop. One name jumped out at me. Ingrid Barnes.

I glanced at Sam, but she was communing with her phone again. I slid the nametag on top of Ingrid's away to see her job title. "Director of Mortgage Operations, Chase Bank."

Warren's Ingrid. She had to be.

I left Sam and went over to the candy counter, now covered with open boxes of baked goods. I'd left the printout of the agenda there. Yep. Other Girlfriend Ingrid was speaking on the panel about mortgages.

Which meant both of my suspects in Warren's murder would be onstage at the Palace that day.

I went upstairs to the balcony, where I knew Callie had set up her film production area. None of the realtors would be seated up there, and it would give her a birds-eye view of the proceedings. I'd expected to see her looking at her monitors or something, but she wasn't there. Two of her ninjas were still setting things up. They didn't know where she was.

I checked the break room, but found only Albert and Marty, who hadn't seen her. I told them about Warren's other girlfriend being on the agenda.

"Oh, dear." Albert blinked rapidly behind his thick round glasses.

"My money's on Callie," Marty said. "If some blonde gets tossed off the balcony this afternoon, I'll know who did it."

"Well, that's just rude." I didn't have to turn to know it was Trixie who'd just spoken behind me. "Some of us are a little sensitive on that subject."

I didn't turn around.

"If you see Callie, warn her," I told the guys. Only then did I turn, giving Trixie a subtle nod to come with me to my office. When we got there, I closed the door and really wished I could hug her.

"Nora, honey, are you okay? I was so worried last night! I saw you two running across the street, and I would have given anything to be able to help."

"I'm fine," I told her, collapsing onto the couch. She perched on the arm opposite me, her feet on the cushion. I rubbed my eyes. "I just have to feed a hundred people, make sure everything goes off without a hitch, keep Callie from having a meltdown when she realizes Ingrid is here, possibly keep Ingrid from having a meltdown when she realizes Callie is here, introduce myself to Stan McMillan and get him to say something incriminating about setting the fire or killing Warren, and hope Lisa doesn't show up to kill McMillan for setting the fire."

Trixie nodded. "That seems like a lot."

"Plus make June so happy that she tells everyone what a great venue the Palace is so we can stave off financial ruin." I took a breath. I had no intention of letting Trixie know the Palace itself was in danger. "Luckily I got plenty of sleep and a hot, nutritious breakfast," I told her.

"Oh, now I know you're fibbing," she said. "Is there anything I can do to help?"

I smiled at her. "I'm just so glad to see you."

I couldn't believe everything that had happened since the scene in the lobby with Callie's mom.

"Callie's mom!" I said. "How weird was that?"

"Oh, Nora, do you think I'll be able to communicate with her? I mean, not like with you, but a little bit?"

"Maybe," I said. "Let's hope so." Then something she said caught up with me.

"Trixie." I looked at her with new eyes. "There is something you can do to help today."

She sat up, clapping. "Gee, that would make me happy. What is it?"

I got up and went to the desk, opening my laptop. "I'm going to show you some pictures of a man. His name is Stan McMillan and he's a realtor. He'll be here today. What?" A look of disappointment had appeared on her face.

"Nothing. It's just that I thought we liked the Latin Lover."

I blinked. "We do like the Latin—Hector," I told her. "This has nothing to do with that. This has to do with eavesdropping on MacMillan today and seeing if he says anything incriminating to anyone about either the fire last night or Warren's murder."

Trixie's mouth formed an O. "You want me to *spy* on him," she said, eyes shining.

"Well, you're in a pretty unique position to overhear things," I said.

"Oh, Nora!" She hopped off the sofa and scampered over to the desk. "Show me his picture! Oh, I can't wait! I know just what to do. I don't even know how many times I've seen *Mata Hari*!"

Since *Mata Hari* (1931, Greta Garbo and Ramon Navarro) had ended with Garbo on her way to a firing squad, I wasn't sure that was the best of all possible training, but on the other hand, I didn't see how Trixie could get into trouble.

She was very excited. "Oh, I wish I could wear a costume! I'll be the best spy ever, why—"

But what she would be was cut off by a quick rap on the door, followed by a voice calling from the other side. "Nora?"

"It's Hector," Trixie said. "Quick, show me the pictures."

I opened the web page that I'd looked at before, wishing Trixie could tap the keys and navigate from there—not that tapping would be the only issue with teaching a hundred-year-old ghost about web surfing. But I got a page of images up as I called "Come in!" to Hector.

He opened the door looking rested and refreshed, as if he hadn't attempted to beat a fire into submission with only his leather jacket the night before. I noticed he wore a different leather jacket this morning, black, over a pale gray cashmere sweater and dark jeans.

"Golly," Trixie said. She was looking at Hector, not the collection of photos.

I tapped the screen to refocus her attention, then looked back to Hector, about to tell him how very busy I was at the moment. Until I caught a whiff of something. "What's that amazing smell?"

He held up a white paper bag. "A scrambled egg sandwich on a multi-seed bagel," he said. "I had a feeling you wouldn't have eaten a decent breakfast."

"I knew we liked him," Trixie whispered.

CHAPTER 23

I had one bite of bagel before Callie appeared at the door.

"The guys said you wanted to see—Hector!" She'd been moving fast. She practically skidded to a stop when she took in Hector lounging against the edge of my desk.

"How nice to see you again, Callie. I hope you're recovered from last night's events?"

Even with everything going on, Callie went on auto-flirt, straightening her spine and lifting a hand to run through her luxurious hair. She then said something to him in Spanish, the only word of which I caught was "*hola.*"

Hector grinned and responded, also in Spanish.

I really did need to make it a point to learn more Spanish.

"What are you doing back in San Francisco?" She switched to English.

"I heard a few things," he said. "First, *mi querida*," he said. "I didn't get a chance last night to give you my condolences on your loss."

She looked confused for a moment, then, "Oh, right. Warren. Thanks."

It seemed her period of heavy mourning had ended.

Hector nodded his head toward me. "I heard a few things about her as well."

"That I have terrible taste in husbands?" I said lightly.

He looked at me. "That your husband has proven himself entirely unworthy of you."

Trixie made a sound that was somewhere between an "ah" and

a sigh.

"Oh," Callie said softly. "That's so good."

I was glad she spoke, because I couldn't have. Something about the way Hector looked at me. "Eat your bagel," he said gently.

I wasn't the least bit hungry.

"Sooo...Nora?" Callie said. "The guys said you were looking for me?"

I glanced at her. Oh, right. Callie. And Ingrid. Right.

"Have you seen the agenda?" I asked her.

"I mean, sure, but what about it?" She'd pulled out her phone and was looking at something.

"The fact that Ingrid will be speaking on the mortgage panel this afternoon."

She looked up from her phone. "*Ingrid* Ingrid?"

"Ingrid Ingrid."

Hector looked confused. "Who's Ingrid Ingrid?"

Trixie smothered a laugh. Not that anyone else would have heard her.

"She's the skank Warren was seeing on the side," Callie told him. "I mean, unless I'm the skank he was seeing on the side. It's all super confusing." She looked at me. "I should, like, talk to her. Shouldn't I? I think I should. I should, right?"

"It's your decision." I glanced at the clock above the blackboard. "But don't take too long to decide, she should be here soon." Yikes. She might be here already. "And you shouldn't talk to her alone." I said. "Let's not forget she may have murdered Warren." I bit my tongue before I finished that sentence with "in a fit of jealous rage." I stood. "Do you want me to go with you?"

She shook her head. "I'm fine. The filming comes first. I'll wait until after everything's over to find her."

"Okay, let me know when you need me." I shot Trixie a quick glance. "We're good, then?"

Trixie nodded, curls bouncing. "I'll find Mr. McMillan, Nora. I'll tell you every word he says."

"We're good," Callie said at the same time.

"Okay, kids," I said, channeling my inner Judy Garland. "Let's go put on a show."

"Hang on," I said to Hector on the way to the balcony stairs. I popped my head into the projection booth where I found Marty explaining the intricacies of some ancient-looking piece of machinery to a seemingly enraptured Sam.

"You two okay?" I asked.

"Go away," Marty told me. "Samantha is asking extremely intelligent questions. I don't know why you made such a fuss about her being here."

Sam, her face turned away from Marty, winked at me.

I went on my way, marveling at her.

From the balcony landing we could see that people had started drifting in. Most everyone stopped and stared as soon as they were through the lobby doors. This didn't surprise me. The usual response from newcomers was to look up at the chandelier and around at the vast expanse of ornate lobby and say something along the lines of "Wow." These were seasoned professionals, used to assessing a space as soon as they walked in, but they behaved just like everybody else. There were a lot of "Wows" and "Whoas" and not a few low whistles. All of which gave me a warm, proprietary glow.

And then it gave me a cold chill. These were, after all, realtors. And some of them worked for McMillan. They were probably seeing condo potential when they looked at my beautiful carved ceilings. Which made me want to kick every single one of them back out onto the sidewalk.

"Where's McMillan?" Hector asked. "And which one's Ingrid?"

I pulled myself together, scanning the crowd. "I don't see him yet," I said. "And Ingrid could be any one of the tall blondes." Which was an issue. Looking down on the crowd I could only conclude that half of the women in real estate were blonde. At least in this neighborhood.

"I'll check the registration table to see if she's picked up her nametag yet," I said. Then I saw June sweep in through the door. "No I won't," I corrected myself. "You do that while I go make June happy. You're looking for Ingrid Barnes."

"Yes, ma'am." I heard a note of mockery in his voice. I didn't have time to answer it.

"June!" I greeted the realtor warmly at the bottom of the stairs. She kissed me on each cheek, something she'd never done before.

"Nora, the place looks great. I was so worried when Cora told me about the bakery last night. But it looks like the fire was contained."

"It was," I said, not wanting to get into the part Hector and I had played in containing it. "We're absolutely fine over here. Can I get you some coffee?"

"Cora will," she said. Which is the first time I noticed the slender middle-aged woman who stood a half pace behind June, checking her watch.

"I don't think we've met," I said to her. "Nora Paige. I manage the Palace. Let me know if you need anything."

"Cora's one of my assistants," June said before Cora could speak. "I'm not sure you've officially met before."

"Hi." The woman seemed a little worn around the edges, but then anyone would look dowdy when standing next to June's polished elegance. I was sure I did. She took June's coat as she slipped it off, first taking her purse, then handing it back to her when the coat was removed. Their movements had the look of often-performed choreography.

Cora's eyes went to her watch again. "We're running a bit behind." She shifted June's coat in her arms. "Is there someplace I can put June's things?"

Albert appeared at my elbow. "Let me take you to the coat rack," he nodded in the direction of the rolling racks we'd placed on the far side of the lobby. "And then let's get you some breakfast."

She gave him an appreciative smile. "I just need coffee for

June," she said as he led her away, checking her wristwatch again. "We'll barely have time for a run-through."

"She seems efficient," I said to June.

"Quite honestly, I'm not sure how much longer I'll keep her on." She rolled her eyes. "Personal issues. You know the way it is." I didn't, but I didn't get a chance to respond before she smoothed her hair, saying, "Now, let's get started."

"Do you want to mingle?" I asked her. "Or shall I show you the podium and get you miked?"

"Let's get to business," she said.

I made an "after you" gesture in the direction of the auditorium doors and followed her through what was turning into a lively crowd in the lobby. Coffee was being drunk, pastries were being eaten, networks were being...networked. We were pulling it off. I caught Hector's eye as we passed the registration table and he gave me a slight shake of the head. Ingrid hadn't checked in yet.

Onstage in the auditorium, Callie's sound ninja hooked June up with a battery pack that clipped to the waistband of her very expensive skirt and a microphone that clipped to the collar of her incredibly chic jacket. Standing at the podium while another ninja tweaked the position of the spotlight, June looked utterly professional and completely at home.

"All good?" I called up to the balcony. I couldn't see anyone, with the lights trained on the stage, but I knew Callie was up there.

"All good," I heard back.

June looked around the stage. "I have to say, Nora, I'm so glad..." Then her smile tightened. She recovered quickly, but something had been there, just for a second, as she'd glanced over my shoulder.

I turned around.

An imposing gray-haired executive type was striding purposefully across the stage. He reeked of money and self-assurance and he was followed closely by an entourage of three guys and the ghost of a bubbly usherette.

McMillan.

"Stan," June said, giving him the same double-kiss treatment she'd given me. It must be her professional-at-a-professional-event greeting.

"June, you're looking younger than springtime," he said. "And who do we have here?"

I didn't immediately realize he was addressing me because I was busy trying to control the jolt of pure rage that surged through me at the sight of him while also doing my best to ignore Trixie waving and pointing at the realtor, as if I might otherwise have missed the fact that she was Mata Hari on the case.

"Nora, I'd like you to meet Stan McMillan," June said. "Nora runs the Palace and Stan runs just about everything else in the city," she laughed, sounding a little forced.

I didn't join the laugh but smiled in what I hoped was a pleasant and not at all hostile way. "So nice to meet you." I shook his hand, resisting the urge to wipe it off immediately after. This is the man who was after my theater. "If you're ready, we can get you miked."

"I'm all yours," he said easily.

"You're all hers," I told him as the sound ninja sprang up the steps to the stage, equipment in hand.

McMillan opened his (tailored, very correct) suit jacket and no incriminating evidence of his guilt in all sorts of nefarious activities fell out of his pockets. Not that I'd expected it to be that easy. But it would have been nice.

Now that I was face to face with him, I realized I had no idea how to proceed. "What were you doing in the early hours of Saturday the Fifth?" seemed a little heavy-handed, and "How dare you think you can go behind my back to buy the Palace?" would let him know that I knew, which might not be the smartest play.

"Have you two worked together for long?" I finally asked both June and McMillan, cursing myself for not having scripted something.

"Oh, years," June said, at the same time McMillan answered, "We don't really work together."

"It's more in the nature of a friendly rivalry, isn't it, Junie?" he smiled with anything but friendliness in his eyes.

I'd been thinking of him as a snake. I was wrong. This guy was a shark. And a patronizing one at that. I was willing to bet June didn't like being called "Junie."

She was spared from answering by the arrival of Cora with her coffee. "Here you are," she handed a cardboard cup with a lid to her boss. "Hello, Mr. McMillan."

He gave her a quizzical look. "Dora, isn't it?"

She blinked. "Cora." She looked at her large, old-fashioned watch. "I think we're a little bit behind schedule."

"Thank you, Cora," June said, in a way that made me think that stating the obvious was not the best way for Cora to keep her job.

Cora might have also gotten that vibe. She pulled her sleeve down and turned to me. "Nora, this man was looking for you."

"This man" was Hector, giving all and sundry a genial smile. "When Nora told me she'd introduce me to a realtor today I didn't realize I'd have my pick of the industry," he said.

Their reaction was something to behold. I watched as June and McMillan performed simultaneous, instant assessments of Hector as a potential client. Even dressed down, as he was today, there was something (that perfect haircut, the manicured nails, the yumminess of his cashmere sweater) that clearly screamed "this guy has money" to them both. They practically fell over each other to shake his hand.

"June Howard." She got there first as McMillan was somewhat hampered by the finishing touches of the sound ninja. June shook Hector's hand, smiling broadly. "What kind of property are you looking for? Residential? Something for you and your wife?"

I was just thinking "Wow, that's a little obvious," when McMillan swooped in as well.

"Stan McMillan," he puffed up somehow as he shook Hector's hand. You could practically see the testosterone. "I bet I know just what you want. Something modern, right? With sleek and sexy finishes, and views that will make them die for it."

Ugh.

"How did you know?" Hector smiled. "That's exactly what I'm looking for."

June was about to say something else, but Stan shifted to put his body between her and Hector. "Let me have my girl set up a few viewings," he said. "We'll slide you into something so smooth you won't believe you ever thought of living anywhere else."

"Sounds good," Hector agreed.

I managed not to vomit.

At this point the auditorium doors slammed open and the realtors of San Francisco began drifting in from the lobby. McMillan leaned in to Hector and said something I didn't catch as June moved into place at the podium. She didn't look at McMillan, but I saw the look Cora gave him on her boss's behalf. It was pure unadulterated hatred.

I left the stage and Hector caught up with me as I went up the aisle to stand at the back of the auditorium. "We have a word in Colombia for a man like him," he said.

"Snake?" I guessed. "He may not be the killer, but he's possibly the sleaziest operator I've ever met. And I worked in Hollywood for a decade." I watched as McMillan worked the room—Trixie hovering close by—while June waited for everyone to take their seats. "Did you see the way he cut June off? What did he say to you at the end?"

"Something my mother would never wish me to repeat," he said. "About you, as it happens. I don't know what it is about me that makes that sexist *cabrón* think I'm a sexist *cabrón*, but there you have it." He was watching the crowd.

I stared at him. I didn't press him about what specifically had been said. I could find out from Trixie later.

"I don't know if he's the killer," Hector went on. "But I sincerely hope so, because I would very much enjoy punching him in the face."

"I think I'd enjoy that, too," I said. "I mean, not you punching him in the face. Me punching him in the face."

"We'll flip for it," he said. "And there..." he put his hand between my shoulder blades and gently turned me a few degrees to the right. "In the pink tweed suit, is Ingrid."

"Oh." She was stunning. If this were Hollywood, every director I knew would be fighting over casting her in something where the camera could linger on her cheekbones. It didn't help that I knew she was a Stanford grad who volunteered for good causes and baked cupcakes in her spare time.

"Oh," I repeated. "Callie's going to want to kill her."

CHAPTER 24

I stayed in the auditorium until I was sure everything was going smoothly. I knew June would speak first, welcoming the crowd and then going into her prepared talk, after which McMillan would give the keynote. The sound equipment worked without a hitch, and June's presentation looked great on the big screen. Or, as great as a presentation on real estate could look. We're hardly talking about *An American in Paris* (1951, Gene Kelly and Leslie Caron.)

Two of Callie's camera guys were at work, one of them on the stage to June's left and another down front, shooting her from below. I assumed the third was in the balcony for wide shots.

Stan McMillan was seated in the front row. Trixie stood in the aisle in front of him, arms crossed, not letting him out of her sight. Nothing would get by her. Of course, even if she heard him clearly confess to coldblooded murder it would never stand up in court. ("Yes, your Honor, this ghost I just happen to know heard everything.") But at least if he did let something slip in front of her we'd know we were on the right track.

Also on the front row, seated three people down from McMillan, was Other Girlfriend Ingrid. I reminded myself that, as much reason as I had to hate McMillan, there was still every possibility that Ingrid had killed Warren because she found out he was seeing Callie. Still, since I suspected McMillan of both Warren's murder and of setting the fire at Lisa's café, he was the bigger target. Plus, I hated him.

Satisfied that everything was under control for the moment, I left Hector watching things and went to the lobby, where Albert had just let in the crew from the party rental company. There was another flurry of activity as I cleared away the remains of the breakfast and the hired crew put up big round tables, eight of them on the ground floor and two up on the balcony landing, with chairs for ten at each table.

Lunch hadn't begun yet, but I started prepping the concessions stand for the mid-afternoon break which would come later. Instead of the chips and cookies that they might have had at any old hotel or conference center, we were going to serve movie-style candy and popcorn. Because "It's movie-time fun when you plan your event at the Palace!" Which was a terrible slogan. I'd have to come up with something better if we were going to make a habit of this sort of thing.

After a while I heard the audience erupt in applause. June must have finished, and they must have liked what she said. A few minutes later I was surprised to see Sam at the top of the stairs.

"Everything okay?" I asked.

She came down. "I was hoping there would still be coffee."

"I just put a fresh pot on," I told her. "And there are still a few doughnuts left if you're hungry."

She shook her head and patted her completely flat tummy. "Better not."

"Is Marty running the projector?"

She made a face. "No need. Stan McMillan is speaking, and he doesn't need slides to hold a crowd's attention." Another face. "That's a direct quote, by the way. He loves telling you how brilliant he is."

"Yeah, I kind of got that vibe," I said, thinking that I might have just found my new best friend. Sam knew McMillan, and she obviously wasn't a fan. "What's he like?" I asked.

She thought about it. "Rich."

Which didn't give me a lot to build on. "He must be good at what he does," I tried.

"Oh, he's good," she agreed. "Just maybe not as good as he thinks." The coffee was ready, and she poured herself a cup with a thoughtful look on her face. "He's one of those guys who lets everyone around him do all the work, and he somehow winds up with the glory. Like today—June put it all together and arranged everything, and he just steps in at the eleventh hour and—there, hear that?"

A roar of laughter from the auditorium.

Sam shook her head. "He turns on the charm and gets all the credit. I don't know why June puts up with him."

"Have they worked together a lot?" I asked.

She didn't get a chance to answer, because just then one of the lunchtime food trucks pulled up outside the theater and tapped their horn. I needed to go out and move the traffic cones so they could park.

"Sorry," Sam said. "I don't mean to keep you from everything."

"No worries," I told her, making my way around the counter. "I'll be right back."

But when I got back she was gone.

As soon as I could, I left Albert overseeing things and went up to the balcony to catch the rest of McMillan's talk. Someone had posted a 'Crew Only' sign on the door but I assumed that didn't apply to me.

Callie was sitting at the table covered with equipment at the front of the balcony. She was wearing a headset with a microphone and had monitors showing her the feeds from the three cameras. Her assistant noticed me as soon as I got near and leapt up to meet me at the end of the aisle.

"Do you need something?" she whispered.

I shook my head, whispering back "I just want to hear this guy's talk."

She nodded and went back to Callie, who glanced in my direction before ignoring me.

McMillan ignored the podium and stalked around the stage as he spoke, working every segment of the audience. He was in the middle of a long story that had the entire auditorium in his thrall. I looked around the crowd, who all seemed to be hanging on his every word. Except for two lone blondes in the front row. One, wearing a pink tweed suit and checking her phone, was Ingrid. The other, wearing a vintage usherette's uniform that caught the light with its rows of bright buttons and gold braid, was Trixie. She was sitting in the seat McMillan had vacated, yawning and buffing her nails.

McMillan, I had to admit, was a good speaker. He was one part Alec Baldwin's sales monster from *Glengarry Glen Ross* (1992, Baldwin, Jack Lemmon, and no women to speak of) and two parts Burt Lancaster's charismatic con artist from *The Rainmaker* (1956, Lancaster and Katharine Hepburn.)

This did not seem like the kind of man who would set a fire in a bakery. On the other hand, he totally seemed like the kind of man who would have a guy on retainer for that kind of thing. Was he the kind of man who would commit his own murders? Or would he have a guy for that as well?

I hadn't really been listening to what he was saying, so I jumped when the audience exploded in laughter and applause. McMillan was done. He put his hand to his chest in a gesture of incredibly fake modesty and jogged to the center of the stage and down the stairs as everyone stood and stretched and began ambling toward the lobby for lunch.

I knew I had to go, but I stayed just for a moment to watch McMillan. Trixie stuck with him as he shook hands and chatted with the circle that had instantly formed around him. I noticed June wasn't part of the circle. I glanced around the theater but didn't see her or her assistant Cora.

They'd disappeared. And so, I realized, had Ingrid.

The lunch trucks were a huge success. I circulated and kept an eye on things until I was satisfied that everyone was happy and the hired crew from the party rental place had everything under control. June and her team reappeared in time to claim one of the tables up on the landing, and McMillan and his flock of acolytes took the other. Positions on the high ground had been established.

I still didn't see Ingrid anywhere. Not in line at the trucks, or at any of the tables. I had no idea where she'd gone after talking to McMillan. I didn't see Callie either.

I slipped up the back stairs to the breakroom, where I found Marty and Albert sharing dim sum from one of the trucks.

"Have either of you seen Callie?" I asked. I didn't like to think of her wandering around alone when I didn't know where Ingrid was. If she had actually killed Warren over Callie, would she go after Callie next? Did people wear pink tweed suits to commit murder?

"She's in the balcony with the film crew," Albert said.

"Eating tacos," Marty concurred.

Okay. Callie was with her crew. Good. But I'd still like to know where Ingrid was.

Albert yawned, which reminded me that he was in his nineties.

"Albert, you should go home when you've eaten," I told him. "I couldn't have done this without you, but the party rental crew will clear up after lunch and Brandon will be here to help out by the afternoon break."

"If you don't mind, I think I'll take you up on that," Albert said. "I'm at a very interesting point in my project, and I'd like to be able to get back to it."

"Are you ready to tell me what you're working on?" I sat at the table for a moment and helped myself to a pork bun from an open container in the middle of the table. Marty watched me, then pulled the rest closer to himself.

"Not quite yet," Albert said. "Not until I'm very sure."

"I can't wait," I told him. "And thanks for coming in today. Both of you. I know it's your day off."

"Of course," Albert said, while Marty grunted something and scattered crumbs.

"Have either of you seen Hector?" I asked.

"He's the one who brought all this," Albert gestured to the food on the table. "He was looking for you."

"I'll check the office." But as I got back to the hallway a timer on my phone chirped, reminding me that the afternoon session would start in twenty minutes. I'd given myself that window to get everything ready for the afternoon's panel discussions.

I took the lobby stairs, glancing in June's general direction. She didn't notice me. She was at her table on the landing, deep in conversation with Sam, while Cora hovered behind. They were the only three still at the table. McMillan's table, by contrast, was crowded and lively with conversation, Trixie in the thick of it. She didn't notice me either.

I found myself feeling sorry for June as I went down the stairs. She was smart and successful, worked hard and was good at her job. I knew she'd built her firm from scratch after her husband's death had left her a young widow. But the minute McMillan had walked onto that stage, June faded into his shadow. I also hadn't forgotten the way he'd swooped in and snagged potential-client Hector right out of her grasp. That sort of thing had to sting. Especially if he'd been doing it for years.

It occurred to me that if McMillan had been murdered instead of Warren, June would probably be my number one suspect. Probably followed by Lisa and anyone else whose property he was trying to snatch.

The concessions stand was swamped. I'd planned to grab a few bottles of water to bring to the stage for the panelists, but I didn't want to fight my way through the crowd. Instead I crossed the lobby and took the employee stairs down to the basement. We had a few cases of water in a storeroom.

I was just rounding a corner when I crashed into someone coming the other direction. A beautiful blonde someone, in heels and a pink suit.

Ingrid.

"I'm so sorry!" we both yelped at the same time.

"What are you doing down here?" I asked.

"I got turned around when I came out of the ladies' room."

The ladies' room was on the other side of the basement. Maybe she was lost, but I chose to believe that fate had put her in my path.

"You're Ingrid Barnes, aren't you? You'll be speaking on the panel this afternoon."

She seemed a little spooked at that. "Who are you?" She took a step back.

"Nora. Nora Paige. I manage the Palace."

She put her hand on her chest, as if to still a racing heart. "Oh. Cool. Can you point me to—"

"I was hoping to get a chance to talk to you," I said. Although I couldn't exactly come straight out and ask if she'd killed Warren in a fit of jealous rage. "Um, I heard about you and Warren—"

At Warren's name she went on full alert again, backing up another step, the color draining from her face. This time she looked beyond spooked. She looked scared to death.

"I'm sorry," I said. "I just meant to say, I heard you were dating Warren and I'm so sorry for your loss."

She held up both hands, as if I were trying to rob her. "Look, Warren and I were totally casual. I'm really sorry if he lied to you, but that has nothing to do with me. Please leave me alone." She started to back away.

"No! Wait—I wasn't seeing Warren!"

She stopped.

"I mean, someone who works here was, but it wasn't me. Look, I'm not—" I took a calming breath. "I'm not accusing you of anything." Yet. "I'm not angry. I just want to talk."

She gave me a hard look. "You swear?"

"Has someone been harassing you?"

She shook her head. "I really need to get back upstairs."

I held my hand up. "Sure. No problem. I didn't mean to frighten you." Which was true, but I did want to get her to talk. "It's just, all we've heard about Warren is rumors. I was just going to ask when you saw him last. If you knew what happened."

And maybe if she'd killed him because she found out about Callie. That's all.

Her shoulders came down a bit. "Sorry. I'm a little jumpy. It's just been so crazy. Everyone on social media has lost their minds."

"I get it," I said. "It must be terrible."

"I mean, as if I wasn't already guilty enough," she said.

My heart leapt. Guilty? Was she confessing?

"I could have done something, you know? If I'd stayed." Her voice cracked.

"Stayed where? At the bar?"

She shook her head. "I didn't go to the bar. I was working late. I told Warren to text me when he was ready to leave, and I met up with him out on the street while he was waiting for his rideshare."

I tried to keep my jaw from dropping. She was confessing! She'd been with him that night!

"You went home with him?" I asked.

She wiped at her eyes, looking up. "If I hadn't had that damn Pilates class the next morning I might have been there. I might have been able to do something. Or maybe, if they'd seen two people instead of one hungover guy..."

"Wait." She was sounding like Callie. This wasn't a killer's guilt. It was a survivor's. "You're saying you left Warren the next morning and he was fine?"

She sniffed and nodded. "I left a little after five, to make my six o'clock class."

I blinked. "So you don't know what happened? Did you see anything...suspicious?"

She shook her head. "I heard Warren lock the door behind me and I went to my class. Then I got pissed at him when he didn't return my texts for two days." She looked at me. "Then the police told me what happened."

"I'm so sorry," I said automatically. And I meant it. It really didn't seem like she was lying.

"So am I." She sniffed again. "Look, I think I'd better check my makeup before that damn panel. Can you point me back to the ladies' room?"

"Sure." I grabbed the waters I'd come down for and took her

back through the maze of halls, trying to wrap my mind around what she'd told me.

If Other Girlfriend Ingrid didn't kill Warren, that left me with one prime suspect.

And he was upstairs right now.

Callie and her team must have finished their tacos, because they were gathered on the stage when I got there, looking at the video displays on each other's cameras and murmuring things about the lighting. I was dying to tell her about Ingrid, but not until we were alone. I called a warning to them before raising the giant screen. They all stood away from it and watched as it rose slowly to reveal the chairs and backdrop behind it.

Which is why none of us were facing the balcony when we heard the scream and the sharp, sickening thump that ended it.

CHAPTER 25

Trixie!

That was my first thought as I turned around and tried to make sense of what I saw.

A woman's body. Blonde hair and a gray suit. An impossible position, lying across the seats just below the balcony railing.

Someone screamed. I think it was Callie's sound ninja. Then one of the cameramen dropped his equipment and vaulted down the stairs and I suddenly understood what had happened.

"Call 911," I yelled for the second time in twenty-four hours. I ran down the stairs from the stage.

The auditorium door opened and one of the realtors stuck his head in. "What—"

"Stay out!" I ordered him. "Call an ambulance!"

So he came in and gawked at what was happening.

"Chris," Callie yelled. "Keep everyone out." I hadn't realized she was right behind me. Her assistant raced to the door and pushed the staring realtor out, closing the door behind him, throwing herself against it to keep it closed. Callie was on her phone.

Then everything went blurry. Everything except the sight of the broken woman beneath the balcony.

Sam Beach.

Someone jostled me and I came back to my senses. I took a step closer to Sam, placing my fingers gently on her neck without much hope. She'd fallen onto the seats to the left of the center aisle. Her back was arched unnaturally, and a thin trickle of blood had appeared at the corner of her mouth.

But beneath my fingers I felt something. Faint, irregular, but it was there. I looked up at Callie. "There's a pulse."

Which is when the next scream came, this one from above.

I looked up to find the balcony railing lined with people. All staring, some already crying and turning away, others demanding to know what was going on.

Scratch that, only one was demanding, loudly and insistently, that someone tell him what the hell was happening.

McMillan.

June was there, her hand over her mouth in shocked disbelief. Cora was next to her, gripping the balcony railing. I saw a flash of bright pink and thought *Ingrid* but lost her in the growing crowd. Callie's crew, gathered below, was yelling at everyone to get off the balcony. "Don't lean on the railing!" one of them yelled, which sent a spark of fear into the crowd. They turned and began stumbling to the balcony doors in fear for their own safety. Cora pulled June away. Eventually they all scattered until there was only one lone figure in the center of the balcony, staring down, her face a mask of unimaginable pain.

Trixie.

I made a sound and reached toward the balcony. She tore her anguished gaze from the broken woman beneath her to meet my eyes.

Then she vanished.

"She's hanging on," an EMT told me before closing the door and taking Sam away. But I'd heard the team of six talking as they'd braced her neck and immobilized her on a board. She hadn't regained consciousness, but that wasn't as concerning as the trauma to her spine.

I stood on the sidewalk, watching the ambulance tear down the street. I didn't realize I was freezing until Hector draped his jacket around me. I hadn't realized Hector was there.

We went back into the theater. Everyone who'd been in the

building was now penned in the lobby, waiting their turn to talk to
the police about what they'd seen and where they'd been when
they'd heard the first scream. They were freaked out, annoyed, and
scared. Every single one of them seemed to be on their phone.

"Nora." A deep voice, coming from my right. I turned to see
Detective Jackson on approach, June and Cora with him.

"I have to go," June was saying. "I have to go be with Sam.
Cora, have you got her emergency contact information? Can we call
someone?" Cora nodded and began tapping on her phone. June
turned to Jackson. "I have to *go*."

"You shouldn't drive," I told her. She was shaking and had a
frantic look in her eye.

"I'll have a squad car take you to the hospital," Jackson said.
"Let me know if you think of anything else." He handed her his card
and signaled to a uniformed officer who came and led the two
women away.

Jackson turned to me. "I'd like to see you in the auditorium."

I nodded and moved to follow him when he seemed to notice
Hector for the first time. "Acosta, isn't it?" He'd met Hector when
he'd investigated Hector's brother's murder. "What are you doing
here?"

"I'm a friend of Nora's." Hector answered.

"Uh huh," Jackson said. "Friends wait in the lobby. Someone
will take your statement."

Hector looked like he was about to object, but I intervened.
"Can you find Albert?" I asked him. "He was already tired out, and
all this..."

I could tell he didn't like being sidelined, but he nodded. "I'll
see to him."

Following Jackson through the crowded lobby I wished it were
just as easy to ask someone to look after Trixie. I couldn't get the
image of her agonized face out of my mind.

In the auditorium, the crime scene people were hard at work.
The area where Sam had fallen was taped off. Jackson led me past
it to the front of the theater, so we could look up at the balcony

where more specialists were measuring, dusting, and taking samples of everything.

"Tell me what happened." Jackson said.

So I did, which didn't take long.

"You didn't look up into the balcony before you heard the scream?" he asked when I'd finished.

I shook my head. "Even if I had, you can't see up there from the stage when the lights are on," I explained. "There could have been a dozen people up there. But I never even looked. Callie and her crew were the only ones who were supposed to be using the balcony today, and they were already down on the stage."

"Show me," Jackson said. I took him up the stairs to the stage. He shielded his eyes, looking toward the balcony, but the spotlights were all still on, and I knew the glare would keep him from seeing anything.

"When was the last time you saw the victim before the incident?" he asked.

I perched on the arm of one of the red chairs on the stage, thinking. "I know she was sitting at June's table on the balcony landing before I went to the break room," I said. "And, yes, she and June and Cora were still at the table when I came back down." How long had I been talking to Ingrid in the basement? Not long. "It couldn't have been more than five or ten minutes before..."

He'd called it "the incident," which was noncommittal in that maddening police way of his. He didn't say "the accident" or "the attack." I didn't know if he thought it had been an attempt at murder.

"You have to think someone pushed her," I said, because I couldn't not say it. "Sam is the same Samantha Beach who was one of the last to leave the bar the night Warren was killed. This has to be connected."

Jackson didn't say anything.

I stood. "There's nothing wrong with the balcony railing," I told him. "I'm up there every day. It's fine. And you can't tell me you think—"

"I'm not telling you anything," Jackson interrupted. "That's not how this works, remember?" He gave me a practiced homicide-detective look.

I took a deep breath, but I didn't give up. "She had to have been pushed."

Jackson paused, then nodded. "Okay. Who do you think pushed her?"

I answered without hesitation. "Stan McMillan."

His eyebrows went up. "Any particular reason?"

"Didn't you get the picture I sent? McMillan was at the bar that night too!"

He nodded. "Which isn't proof that he killed anyone."

"But I saw him up in the balcony right after Sam was pushed!"

"Right after?" he asked. "You've just proven that you couldn't see the balcony from the stage."

Maddening! "Okay, not right after, but as soon as I got to Sam." That wasn't quite true, I realized. "I felt for her pulse and looked up right after I realized she was alive."

"And you saw McMillan at the balcony railing. Was he the only one there?"

"Well, no, but—"

"Who else did you see?"

I wanted to scream in frustration, but I kept it together. I tried to visualize the crowd looking over the balcony railing. "June and Cora, the three guys who were with McMillan all day. Maybe Ingrid Barnes—or someone else wearing pink—and a couple others whose names I don't know." Plus Trixie, I didn't add.

He nodded. "Any of whom could have pushed Sam just as easily as McMillan."

"Sure, but he's..."

Jackson waited to see how I would finish.

"...Awful."

Even I knew that wasn't exactly evidence that would hold up in court.

"What did June say?" I challenged him. "Was McMillan

already in the balcony when she and Cora got there?"

"You know I can't share other witness's statements with you."

"But she must have said McMillan was there first! She must have!"

"Nora." Jackson used his rich, deep voice to full effect. "You need to take a beat." He nodded in the direction of the crime scene teams. "All these people are gathering evidence. A whole bunch of other people are gathering statements. I'm personally going to talk to anyone who saw anything. We're going to get to the truth here."

I was just about to hit him with a pithy answer when his phone rang. He gave me one last look before walking out of earshot to take it.

I was dismissed.

I stormed up the back stairs to the break room. I'd never felt so frustrated. I *knew* McMillan had pushed Sam off the balcony. And I knew I had a witness. Trixie. She'd been glued to her target all day. She must have been with him in the balcony. She must have seen everything.

But that was exactly the problem. She'd seen everything. She'd seen a young woman get pushed from the same balcony she herself had been pushed from on the night she died. How horrible it must have been for her, like watching her own death again. Incapable of stopping it again. No wonder she'd been so traumatized she'd vanished.

My heart went out to her. She was my friend and there was nothing I could do to comfort her. I had no idea how long it would take her to recover. If she'd be able to recover. I had no idea when I'd ever see her again. Or if.

I'd never wanted to see her more.

CHAPTER 26

My office was crowded. Callie, Marty, and Brandon had assembled and were exchanging notes on what they'd heard from the police.

"Are you guys okay?" I asked. "Where's Albert?"

"He and Hector are just finishing up with the cops," Callie said. "Then Hector's going to give him a ride home."

"Good." I sank into the chair at my desk. Callie and Brandon were on the couch. Marty was pacing like a caged yeti.

"They shouldn't even be talking to Albert," Marty said. "We were both in the break room when we heard the scream. I went looking to see what the hell was happening, but Albert stayed behind. They should just let him go home."

"I'm sure they will."

My attempt at soothing words earned me a glare.

"What have you heard?" I asked the others. "Did any of you see anything?"

"I just got here," Brandon volunteered. "The police weren't even going to let me in, but Detective Jackson said it was okay."

"The cops wouldn't tell me anything," Callie said. "But everybody's saying, like, the balcony railing gave way."

"Like hell it did!" Marty fumed, at the same time I protested, "It did not!"

"Somebody pushed her," I told them. "They must have. Callie, when did you first look up to the balcony? Who did you see there?"

"That's exactly what the cops wanted to know." She scrunched her forehead. "But I wasn't really paying attention." She made a face. "I'm, like, the worst. I was just looking at my setup and thinking those idiots were going to break all my equipment."

Her production station had been in the front aisle at the center of the balcony. From the position of Sam's body, she must have been just next to it when she was pushed.

"Which idiots?" I asked her. "Did you notice anyone in particular?"

"I mean, that guy," she said, thinking. "The one who was yelling at everyone."

"Stan McMillan," I nodded. "Was he alone when you looked up? Was he the first one there?"

She concentrated. "I don't know. There were a bunch of people. June, for sure, I saw her streak of white hair. And some more people I don't know."

"What about Ingrid?" I asked. "Pink tweed suit?"

"I don't think so." Callie looked distressed. "Honestly, I kind of forgot about Ingrid. Is it wrong that I don't want to go downstairs and, like, find her after all of this?"

"Of course not," I told her.

"Attempted murder trumps boyfriend issues," Marty agreed. Then he unhelpfully added, "Even dead boyfriend issues."

"I talked to her," I told Callie. "Ingrid. She seemed...nice."

Callie winced. "I was, like, afraid of that."

Marty cleared his throat. "If we could get back to the attempted murder?" He turned to me. "What about you? Who did you see when you looked up to the balcony?"

"It seemed like there were dozens," I said. "But, honestly, the only people I *know* I saw were June and Cora and McMillan. And those three guys who seem to be permanently attached to McMillan."

"His bodyguards," Marty said.

"His what?" I turned to him.

"At least one of them is a bodyguard. Sam told me when we were watching him from the booth. McMillan's had some death threats over some project he's doing in North Beach." He flung himself into a chair, biting his thumbnail. "I could understand it if *he'd* been pushed from the balcony. Thousands would cheer."

"What else did Sam say?" I asked Marty. He'd spent the most time with her that morning, bonding in the projection booth. "Anything else about McMillan? Was she afraid of him?"

"She thought he was a tool," he said. "My word, not hers. She clearly despised him, but I don't think she was afraid of him."

But he'd been afraid of someone. Afraid enough to hire a bodyguard. Who?

"If Sam hated him so much, maybe she did try to push him from the balcony," Callie suggested. "I mean, they could have argued, she could have shoved him, he could have shoved back...?"

"Where was the bodyguard during all this shoving?" I wondered. "Marty, when you came out to the landing, were McMillan's guys still at the table?"

He shrugged. "The entire building was filled with white guys in suits. Who can tell them apart?"

He could have told them apart if they were Alan Ladd and Glen Ford. Or even if they were bit players like Donald Crisp or Fred Clark. But as these white guys in suits were real people in the real world, they had Marty flummoxed.

"Did David tell you anything?" I asked him.

Another glare. "Our relationship does not make me privy to any information."

I assumed that was a direct quote from Detective Jackson. Which was fine and honorable and everything, but if you weren't going to get good information, what was the point in dating a cop?

The cop in question chose that moment to knock briskly on the open door. We all turned to him.

"Nora," he said. "A word?"

I stood, but Marty protested. "Oh, come *on*. Whatever it is, she's just going to tell us anyway."

Jackson looked at me and I shrugged. "Odds are," I agreed.

He sighed. "While a preliminary examination doesn't reveal any obvious structural flaws, the balcony will need to pass a city safety inspection. That's after it and the area below are cleared by the techs as an active crime scene."

I sank back down into the chair again as Marty stood. "You've *got* to be kidding me. David—"

"It's not my call," Jackson said firmly. "It's procedure."

"What does that mean?" Brandon turned his stare from the detective to me. "Do we have to keep the balcony closed?"

"It means," I said heavily. "We can't let anyone sit in it or below it." I looked at each of them, Marty scowling, Callie with understanding dawning, and Brandon still in confusion.

"It means we need to close the Palace."

I sent everyone home, but I stayed until the party rental crew had cleared their tables and chairs from the lobby and until every last realtor had left the Palace. Also every last cop. I knew they were all gone because after they left, I made a full sweep of the building from basement to offices. Talking to Trixie.

I said anything I could think of to give her comfort. I told her how sorry I was, how awful it must have been for her to see Sam fall. I didn't know if she could hear me, but it was the only possible thing I could think of to do for her.

She didn't answer.

After that I finished up in my office, where I finally did what I'd been putting off all afternoon. I called Robbie to let her know what had happened. I started with the news that the theater she'd entrusted to me was being closed until further notice, and then worked backwards to the attempted murder that had happened right under my nose.

"Wait, what?" she said. "You're telling me there was a three-person camera crew and a hundred people in the theater and nobody saw anything?" Her voice was incredulous.

"If they did, they aren't talking," I told her. "And the police took all the cameras and recordings." Much to Callie's dismay.

"Okay," she said, and I could tell from that one word that she'd switched to her this-will-not-defeat-me voice. She'd once told me that this voice was her magic superpower. It's what enabled her to rule her TV empire. I relaxed a little. Nothing bad could happen when Robbie used her this-will-not-defeat-me voice.

She spoke. "Let's think of this like the writers we are and ask a character question: Who's your gutsiest suspect? Because to do something like that, in that amount of time, with all those people around, you have to be either crazy sure of yourself or just plain crazy."

"First," I said. "Thank you for putting this in fictional terms. When I think of it like that, I still have to say Stan McMillan. He's got an ego the size of Montana. That could read as gutsy in the right circumstances."

"Uh huh. And he was on the balcony landing when you went past?"

"Yes, but to be fair he wasn't alone. In fact, I didn't see him alone all day. He has henchmen."

"Henchmen?"

"Okay, a bodyguard and two hangers-on. In any case, I don't know if he could have shaken them."

"Maybe he didn't need to. Maybe he got them to do his dirty work. I mean, *henchmen*. It's what they do."

I blinked. "You're a genius. I've been worried about how he could have gotten into the balcony unseen, but maybe he didn't have to."

"Did you hear Sam arguing with anyone before she...before it happened?"

"No." I sat up. "And I would have. If there had been raised voices—or even normal voices—coming from the balcony, we would have heard them on the stage." Score one for the theater's acoustics.

"Wait, didn't you tell me you were raising the screen? Is that loud enough to drown out voices?"

I blew out a breath. "Maybe," I admitted. "Probably not enough to drown out yelling, but maybe enough to cover whispers. I'll try a test tomorrow when someone else is here."

"Who's coming in if you're closed?" she asked.

"Right. Well. I wanted to talk to you about that," I said. "Everyone on the payroll is hourly, so if we're not open, they don't get paid."

"I hear that's how work works," she said.

"Sure, but everyone really needs their paycheck," I told her. "I mean, Callie's parents are loaded, but she doesn't live off them. And I don't know how Marty makes it in this city on what—"

"You want to keep paying them?" Robbie asked. "Done. I can talk the other partners into that. I'll stress that we don't want them going off to get new jobs and then being stuck with nobody to work when we reopen. How long will it take to get the inspection, anyway?"

I'd called the city building inspector's office about that earlier, as soon as I'd sent the gang home. The news was not good.

"We're in the queue," I told Robbie. "But they couldn't give me an exact date." They'd given me a range, which extended into the next month, but I didn't share that with Robbie. I figured I'd head down to city hall and plead my case in person the next day.

"We can pay people for a week or so," Robbie said.

"Thanks." One tiny knot in my chest loosened. "And it won't be for nothing. The theater is closed, but it's not red tagged. We can still be in here as long as we're not in the balcony or the taped-off area. I'll come up with a list of chores we can catch up on until we open to the public again." The Palace had deferred a lot of upkeep in the past few years. Coming up with a task list would not be a problem.

"Perfect," Robbie said. "I've got to go, but, um..."

Okay, her voice had changed again. This was her I'm-about-to-say-something-I-really-don't-want-to voice.

"What?" I asked her. It could only be one thing. "What's Ted done now?"

She paused. "He's packed up all your things."

I blinked. "What does that mean?"

"Well, he sold the house, you know? So he's packed everything up. And he's sending you everything of yours."

Everything of mine. "Everything? You mean like the life I was stupid enough to think would go on happily until death us did part?"

"More like your clothes," she said. "And shoes and stuff."

"Well." I cleared my throat. "That would be easier to pack."

"Oh, Nora." This was said in her best-friend voice. Which was my favorite Robbie voice of all.

I stared at my phone for a while after hanging up. I thought about getting all "How *dare* Ted decide what's mine and what isn't?" about it, but honestly, I didn't have the energy. In the vast scheme of "How dare Ted?" behavior, this wasn't that monumental. I was mulling that sad fact over when someone spoke, startling me half out of my chair.

"Nora? Don't be alarmed. It's just me."

Hector.

He stood at the open doorway, hands up. I should know better than to expect locked doors and a burglar alarm to keep him out.

"Are you all right?" he asked. "You look a little..."

"I am a little." I waved him in. "How's Albert?"

"Home, drinking tea by the fire with a book."

"Wow, does that sound good."

He sat in the chair opposite my desk. "It could be arranged."

I smiled. "How was your chat with the police?"

"Not my favorite activity, but it had the advantage of being brief."

"Did you see anything? Where were you when it all happened?"

He ran a hand over his stubbled face. "I knew you'd be busy until after the lunch break, so I went across the street. I wanted to check something out at the café."

"Right. The other crime scene." Had the fire just been the night before? "Did you find anything?"

He frowned. "Remember when the police asked me how many

locks I'd undone when we broke in to put out the fire? I only had to unlatch the door handle, which would have locked the door automatically when it was closed. But I saw today that there were other locks, deadbolts. They weren't damaged, except for the smoke, and they can only be bolted from the inside."

I sat up. "Lisa usually locks up and then leaves by the back door," I said.

"Right, but our arsonist set the fire in the back. They had to leave by the front door."

"It was the front door opening and closing that caught my eye."

He nodded. "It seems we can conclude that the arsonist, if they were trying to make it look like an accident, miscalculated by leaving those bolts unlocked."

"So maybe it was someone who wasn't familiar with the store?"

"Or they assumed the whole building would burn down and it wouldn't matter. In any case, I was over there poking around when I heard the sirens coming up the street and cursed myself for having left you." He grimaced, but even a grimace looked good on him. "By the time I got back over here it was a madhouse. Everyone was saying someone had fallen to her death from the balcony." He met my eyes. "I thought it was you."

I couldn't look away. "I'm fine."

"This time. But the fact remains that I left you alone with your prime suspect in a murder and an arson. That won't happen again."

I blinked. I couldn't tell if his promise made me feel protected or stalked. "Okay," I said slowly. "Three things: I wasn't exactly alone, it's not your job to take care of me, and I can take care of myself."

"All good points," he said. "Nevertheless." Something flashed in his eyes. "And now, if you're finished here, we should get you something to eat before I take you home to that cup of tea by the fire that I know you won't have."

I stood. "You're always trying to feed me."

He shrugged. "I have to do something, and you won't let me kill your husband."

Okay, then. Dinner it was.

CHAPTER 27

The next morning I woke to find the Palace all over the news.

"A near-catastrophe at the landmark Palace Theater yesterday when a moviegoer fell from a faulty balcony..."

What? I stared at the Channel Five newscaster in horror.

"A local realtor is in critical condition today after plunging from the faulty balcony of the historic Palace Theater..."

No!

It was the same on every channel. I dove for my laptop and checked the *San Francisco Chronicle* online.

The historic Palace Theater is closed today, following an accident yesterday in which local realtor Samantha Beach was critically injured in a fall from the ninety-year-old theater's balcony.

It went on from there, not as accusatory as the TV news had been, but also not raising for a moment the possibility that Sam had been pushed. Until I got to the comments section after the article.

She was a realtor? Somebody probably did us all a favor and pushed her.

OMG everyone knows that place is haunted! The ghost did it!

HaHa right! The ghost pushed her. Woo!

My phone rang and I grabbed it, seeing Callie on the caller ID.

"Nora, it's all over Insta. It's literally everywhere!"

I hadn't checked social media. "What are they saying?"

"That the ghost is back at the Palace," Callie said. "And she's, like, super pissed."

I was super pissed. I shouldn't have been surprised that the hive mind of the Internet would grab on to the legend of the ghostly usherette and run with it. I felt horrible for Trixie, but she had the distinct advantage of being on an alternate plane of existence, presumably with no Wi-Fi access. She was spared hearing what they were saying about her, at least until she came back. Now I was kind of hoping she'd stay "away" until it all died down.

But what I was really furious about was the way the supposed-to-be-professional journalists had all piled on to the notion that the balcony railing had given way. The Palace could recover from stupid social media blather about a vengeful ghost. That would probably even increase attendance, at least for a while, at least from gawkers, before naturally fading away. But a rumor reported as fact in the legitimate press? One that declared the building structurally unsafe? That could really hurt us.

And I couldn't think of a damn thing I could do about it.

Wait. Yes, I could. I knew half a dozen public relations specialists in LA. The kind of people who made a celebrity's stint in rehab or inconvenient DUI disappear from the press, or—even better—turn into an inspiring redemption story rather than a public flogging. Why couldn't they protect the reputation of the Palace the same way they did the latest Real Housewife?

Of course, hiring someone like that would be excruciatingly expensive, but if word hadn't gotten out about how Ted had stolen all my money (and he probably paid just such a PR flack to ensure that it hadn't, as it might make him look bad) the general assumption that I had access to millions should still be in place. I should be able to hire someone now and worry about paying them later.

I made a few calls.

Then, because I had to fight the battle to save the Palace on all fronts, I summoned a rideshare to take me down to City Hall.

Okay, so the Department of Building Inspection wasn't at City Hall. It was about a mile away, in a generic office building on Mission. The Inspection Services department was on the third floor, and I followed the signs to the office where they handled Special Inspections. The Palace, in this context as in all others, was Special.

I told the guy handling walk-ins what I was there for, and he pointed me to a hard plastic chair where I could wait.

The room was a hellscape of bureaucracy lit with energy-efficient bulbs. I had plenty of time to take it in because I waited four and a half hours, draining my phone's battery as I obsessively checked what was being said online about the Palace. Finally I was handed off to a middle manager named Alice who appeared to have been sapped of any visible will to live quite some time ago. She told me that an inspector would be probably be available in three- or four-weeks' time.

But I hadn't spent the past decade negotiating contracts on behalf of my undeserving husband for nothing. I looked Alice in the eye, and I explained, then I cajoled, then I wheedled. Then I agreed to take a look at her son's screenplay and get it to the right Hollywood agent. By the time I left I had an appointment with an inspector for the following Friday afternoon.

I've said it before, and I'll say it again: everybody has a screenplay.

Back in the elevator I resisted the urge to collapse into a puddle of exhaustion. Which was just as well, because the elevator stopped on the second floor and a guy in a well-cut suit got in. He was quite obviously not in his happy place. He was glowering. He fired up his phone immediately and indulged in a string of profanities the likes of which I'd only heard from thwarted paparazzi. Apparently, whatever he'd been working on was caught up in the machinery of local government.

Which was only interesting because the guy in question was one of McMillan's henchman.

Once we hit the ground floor, he stormed out the door and climbed into a waiting SUV. I watched him leave, still ranting into his phone. He hadn't once looked over toward me. I went to the building directory by the elevator doors.

The second floor, where he'd been, was home to Plan Review Services.

So what plan of McMillan's had just been denied?

"I don't know," I told Lisa. "But here's hoping it was the plan for tearing down the neighborhood."

I was back at the Palace, and I'd called Lisa to tell her what I'd seen. I wanted to believe it meant that her café and my theater were both safe. At least for a while.

"That would be so amazing," she said.

"It would, but we can't count on it," I cautioned her. "The guy probably has half a dozen projects at the planning stage. We don't know which one has been denied."

"I just want to believe there's hope," she said. "All I can think about is rebuilding. And I'll be damned if I'm going to get everything back up and running just to be forced to sell it to that snake McMillan."

I didn't tell her he was more of a shark. To each their own.

Around three that afternoon I was down in the lobby with a clipboard, making an inventory of all the little tasks we could take care of while the Palace was closed. Areas that needed touch-up paint, or a thorough cleaning, or a minor repair.

The list was not short.

I was interrupted by a rap at the glass lobby doors. It was

Brandon, waving and grinning hopefully.

"I thought you'd be here," he said when I opened the door. I was alone in the theater, so I'd kept everything locked up.

"And I thought I told you guys not to bother coming in until tomorrow."

He shrugged. "It's on my way home from school. I just thought I'd ask if there was anything you needed help with." He glanced around the lobby. "Anyone else here?"

The penny dropped. "Callie isn't in," I told him.

"Oh, I didn't mean...um..." He tried to cover, but the rising flush on his face confirmed that he'd come here looking for the object of his infatuation.

I gave him a look and he abandoned his pretense with a sigh and a shrug. "The heart wants what the heart wants," he said plaintively.

"So I've been told. Come on. There is something you can do for me as long as you're here."

I put clipboard and pen down on the candy counter and crossed the lobby to the auditorium doors. "The furniture rental people will be here first thing in the morning to pick up the chairs and the podium. You can help me wrap them back up in their plastic and blankets and take them downstairs to the back alley door."

"Cool." Once in the auditorium, he shrugged off his jacket as he followed me down the darkened aisle to the stage. "Um, the police are okay with us moving things?"

"As long as it's not in the taped-off area." I'd checked. I went up the steps and flipped on the stage lights. The screen was still raised from the day before, which reminded me I had to try something out.

"Brandon, there's something else you can do after we get the chairs out of the way. I want to see if I can hear someone talking from the balcony while the screen is coming down."

He gave me a doubtful look. "Are we allowed in the balcony?"

For a self-confessed stalker and boyfriend spy, the kid was a stickler for the rules.

"Not strictly speaking, but I won't tell if you don't. Let's take care of the furniture first."

"I'm on it. Where's all the wrapping?"

"In a pile behind the backdrop, unless somebody's moved it." I started for the podium. I'd have to take the microphone off and pack that up as well. The audio equipment had been rented from yet a different vendor.

"Have you heard anything about how that lady is doing?" Brandon asked. "The one who fell?"

"Just on the news," I told him. "This morning they said she was still in critical condition. I texted June earlier, but she hasn't gotten back to me." Looping the microphone cord around my arm, I glanced over at him.

"Who do you think—"

But the rest of his question was cut off with a yelp of surprise as the floor went out from under him and he plunged through the stage into darkness.

CHAPTER 28

"Brandon!" I ran to the hole that had appeared in the floor. One of the ancient trapdoors had given way. I peered over the rim to the dark room below. "Brandon, are you okay?"

"Callie?" I heard him say, sounding dazed.

I felt a rush of relief. "It's Nora," I yelled. "Don't move. I'll be right there!"

I dialed 911 as I raced for the stairs. I should have put them on speed dial.

Brandon had broken his leg. That much was clear when I got downstairs and found him on the floor of the prop room beneath the stage.

"Nora, hey," he greeted me when I flipped on the lights. "I'm sorry. I think I fell."

He was dazed, but he didn't seem to be in the kind of pain I'd expect from the very wrong angle his left leg was in. Maybe he'd hit his head. Maybe he was in shock.

"You'll be okay," I told him, hoping it was true.

His face scrunched in concentration. "I think I hurt something." He struggled to get up, but I restrained him with a hand on his shoulder. "Don't try to move." Aside from the fact that his neck or spine might be injured, I didn't think it was the best idea for him to see his leg like that. I heard the faint wail of sirens. "I'll be right back."

I ran back up the stairs to let the professionals in.

The EMT team included the good-looking young man who'd taken Callie home the night of the fire. He grinned as I opened the door. "This is getting to be a habit."

"You're hilarious," I told him. "We're going to the basement."

The pain had hit by the time we got back downstairs to Brandon. He was completely drained of color, his eyelids fluttering.

"What happened?" he asked me as the medics assessed his injuries.

"The trapdoor gave way," I told him. "Which should have been impossible. It's been nailed shut for years. Somebody did this deliberately."

It was right above us, and one look revealed that, while the other trapdoor was still boarded over and nailed securely shut, the one that now gaped open had damage all around it where the nails had been pulled out.

"Who would do something like that?" the EMT asked.

His partner glanced up at the open trap. "Maybe it's the ghost again."

"There is no ghost," I said forcefully. Which wasn't true. What I meant was that the ghost hadn't done this.

"There's a murderer," Brandon said. Then he passed out.

They let me ride along in the ambulance for the few blocks to the hospital. Brandon came around once the truck began moving. He looked at me, his eyes wide. "Don't tell Callie I fainted," he begged.

"Never." I squeezed his hand.

"How *is* Callie?" the EMT asked. Whereupon Brandon looked from him to me in a stricken sort of way and I changed the subject.

"Are the police on their way?"

"They should be," the EMT said.

I pulled out my phone and texted Marty.

I need you to call David and get to the Palace. Now.

Because Brandon was right. Someone had deliberately opened that trapdoor. Someone whose intention was murder.

"A clean break to both tibia and fibula, a sprained wrist, and a mild concussion." This is what a doctor told us a while later. I was standing by Brandon's bed in the ER, and whatever drugs they'd given him were very much working. "We've set the leg, but we'll leave it in a splint for a while to let the swelling go down before we get him into cast."

Brandon gave her a thumbs up. His eyes were glassy.

"Your son will be fine," the doctor said. "You should get some rest."

"He's not—" I began to protest, but she'd already moved on.

Son? Ouch. I realized that at thirty-nine I was technically old enough to be a teenager's mother, but still.

Brandon snickered. "They think you're my mom." His eyes widened. "Do we have to tell my mom? She's going to kill me."

"She'll probably figure it out when she sees the cast," I said. "Plus she'll be here any minute." I'd used his phone to call her as soon as we'd gotten to the hospital.

"You're way hotter than my mom," he mumbled. Then the small part of his brain that wasn't soaked in painkillers realized what he'd just said, and his face flushed its familiar shade of crimson.

"I'm going out to the waiting room," I told him. "And we will never speak of this again."

He nodded.

I had to go to the waiting room because I had to make some calls, and cell phone use was forbidden in the ER.

Marty answered on the first ring. "How's the kid?"

"He'll be okay," I said. "He was lucky."

I knew Brandon's fall could have been much worse.

"What does Jackson think?" I asked Marty.

"That someone sabotaged that door with an intent to kill

someone," he said. "Which seems like a completely insane way to plan a murder. How would you know who'd fall?"

"Maybe they didn't care," I said.

"What do you mean? Are we talking psychopath? Because I could one hundred percent get behind that idea. I have a few contenders."

"No, that's not what I mean." I'd had time to think about it while waiting for Brandon's results. "What if the point wasn't to kill someone specific? What if it was just to cause another "accident" at the Palace? Maybe the point was to promote the whole idea that the theater is unsafe."

Marty paused, then he swore. Elaborately. And at length.

"I think it was McMillan," I said when he paused for a breath. "He's trying to drive down the price before he swoops in to snatch it."

"What do you mean, snatch it?"

"He's made an offer for Tommy May's quarter share."

There was a strangling sort of sound, then, "I'll kill him," Marty said. "That—"

"You really shouldn't threaten murder in front of your boyfriend the homicide detective."

"He's not—oh, *fine*. He wants to talk to you."

Marty passed the phone to Detective Jackson.

"Nora. How's Brandon?"

"Worried that his mom will kill him," I said. "What do you think about the door?"

"Obviously someone deliberately tampered with it," he said. "When did you last see it secured with planks?"

"I'm not sure. I was in and out of the prop room on Sunday and Monday, getting things ready for the event," I said. "But I don't know if I actually looked up." Then something occurred to me. "Hang on. The trapdoor must have still been secured on Sunday, because I put something on it when Callie and I were setting up. If it had already been sabotaged, the backdrop would have fallen through." And so would I, I realized with a shiver.

"We'll need to talk to everyone to find out who had access on Sunday or Monday," Jackson said.

"It had to have been Monday," I told him.

"Why?"

"Because that's when Stan McMillan was in the theater." I filled the detective in on my theory about McMillian using criminal tactics to get the Palace at a bargain price.

He heard me out before replying. "I don't suppose you have any evidence to support that?"

I'd already thought of that. "Would he have to file plans?" I asked. "If he wanted this block? Is that something that would be on file with the city? And would you be able to subpoena it or something?"

"Even if he did, I couldn't get a court order without a shred of evidence. But I appreciate you thinking I might have some small part to play in solving this series of violent crimes."

I took a breath. "Okay, sarcasm noted. But I'll bet you anything that you'll find McMillan's fingerprints all around that trapdoor. Or at least his henchman's."

"Henchman," he said. "Uh huh. I'm handing you back to Marty."

"Are you on your way here?" Marty asked when he got the phone back.

"Not right away," I told him. "There's something I have to do here first."

I needed to go back to Brandon and make sure his mom had arrived. But first I needed to visit Sam. According to the news, I was at the hospital where she'd been taken yesterday.

A helpful volunteer told me I should ask at the desk on the fourth floor and pointed me to the elevator, which let me out near the intensive care waiting area. The first person I saw was June's assistant Cora.

She was absorbed in her phone, texting rapidly. I crossed over to her, looking around for June, but Cora was alone.

"Cora?" I wasn't sure she'd remember who I was. "I'm glad to see you. Do you know—"

But I didn't have to finish. Because the tears streaming down her face when she turned to me told me everything before she said the words.

"Sam's dead."

I sank down next to Cora on the waiting room couch, not quite believing what she'd said.

"She died of her injuries." Cora wiped her face with her sleeve. "She never woke up."

I couldn't take it in. I knew how badly Sam had been hurt. I knew that Trixie had died falling from the same balcony. But I'd thought once Sam made it to the hospital, they'd be able to save her.

"Even if she had woken up, she never would have walked again." Cora's voice sounded artificial, like one of those robots on the telephone. She looked at me, with something like desperation in her eyes. "June says Sam wouldn't have wanted to live like that. Do you think that's true?"

I thought it was an awful thing to say. My mind flashed to Hector's cousin Gabriela in her wheelchair. Smart, successful Gabriela who certainly wanted to live "like that."

I looked away from Cora. "Is June here?"

"She went back to the office," Carla's robot voice answered. "She has to message everyone, tell them what happened before they see it on the news."

The news. I knew I should care about it being on the news. I just couldn't yet.

"When did it happen?" I asked.

Cora blinked. She looked at her watch. "About half an hour ago."

I'd been downstairs with Brandon.

"June brought her flowers." Cora was still speaking. "I told her I could take care of it, but she wanted to bring them herself. She wanted Sam to have something nice to wake up to." She turned to me. "She stayed with Sam all night. Sam's family is all on the east coast, and June didn't want her to be alone. I had to beg her to leave this morning to get some rest, but she came back with those flowers." She blinked. "At least Sam wasn't alone when she..." Her voice trailed off.

"Let me give you a ride home," I said.

She shook her head. "I'm waiting for Sam's family. They're due in soon, and June had to go, but she wanted someone from the office, someone who knew Sam, to be here for them when they found out."

I swallowed.

Samantha Beach was dead. She'd been murdered in my theater. And every instinct I had told me I knew who had killed her.

CHAPTER 29

"I'm here to see Stan McMillan," I told the receptionist.

It was mid-morning the next day. I'd spent a sleepless night thinking about Sam, about Warren, and about everything that had happened since the night of Warren's party. Then I did what I should have done before meeting McMillan on Monday. I wrote a script.

"Do you have an appointment?" The polished young woman gave me half-raised brows of polite inquisitiveness. She fit right in with the gleaming minimalism of everything else in the lobby. What didn't fit in was the guy in the dark gray suit standing not-quite-at-attention to the left of the desk. Henchman Number Two, I labeled him. Not the same one I'd seen coming out of the city planning offices, but he'd been at the Palace on Monday.

I smiled at the receptionist. "No, but please tell him it's Nora Bishop. I think he'll see me."

I deliberately used Ted's name, my married name, and it registered with her. I could tell by the way she reassessed me as she spoke in hushed tones into the microphone of her headset. Henchman Number Two also flicked an appraising eye over me.

That was fine. I'd dressed for the part of Nora Bishop. Instead of my usual comfy jeans and a sweater, today I wore the Hollywood Wives equivalent of a power suit: designer jeans, an ivory silk blouse, murderous Valentino heels, and a buttery soft burgundy leather jacket. I'd borrowed most of it from Robbie's closet in her main house. I was sure she'd approve. I also carried one of her handbags. A really, really, good one.

I couldn't count on McMillan making time to see Nora Paige,

the financially strapped theater manager he'd met two days ago, but I was willing to gamble that he'd have time for Ted Bishop's soon-to-be-ex-wife. Particularly if he, like June, assumed that a hefty divorce settlement was in my near future. I still hated the way the Palace had been in the news since Sam's death, but at least it meant McMillan would probably know who I was by now.

I was right. It took roughly forty-five seconds for McMillan to appear in the lobby. "Nora! It's so good to see you again."

At the theater on Monday I hadn't been the recipient of his full-wattage charm. But today teeth flashed, eyes sparkled, and his entire demeanor told a story of him being thrilled beyond words to have me show up unannounced. He took my freshly-manicured hand in both of his and, without taking his eyes off me, spoke to the receptionist.

"Cat, go ahead and cancel my next meeting. I have a feeling Mrs. Bishop has something important to talk about." He gave my hand a squeeze before releasing it. "Now, Nora. How about we get you a coffee and you can tell me what brings you here today?"

Mata Hari, I told myself. My script called for a dazzling smile at this point, so that's what he got. "Why, Stan, I'd love to."

McMillan's real estate office couldn't have been more different from June's. Hers was a neighborhood storefront, crowded but comfortable, a warren of small rooms that had been retrofitted inside a rambling Victorian house. Stan McMillan's place of business was a vast expanse of cold modern spaces on the forty-second floor of a new glass tower. The floor-to-ceiling windows of his office looked out over the Bay Bridge and waterfront. Everything was calculated to impress.

I'd just taken a seat in one of his low-slung guest chairs when there was a rap on the door, followed by the entrance of a ruthlessly groomed young woman carrying a tray laden with coffee and pastries. The sleek pitchers and cups could have been displayed at the Museum of Modern Art. The pastry didn't look half as good as what I got daily at Café Madeline, the business that I assumed the man sitting across from me had tried to burn down.

I took a croissant I had no intention of tasting. "Yum."

He smiled his shark smile. "Things ended so abruptly on Monday. I didn't get a chance to really talk with you. I didn't even realize who you were until after...well...after everything."

After Sam was pushed from the balcony, he meant. After he or one of his henchmen had pushed her. They guy I'd just passed in the lobby?

"It was a terrible thing," I said.

"Terrible," he agreed, then he swept past Sam's death. "But, as I say, I didn't know who you were until one of the news stories mentioned it." He gave me the kind of elaborately sincere look that it takes years of practice to perfect. "I was so sorry to hear about your marriage. But I'm sure a beautiful woman like you will be just fine. And, please, don't hesitate to call on me if there's anything I can do to help. I know you're new in town and I'd love it if you considered me your friend."

Okay, first...yuck. But I couldn't focus on how obvious or patronizing he was. I had to focus on the offer he'd just made. Because that offer triggered the next part of my script.

"Well, this is a little delicate," I told him, wiping my fingers on a linen napkin embroidered with his company's logo. "You know I'm working with June on finding a house here in the city?"

"She mentioned something about that, yes." A touch of greed infiltrated his smile. He thought I was about to trade June in.

"Of course, I'd never think of leaving her," I said, popping that particular bubble. "But since we met the other day, I've been doing a little research on you." Pause for eye contact. "I've heard you're the man to see if I'm looking to invest in commercial development." Sip coffee. "If I'm looking to invest substantially."

There's a phrase that one of my screenwriting mentors used to describe the moment when an audience becomes fully invested in your story. The moment when they're hooked. When you know you've got them for the rest of the movie—as long as you don't screw it up. This moment, she'd said, was when the audience was all aboard your train.

With the words "invest substantially," Stan McMillan was all aboard. "You heard right," he smirked. "I'm definitely the man."

Ugh. Smile. "I'm so glad. Because a little birdie told me that you're planning something in my neighborhood?"

He leaned forward, legs apart, elbows on his knees, hands loosely clasped. "Well, now, I don't know who your little birdie is," he began, "but I'm planning a lot of things in a lot of neighborhoods."

"I'm sure you are," I said smoothly. "But you understand why I'm particularly interested in mine. In fact, I have it on fairly good authority that you're planning something for the Palace."

He blinked, then cleared his throat strenuously. If this were a comedy, I'd have timed it so he did a spit-take with his coffee. But this was very much not a comedy. He eyed me, recalculating.

I held his gaze, doing my best to channel Rosalind Russell in any one of her smarter-than-any-man-in-the-room roles. Eyebrow a little arched, keen gleam in the eye, chin raised expectantly.

He finally answered me. "Nora, I'm sure you're aware that if I was interested in the Palace, there are four owners I'd have to convince to sell."

"Three, really," I shrugged. "Probably two if you played your cards right. And I suspect you always play your cards right. I assume I'm correct in thinking you've already approached Tommy May?"

I spoke quickly, intending to keep him off guard. I was rewarded with a flash of surprise on his face, followed by a resigned grin. "Well, I suppose I haven't been as discreet as I should have been." He tried for a look of sheepish bad boy, which he'd probably put to good use in his younger days. But he'd aged out of its effectiveness. At least on me.

"Nobody is ever as discreet as they should have been," I told him, because it was my turn to be patronizing. I'd just won. I'd gotten confirmation that he was after the Palace.

Now I just had to thwart him.

He went into damage control mode, leaning forward and hitting me with full-force sincerity. "Nora, you have to understand that it's nothing personal. I had no idea you were involved with that movie theater."

"Of course." I leaned forward conspiratorially. "But now that you do know, I'm sure if I ask you nicely, you'll drop your plans and go find somewhere else to develop, won't you?"

He flushed. "Well, um, it's not quite that simple…"

I laughed, sitting back and crossing my legs. "Relax. I'm kidding."

He was officially discombobulated. It was time to wrap up Act One.

"Stan, do I strike you as the sort of woman who would be happy spending the rest of her days making popcorn for a bunch of elderly film buffs?"

"Well…"

I held up a hand. "I am not. I am the sort of woman who would like to leverage her capital in a winning investment." I looked him in the eye. "And I think you're a winner."

He cocked his head. "Are you saying…?"

I gave a tiny shrug. "I want in. I like the area around the Palace. I like the ratio of residential to commercial properties, the demographics are great, and the current zoning makes it very compelling." I'd practiced these real-estate phrases in the wee hours of the morning until they rolled right off my tongue.

McMillan sat back in his chair, stroking his tie and regarding me in a new light. "Why, Nora," he grinned. "Aren't you just full of surprises?"

"Isn't everyone?"

"Of course this would have to be completely confidential."

I drew an X over my heart. "Of course."

He shifted forward again, moving into his pitch with the practiced patter and smooth hand gestures of a lifelong huckster. "Then what would you say to an entire city block? High-end retail on the ground floor, commercial offices above, topped with two stories of luxury residential for a total of sixty-four prime units."

"I'd say that sounds pretty compelling."

Smug couldn't begin to describe the look on his face. Which was good. Smug wasn't cautious.

He rubbed his hands together. "Excellent. Of course, these things take time, but with your help in persuading the other owners..."

"You can count on me," I said. He could count on me to persuade them never to sell to this evil snake. But he didn't know that. "You haven't approached the other three?"

"Not yet," he said.

"Good. Hold off on that. And don't pressure Tommy. Just leave it with me." Which should buy me some time. Hopefully enough time to see him behind bars for two murders.

He smiled expansively. "We should probably discuss the finances..."

I waved a manicured hand. "I'll let the lawyers and accountants handle that. My team will be in touch. I just wanted to speak to you first. To come to an understanding." I put my coffee cup on the tray, looking like I was preparing to leave. I was preparing for Act Two.

"Stan, there's one thing I have to ask you," I said, as if it had just occurred to me. "This business with the realtor who fell on Monday..."

His smile wobbled. "Yes, it was terrible."

"Terrible," I agreed. "But also..."

He didn't seem to know where I was headed, which was unfortunate. I'd have to lead him there.

"All the negative press," I said. "I'm sure you've seen it. All the stories about the Palace being unsafe..."

His gaze had sharpened, but he still didn't take the bait.

"I was just thinking," I said. "That kind of press will be very helpful in convincing the owners to sell. It couldn't have been better timed if you'd planned it yourself."

"Oh." The penny finally dropped. "Well, I wish I could say I was that clever," he shrugged.

"Of course I'm not saying you had anything to do with the *accident*," I lied. "It just seemed like afterwards someone was telling a very consistent story to the press..."

Another shrug. "Sometimes things just align," he said.

Sometimes they have help. "So you haven't spoken to the press?"

"Me? No."

"But you have spoken to the police," I said. "We all did, and I'm sure they were interested in what you'd seen. You got to the balcony fairly quickly, didn't you? After she fell. You and your...associates?" I stopped myself, afraid I'd started to ramble. I'd only just caught myself before saying 'henchmen.'

He shifted in his seat. "Yes, we were just outside the balcony door. Of course we rushed in when we heard the scream."

"Of course. All of you?"

He gave me a quick look.

"It's just that I noticed your table was quite lively at lunch. Do you remember if everyone was still there when you heard..."

"I wasn't exactly keeping tabs on everyone," he said. "People came and went."

"Of course," I repeated. I had to admit it seemed unlikely that he had excused himself from the crowded table to murder Sam, but I was still sure he was behind her death. I wanted to know which of his henchmen he'd sent to do the deed.

"You were probably one of the first to get to the balcony," I said. "I mean, after..."

He frowned. "No, there were others. I'm sure someone saw what happened."

"Do you remember who was there?" I asked, probably too eagerly. "I mean, that's what the police asked me, but I was down below and couldn't see anything up in the balcony." That should reassure him.

He shook his head. "I wasn't paying attention. I saw June and that assistant of hers, and a couple of the junior realtors were screaming and crying, a few people I didn't know, but that may have been later, after we'd been warned away from the railing and we all turned to go. As I told that detective, I'm not really clear on who got there when."

Well, that was no help. I was about to press him when he spoke again.

"I'm sure the police will figure it out," he said. "It was probably just an accident." He grinned conspiratorially. "From that faulty railing."

I wanted to slap that grin off his face. Instead I smiled. "I'm sure they will." I reached for Robbie's handbag, as if preparing to leave, having no intention of leaving. "I'm sure Sam's death was an accident, and I'm sure Warren's death was just a random burglary."

He'd been about to stand, to see me out, but now he froze. "Warren?"

"Oh," I smiled quickly. "He worked for June. He was killed a week or so ago. I assumed you'd heard?"

"I had," he frowned. "Are you saying you think his death is connected to the accident at the theater?"

I widened my eyes. "How could it be?"

He blinked. "Right. Sure. How could it be?"

"Well, I mean..." I flashed him a smile. "Forgive me, I'm a recovering screenwriter. Warren and Sam both worked at the same real estate firm and both died suspiciously within two weeks of each other. If this were a movie they'd have to be connected."

He swallowed. "Good thing this isn't a movie." He stood, signaling it was time for me to go.

I lingered. "If it were, the police probably would have asked everyone who was there when Sam died where they were on the night Warren died."

"Are they?" he asked sharply.

"Why?" I looked up at him, my voice teasing. "Don't you have an alibi?"

He sank back down, rubbing his face. "As a matter of fact, I happened to be at the same bar as this Warren kid on the night he was killed."

I gave him shocked fascination. "Really? You knew him?"

"No! It was just a coincidence. A lot of the same people were there that night and at the event on Monday. It was a bunch of realtors."

"Oh, so you were with that party? With the realtors?"

"No, not with them," he said. "I was meeting a colleague. We didn't join the others. I don't think they even saw us."

They wouldn't, what with him hiding in a dark corner and everything. Except Warren had.

"Your colleague knew Warren as well?" *Who was the mysterious colleague?*

"Yes, I mean," he looked flustered. "She—" Then he opened his mouth and closed it again, looking out the window. When he turned back to me something had changed. There was something new in his eye. Fear.

"Nora, as much as I enjoy your company, I'm afraid I'm going to have to cut this short. I'm sure we'll be speaking again soon."

"What is it?" I asked him. "You look like you've seen a ghost."

"It's nothing." His smile was completely false. "I've just remembered that I have someplace to be. And as my newest partner, I'm sure you'll appreciate that I never cancel on a commitment."

I stood. "Your newest partner. I like the sound of that." I hated the sound of that, and I hated that he'd stopped himself from telling me who had been with him at the bar that night.

Something had stopped him. He'd realized something. What was it? What was I missing?

CHAPTER 30

"What isn't he telling you?"

This was Hector's greeting when I exited the building and got into his waiting car.

"I wish I knew." McMillan had completely closed up, barely saying a word as he'd led me back to the elevator. As the doors had closed, I'd seen him motion to Henchman Number Two on his way back to the office. "Why didn't you give me one of your famous bugs to plant under his desk or something? We could be listening to him right now."

"Or he would have caught you and I would now be explaining to Detective Jackson why you became McMillan's third victim," Hector said.

He'd been waiting for me because I'd called him at an insanely early hour that morning to ask if he could loan me a recording device to wear during my confrontation with McMillan. I probably could have used my phone to record it, but I assumed a (former) criminal mastermind would have access to something a little more high-tech. I'd been right. Hector's one condition was that he come along and listen in just in case McMillan got out of hand. He'd heard every word.

Now he pulled away from the curb as I unclasped a tiny oblong device from the underside of my jacket lapel. "Is there anything on this I can take to Jackson?"

"Not unless he's looking to invest in real estate," Hector said.

"I didn't get proof of a damn thing."

"No, but it was never likely that a multiple murderer would pour his heart out to you just because he thinks you're investing in his latest project."

"I didn't think he'd pour his heart out," I said. "But I hoped he'd be so arrogant, once he thought we were on the same side, that he might let something slip."

"Maybe he did," Hector said. "Maybe we're just looking at it wrong. Tell me again why you think he's behind all of this."

I took a breath. "I think he killed Warren because Warren saw him with someone at the bar that night. He killed Warren because he had something to hide."

"I would imagine a man like that has many things to hide," Hector said. "He can't go around killing everyone."

I stared at him. "Are you saying you don't think he did it?"

"I'm keeping an open mind. He said he was with 'a colleague' that night, yes?"

"Yes." Then it hit me. "If it was a colleague, it was probably someone in real estate. And we had a hundred realtors at the Palace on Monday."

"You think the colleague was there?"

"They could have been. *She* could have been. At least he let that much slip. The colleague is a woman."

"Maybe this woman is the killer, and not McMillan."

"Is that what he realized?" I asked. "When he stopped himself from telling me anything else? Did it just occur to him that he knew someone else who had been at the bar and on the balcony?"

"If so, that could account for his change in behavior."

"He was afraid," I said.

"Quite possibly with good reason."

Possibly. But I wasn't willing to give up on casting McMillan as the killer just yet.

"I'll look at the social media posts again." I tugged at my seatbelt. "I know Warren saw something that night, and I think Sam must have, too. Something that she might not have realized was significant until later. Maybe someone else saw something. I think we should talk to anyone who stayed late at the party. We have to find out who the colleague is."

"If anyone saw what Sam and Warren saw, they could be in danger," Hector said.

"They could. I'm just glad Callie left early. I wouldn't want her to be next on the list."

"And I don't want you to be."

I stared at him. "Why would I be? I had nothing to do with anything. And I'm now officially McMillan's new best friend. Or did you miss that part?"

"No, I heard that part. That part went just as you said it would."

"Damn right it did." I stared out the window. "At least the Palace is safe for now, assuming McMillan doesn't find out that I'm not getting the fat settlement he thinks I am."

"You don't need a settlement. You don't need anything from any man who was foolish enough to betray you."

"That's sweet," I said. "My bankers would disagree."

"Returning to you being next on the list," he said. "I think you're forgetting the trapdoor."

I blinked. I had forgotten the trapdoor. "You think that was meant for me?"

"Who else is in the habit of wandering around on your stage?"

"That depends on when it was tampered with. There were plenty of people wandering around on it Monday. You, for instance. Both June and McMillan. And Callie's film and sound people. And June's assistant Cora and McMillan's entourage of baddies. In the afternoon all those same people plus the panelists were scheduled to be around. Maybe the trapdoor was meant for someone specific, but I still think it would be really difficult to predict who'd be on it when." Then I saw it. "Except," I said. "One of the panelists was Other Girlfriend Ingrid."

"Where does she fit in?" Hector asked.

"It could have been meant for her," I admitted. "She told me she wasn't at the bar that night, and I believed her. But she could have been lying. Recent history has shown me to be quite gullible when it comes to liars."

Hector shot me a look but spared me from commenting.

I went on. "If Ingrid actually did come late to Warren's party, after Callie had already left, she might have seen something. Or even if she wasn't lying about that, she still might have seen something on the street outside the bar, and she might not even realize it's important."

Or she could be the killer. Was she? I wasn't sure of anything anymore. Except. "She was in the basement," I told Hector. "She was wandering around the basement on Monday."

"Which means she could have sabotaged the trapdoor."

I frowned. "Theoretically, sure. But you saw how she was dressed. She had on heels and a pink suit. I don't think I see her rummaging around in the prop room, finding a ladder and a crowbar, ripping down all those boards, and still looking fresh as a daisy when I ran into her. Besides, why would she sabotage it? Who was she trying to kill? And how would she even know there was a trapdoor?"

"How would McMillan?" he asked. Which was a point. I'd have to think about that.

"If Ingrid isn't the killer she could be in danger," Hector went on. "If she saw something. If McMillan knows about her. If he's the killer."

"He could have sent one of his henchmen downstairs to open the trapdoor," I said, considering. "Assuming he knew it was there. Could he have seen it earlier that day when we were putting the mic on him? But, again, how would he know who was going to step on it?"

"Unless he planned to guide his victim to it," Hector shrugged. "These things can be arranged."

I chose not to think about what Hector might have arranged in his pre-retirement past.

"It's pretty farfetched," I said. "Am I just trying to make the puzzle pieces fit because I want the killer to be McMillan?"

"It's clear that's what you want." Hector glanced in the rearview mirror before changing lanes. "Why?"

I thought about it. "He's such a snake," I finally said. "And a shark. I mean, when he went into his sales pitch he was as polished as the slickest Hollywood agent. He practically oozed. He was..." I tried to think of the ultimate flim-flam man. "He was Professor Harold Hill, without the charm or the musical ability."

Hector shot me a glance. "Who's Professor Harold Hill?"

"Professor Harold Hill. From *The Music Man*." (1962, Robert Preston, Shirley Jones, and the good people of River City, Iowa.)

"I haven't seen it."

I blinked. "How does a person go through life without having seen *The Music Man*?"

"Fairly easily, if the several million Colombians I grew up with are any measure," he grinned. "You'll have to show it to me some time."

"Damn right I will. There are some movies that are just *necessary*. I'll put together a list."

"Marty is already making me a list," he informed me. "He feels much the same way as you. He also referred me to a website."

I stared at him. "Let me guess. *Movies My Friends Should Watch*? By Sallie Lee?"

"I believe so. Are you familiar with it?"

"Vaguely."

We were a few blocks away from the theater when I got a text from Callie.

I'm at the Palace. Where are you? I thought you might want to hear about my chat with Ingrid...

The girl had a flair for the cliffhanger.

As we pulled up I saw her in the ticket booth, taking down the deep blue velvet curtains that lined the interior of the glass enclosure. I tapped on her window as Hector drove away.

"You found my list," I said when Callie opened the door.

Taking the dusty drapery down to be dry cleaned had been one of the many tasks I'd come up with to take advantage of the downtime until the building inspector cleared us to reopen. I'd left the list on the candy counter before Brandon's fall the day before.

"Can you, like, hold the bag open?" Callie spoke from behind an armload of fabric.

She'd brought several large plastic garbage bags out to the booth. I grabbed one and she stuffed the curtains in as I held it for her. By the time we got everything bundled up into four bags we were both sneezing.

"I mean, now what?" She regarded the bags, heaped on the tiled walkway that led from the ticket booth to the lobby doors.

"Good question." Neither of us had a car, and even if Hector had stayed, he probably wouldn't have wanted the grimy bags anywhere near his lush leather upholstery. "Shall we walk it?" There was a dry cleaner two blocks down. "While you tell me every single detail about talking to Ingrid?"

She hefted two bags and I grabbed the others.

"What happened?" I asked as we hit the sidewalk. "How did it go?"

"She's, like, nice," Callie said. "You were right. I messaged her this morning and we ended up meeting for coffee. She's super chill."

"Chill about you and Warren?" I asked. "Did she already know?"

She shook her head. "Not until after he died. She figured out about me the same way I figured out about her, because of everything that everyone was posting. But guess what?" She shifted the weight of the bags. "We weren't the only ones."

"What?"

She nodded. "He was seeing this other girl named Tabatha from San Francisco State."

Where did he find the time? "Did Ingrid know about *her*?" I asked.

"Not while Warren was alive. But after he died Tabatha found out about Ingrid and came pounding on her door all freaked out and yelling." She shifted the weight of a bag. "She told me that when you ran into her in the basement, she was trying to get away from someone she thought was following her. Someone who was staring at her when she was putting on her lipstick in the ladies' room. She was afraid there was another one."

"Oh," I got it. "That explains why she was on the other side of the building. And so jumpy." Or it was a very convenient story, I reminded myself.

"I know I'm the worst," Callie said. "But I'm, like, so glad this Tabatha found out about Ingrid instead of about me. Ingrid said she was legit crazy."

"And we're sure she didn't find out about Ingrid *before* Warren died?" A legit crazy Other Other Girlfriend sounded like a legit suspect to me.

"You mean, are we sure she didn't find out and kill him?" Callie asked. "Pretty sure. She thought she was his only girlfriend until after he was killed. But so did I." She stopped at the corner, setting the bags down on the sidewalk and flexing her hands. I did the same. "Tabatha said she had a date with him on the Saturday he died. She told Ingrid that she waited for him for an hour at the Ferry Building. They were supposed to meet for the farmer's market. When he didn't show she sent him a million texts, getting more and more crazy because he didn't respond."

"For obvious reasons." By that time on Saturday, Warren had already been killed. "If his phone ever turns up, we can see if her story checks out." We picked up the bags and started walking again. "How many phones did that guy have?" I wondered. "Just the two we know about, or one for every girl? And where are they all now?"

I wondered if Detective Jackson had any leads. Not that he'd tell me anything.

"I mean, I can't believe how into him I was," Callie said.

"Don't blame yourself. Clearly he was very good at convincing women they were the only one."

"I mean, he was with me early on Friday, and then with Ingrid late Friday, and all the time he knew he'd be seeing Tabatha Saturday morning."

By this time we were in front of the dry cleaner, but we didn't go in yet. "Did Ingrid tell you she met up with Warren outside the bar?"

Callie nodded. She'd heard the same story I had.

"Did she say if there was anything weird? If she noticed anything when they were waiting for the car?"

"The only thing she remembered was that there was this woman who was also waiting for a car. She was super drunk, and Warren knew her, but he didn't want to talk to her. He didn't want her to see him, so they went around the corner." Callie gave me a look. "He told Ingrid that he'd be so in with June if he told her about it."

"Holy hell, Callie, way to bury the lead! That must have been who he texted you about. Who was she?"

"Ingrid didn't know. But she said she was, like, older. Not old-old, but older. Probably older than you."

Great. At least I wasn't old-old. "Anything else?"

"Ingrid told me the woman was wasted, but still seemed to be super uptight."

"Was she alone?"

"She was by the time Ingrid got there, but who knows what went on before? Do you think she's the one who was with that creep McMillan?"

"I don't know," I admitted. But the way Ingrid had described her did call someone to mind. A middle-aged uptight type. I'd met someone like that recently.

June's assistant Cora.

Was she the mysterious colleague?

CHAPTER 31

Callie and I went our separate ways after dropping the curtains at the dry cleaners. She walked back to the Palace and I headed down the street in the opposite direction, toward June's office.

I'd already sent June two texts, one the day before, right after Cora told me about Sam, and one that morning, asking if we could talk. She hadn't answered either, which is why I'd decided to just show up.

It was mid-afternoon on a Wednesday, so I was surprised to see a Closed sign in the window when I got there. Inside all the lights were off. Which didn't seem right. I would have totally understood if June and some of the other people in the office who'd been close to Sam hadn't come in that day. That would only be natural in light of Sam's death. But shuttering the whole office? If June had taught me anything about the San Francisco real estate market it was that snoozers were losers and closings waited for no one.

So why was the office shut up tight?

I rapped on the door, but nobody appeared from a back room. It looked like the whole place was deserted. Which had me worried. Specifically, I was worried about Cora. If June's assistant had been the mysterious middle-aged woman at the bar that night, she could be the next person in danger.

Or she could be a killer.

I walked back to the Palace, thinking everything over, not figuring anything out. I was still wearing Robbie's borrowed clothes, including her ridiculous heels. I didn't know how people walked around in those things all day. I'd probably be limping by the time I got back.

It was a drizzly afternoon, the kind of afternoon that was a perfect San Francisco backdrop for the warm glowing lights of the Palace marquee. So it was especially bleak to look down the street and see the lights were off and the marquee was dark. I'd asked Marty to take the Tuesday lineup down and replace it with "Reopening Soon!" but he'd used a little editorial license. When I got closer, I saw the unlit marquee read "Reopening As Soon As The City Comes To Its Senses."

I'd have to have him change it before the building inspector came on Friday. There was no need to preemptively antagonize a city official. Now that I thought about it, I'd have to remember to tell Marty to stay home on Friday.

Inside, the Palace was bustling. Not with paying customers, but with most of the staff checking off the items on my let's-spruce-this-place-up list. Mike and Claire, the brother-and-sister teenagers who sometimes worked after-school and weekend shifts, each had cans of paint and small brushes and were touching up all the scuffs and dings along the wall going up the balcony stairs. Callie had just lowered the enormous chandelier down from the lobby ceiling and was on a stepladder, ready to begin polishing each individual crystal. I had no idea what Marty was up to, but I saw that Albert had taken all the candy and snacks out of the vintage glass-and-wood concessions stand that ran almost the full length of the lobby. He was cleaning the glass, section by section, inside and out. It was one of the less physically-taxing jobs, but I still wasn't crazy about him exerting himself beyond his normal duties.

"Hey everyone," I called out as I closed the lobby doors behind me. "The place is looking great. Thanks for everything. I'm sure we'll be open again by the weekend."

This earned me a somewhat lackluster response, which is all it really deserved. I was sure the balcony was sound, and that the city inspector would find nothing wrong with it. But now there was also the issue of the boobytrapped stage being a potential deathtrap. I wasn't entirely optimistic that we'd be able to open again for the weekend, when we were scheduled to show a triple feature of *Broadway Melody of 1936* (1935, Eleanor Powell and Jack Benny), *Broadway Melody of 1938* (1937, Eleanor Powell and Robert Taylor), and *Broadway Melody of 1940* (1940, Eleanor Powell and Fred Astaire). I was raised to believe there's no such thing as too much Eleanor Powell, but this might not turn out to be her weekend.

I went over to the candy counter. "Albert, I want to hire a carpenter to take out those trapdoors for good." Inspector or not, I didn't want to worry about another accident. "Do you know who we've used in the past for that sort of thing? Someone familiar with the building?"

He stopped polishing and adjusted his round glasses. "I believe the fellow that we used has retired, but I wouldn't be surprised if he'd still be willing to come help us out. At least to tell us what our options are. Let me see if I can find his name in my notes."

"You have notes?"

He caught himself, then smiled. "Perhaps it's time for me to tell you about the project I've been working on."

Since my main objective for this conversation was to get Albert to take a break, I agreed. "Come upstairs. Tell me over a hot cup of tea."

"I'm writing a memoir," Albert told me once we'd settled in the break room with steaming mugs in front of us. I eased off Robbie's shoes under the table.

"That's great," I told him. "You've had such an interesting life."

He shook his head, smiling indulgently. "It isn't a memoir of my life. It's a memoir of the Palace."

"Oh." Then I realized what that might mean. "*Oh*. Albert, that's amazing."

He sipped, pleased with my reaction. "What's unique about the Palace is the lives she's touched. I want to tell people how important this theater has been in my life, and my family's. How it was a place of joy and community during the Depression. How it was a respite from worry for women like my mother, when my father and I were both off at war. How the generations who grew up in this neighborhood passed their favorite films down like family heirlooms."

"That's lovely," I told him.

"But I also hope it will shed an interesting light on life in this city, and in this world, as the decades changed and the Palace adapted."

"Or didn't," I said wryly.

"Or didn't," he agreed. "I have to say, I've been having the most wonderful time digging into the archives and hunting down old information. Do you know, I've unearthed the original plans for the building."

"Seriously? Can you show me?"

"I'd be delighted," he said. "I've found out so much about the building. For instance, those trapdoors we need to seal up? They were always causing problems. From the beginning, people broke collarbones and arms from being launched up through them too forcefully."

"Really? I never thought about anyone making an entrance through the traps, just about making a quick exit."

"They worked both ways," Albert said. "At least, most of the time they did."

"How did anyone ever drop so far without breaking their legs?" I asked, thinking of Brandon. "Were there giant mattresses or something?"

He shook his head. "They didn't drop that far. Originally there was something like a loft or a platform under that part of the stage. So the players were only raised or dropped a few feet. I imagine the loft was removed at the same time the traps themselves were boarded up."

"Wow," I said. Then I had a thought. "I wonder if people would be interested in Palace tours once your book comes out."

His eyes gleamed. "I had the same thought. Of course it won't all be about architecture and history. There will be a great deal about the legends of the Palace as well."

I looked at him. "You mean the ghost."

Albert had known Trixie in life when he was just a boy going to kiddie matinees every weekend. He'd also seen her, just a glimpse here and there, since she died.

Albert, like Callie's mother, was a believer.

He nodded. "Of course, I'll dispel the rumor about the knife thrower's assistant," he said. I knew he meant the legend about a vaudeville act gone awry, resulting in another ghost story. But that one really was just a story. Albert had reliably informed me that the showgirl in question had in fact choked on a sandwich and hadn't even died at the Palace.

"But you'll talk about Trixie," I said. Then, quickly. "About Beatrix George. The usherette. Will you say you've seen her yourself?"

Maybe he wasn't as afraid as I was of being carted off to some very relaxing spa with bars on the windows and the kind of robes that tie in the back.

"I will," he said. "And I've found a few others who have had similar experiences." He peered at me, and I had the feeling he was waiting for me to confirm his suspicions. I suspected he'd suspected something from the first time I'd seen Trixie. I just couldn't bring myself to say anything.

He blinked and looked away. "I wish there were some way of communicating with Trixie," he said. "I've spoken to Lillian— Callie's mother—about the possibility of a séance." He tilted his head, regarding me. "What do you think?"

I swallowed. "What would you want to say?"

"I'd want her permission," he said simply. "And perhaps her blessing. After all, if the story of the Palace belongs to anyone, it belongs to her."

This was the point at which I would have loved to hear Trixie's voice ring out behind me, saying something like "Well, I'll be darned," or "Gee, that's a grand idea."

But the ghost of the Palace remained silent.

CHAPTER 32

"You look different," Marty accused. He'd found me at my desk in the office after I left Albert.

"I'm wearing nice clothes," I said. "I borrowed them from Robbie."

I'd also put on makeup and gotten a manicure and a blowout in an attempt to look Hollywood wealthy for McMillan that morning. Not that it had lasted. I'd ruined the hair by wandering around in a drizzle all afternoon. It was now pulled into its customary ponytail, and I was wishing I had some sneakers to change into.

Marty made a face. "You don't belong in nice clothes." Before I could ask him what exactly he meant by that he flung himself into a chair. "I heard from Brandon. He's home from the hospital but he'll be in a cast for at least six weeks. He may try to come in after he gets the hang of his crutches, but until then I'm *not* covering his shifts."

"I wouldn't dream of asking you," I said. "Brandon interacts with the public."

Marty scowled.

"I'll talk to Claire and Mike about splitting up his shifts until he's back," I said.

He snorted. I could only assume it was in agreement.

"Has Detective Jackson told you anything about the investigation since Sam died?" I asked. "Are they taking the possibility that someone pushed her any more seriously?"

He shrugged, chewing on a cuticle. "We're having dinner tonight, unless someone else gets murdered. But I'm sure he won't tell me anything. Nobody ever tells me anything."

"Did someone say 'dinner?'" Hector stood in the doorway, a pleased look on his face and a shopping bag in his hand. The man was like a cat. I never heard him coming. I mean, he was like an incredibly handsome and charming cat, with a sexy Spanish accent, but still.

"It's a little early for me," I told him. "What brings you here?"

"I thought you might like these." He dropped the shopping bag on my desk. "And I hoped to invite you to my new home for dinner. Gabriela will be there and as we speak, she is making her famous *ajiaco*." He took a seat in the chair next to Marty and crossed his legs. "It's a soup. With chicken and potatoes."

Marty looked from Hector to me and back again. "Well, isn't that just domestic."

I gave him a look. "I think you have things to do."

He grimaced and stood. "I'll be in the projection booth." He pointedly closed the door behind him.

"What's in the bag?" I asked Hector.

"Open it and see." He watched as I peered in, then pulled out a shoebox.

"Sneakers?"

"I thought your friend Robbie's heels might grow uncomfortable as the day went on," he said. "There are also socks."

I looked at the label. "How did you know my size?"

"I have an eye for such things. Will you join me for dinner? Gabriela's *ajiaco* is not to be missed."

"Sure, I mean, wait—" Something he'd said had just caught up with me. "Your new *home*? What do you mean your new home?"

"I told you I was considering staying in San Francisco."

"You told me that three days ago! Don't tell me you've already got a place."

He shrugged. "Only a rental, for now, but it suits my needs." He rose. "I'll be back to pick you up at six thirty."

I continued to stare at the space where he'd been after he left, thinking something along the lines of "How does he *do* that?" Then

I tried on the sneakers.

They were a perfect fit.

I still hadn't heard back from June. I checked her website to see if she'd posted anything about the office being temporarily closed. There was nothing on her home page except a photo of a welcoming front door. Nothing about an office closure anywhere, just photo after photo of homes I was sure I could no longer afford. Thank you, Ted.

Thinking of Ted, I realized my lawyers had been ominously silent for a few days. Were they still trying to figure out how to prove Ted had squirrelled all our money away somewhere, or had they moved on to their next high-profile split? And when should I expect a truck containing all my earthly possessions—or at least the ones Ted had identified as such—to pull up outside the theater door? And where the heck was I going to store everything until June found me a house? Assuming June would resurface to do that. Assuming I could scrape together sufficient money for a meagre deposit on anything.

Okay, enough self-pity. I needed to pull myself together. After which I needed to hit social media and start sifting through Warren's friends' posts from that night at the bar again, this time looking for Cora in the background. For that task I would love some company. Some very specific company.

"Trixie?" I said out loud. "Don't stay away too long, okay? I miss you."

I held my breath for a moment but didn't have any sense of her presence. All I could do was wait.

I turned to the laptop. When Callie and I had looked at all the photos of Warren's party before, neither of us had met Cora. Now that I knew I was looking for her, or at least someone who looked like her, things should be easier.

An hour and a half later I thought I had her.

*   *   *

"I think it's her watch."

"Her watch?" Hector repeated. I was back in his car, this time being whisked to his new mystery house for soup with cousin Gabriela. Marty was right. That did sound pretty domestic.

"I noticed it on Monday. Cora kept checking it to keep June on schedule. I noticed because most people who obsess about their watches have those high-tech ones, but this was an old-fashioned men's wristwatch." I told him. "It caught my eye. And I'm sure it's the same watch that's on the arm of someone in the background of a selfie Warren posted that night."

"All right," he nodded. "Let's assume it's Cora's watch in the photo. Does that mean she was the colleague who was there with McMillan? From what I saw of them the other day she despises the man."

"To know him is to despise him," I said. "But who knows if that was an act? Maybe it was a case of the lady protesting too much. She could have been covering for their scheming." I ignored his raised eyebrows and continued. "It's just too much of a coincidence otherwise. And it ties in with Warren being so smug about having seen someone that June would freak out about. Cora is June's assistant. She must know everything that's going on at June's agency. What if she was secretly feeding information to McMillan? She can't be earning much as an assistant. What if he was paying her to tell him what the competition was up to? Or to undermine June's business? That would seriously make June freak."

"You think Cora killed Warren and Sam to keep them from saying anything to June?" Hector asked.

"Maybe. Or maybe she and McMillan did it together. Since McMillan apparently has witnesses that he wasn't in the balcony when Sam was pushed, maybe Cora murdered Sam. But McMillan could still have murdered Warren."

"That's a lot of maybes," Hector said, pulling into the garage of a modern glass-fronted house on a block of tall Victorians.

"We're here already?" We hadn't been in the car five minutes. "You're living in the neighborhood?"

"It's a great neighborhood," he said. "I hear all good things about the demographics and zoning and so on."

I recognized the buzzwords I'd used on McMillan. "You're hilarious." I told Hector.

"I am many things."

I couldn't argue with that.

The house was amazing. Four floors of gleaming surfaces and tasteful neutral furnishings topped by a roof deck with literal million-dollar views. There was an elevator, just in case the modern glass stairs were too much. There was a kitchen that would have made grown chefs weep with envy. And there was Cousin Gabriela, in her chair at a table-height section of the vast kitchen island, wielding a knife like a pro.

"Nora, I'm so glad you could make it." Her smile provided the warmth that the ultramodern kitchen lacked.

"I'm so glad you invited me." I bent to give her a hug, staying clear of the knife. "Something smells incredible."

"It's our grandmother's recipe," she said. "But that's for later. First, a glass of wine and some of this gorgeous cheese I got from that shop down the street."

Hector was already opening a bottle of red, and the island was laden with platters of cheeses, crackers, grilled vegetables, and fruit.

"Nobody ever goes hungry around the Acostas," I said.

Hector grinned. "We should adopt that as our new family motto."

"What was your old one?"

"Something grim about revenge," Gabriela said.

Which really shouldn't have surprised me.

*   *   *

"I've never eaten that much in my life," I said later, pushing back from the table. "Or that well."

Gabriela waved a dismissive hand. "You should see us at the holidays."

"I don't know if I could take it."

The conversation had been as good as Gabriela's cooking. She'd told me more about her work, developing technology to make the world more accessible to people with all sorts of disabilities. She spoke passionately about bridging the gap between humans and computers, of using tech to enable all sorts of things that weren't possible just a few years before.

Listening to her, I had a crazy thought about using technology to help Trixie. If Gabriela's research could help a veteran who'd lost his arm to "feel" his robotic hand, was there something she could do for someone without an entire body?

Hector noticed that my mind had wandered. "I fear we're keeping you up too late," he said.

"You should take advantage of the theater being closed to catch up on your rest," Gabriela advised. "Hopefully it will only be for a few more days."

"The inspection is Friday," I told her. "Fingers crossed that the inspector doesn't ask me about the giant gaping hole in the stage."

"What are you going to do about that?" Hector asked.

"For the balcony inspection, my strategy will be to lower the screen and not mention it," I confessed. "But long term I'm calling in a carpenter to take out both of the old trapdoors and repair the stage."

"That seems safest," Gabriela said.

"Meanwhile, we've got those orange traffic cones around both traps, and the public isn't allowed onto the stage, so there shouldn't be any danger." *Famous last words*, I didn't add.

"Well, I can't wait until you're open again." Gabriela folded her napkin and placed it neatly over her dessert plate. (Did I not mention the dessert? Rice pudding. Amazing spices.) "I've been looking forward to your Eleanor Powell movies this weekend. You know how I feel about musicals."

"I sincerely hope we don't disappoint."

I'd managed to put the troubles at the Palace out of my mind for a while, but now they all came rushing back. Hector must have read my thoughts.

"Gabby," he said casually. "Nora has a theory about the people who might be behind all this. I don't suppose you could do something magical on your computer and see if there's any connection between our two main suspects?"

Her eyes flashed. "I thought you'd never ask."

"Cora used to work with McMillan?" I repeated.

Gabriela was looking at her laptop screen. Hector and I had cleared the table while she'd tapped away at the keyboard. By the time we got back from the kitchen she had our connection.

"Until six years ago she was the office manager for a real estate firm in Noe Valley where he was the top salesman," she now told us. "They both left at about the same time. He opened his own firm in the Financial District, and she...I don't know what she did until she showed up working for June."

"When was that?" I asked.

Gabriela tapped again. "Three years ago."

"I can't believe you found all that out so fast," I marveled. "You're a genius."

"I'm really not," she grinned. "Everything I told you is right there on LinkedIn." She didn't say "any fool could have found it," but she didn't have to.

"Still," I said. "Thank you. I hereby grant you free passes to the Palace for life."

She laughed. "For free passes let me keep digging. I'm sure I'll be able to come up with something more."

"A secret video of McMillan killing someone would be useful,"

Hector said.

"Don't get too ambitious," I said, then, in my best Bette Davis voice: "Don't let's ask for the moon, we have the stars."

Blank looks from both of them. They didn't recognize the line from *Now, Voyager* (1942, Bette Davis and Paul Henreid).

"Sorry," I said. "I tend to channel Bette Davis after a few glasses of wine."

Hector was looking at me with something in his eye. "Perhaps we should call it a night."

Hector walked me to the door of Robbie's guest house and waited until I was inside with the bolt in place before calling "Goodnight, Nora" and walking away.

There was no goodnight kiss. Hector had never tried to kiss me. He hadn't even so much as paused and lingered and looked at me like Paul Henreid lighting that cigarette for Bette Davis. Sure, Hector smoldered now and then, usually from a safe distance, with a table or a desk between us, but that was as far as it had gone. And to be fair, he probably couldn't help but smolder. It seemed like his natural state.

But no, there had been no moves. And that was a tremendous relief.

I liked him. A lot. And I was attracted to him. Any woman would be. Any woman with a pulse. And at least one without. But no amount of attraction made up for the fact that I wasn't ready. I wasn't ready to let another man into my life. Not after Ted's series of brutal betrayals. No, I wasn't ready to start thinking about a life with someone else. Not until I'd established a life just for me.

I could only see about five minutes into my future, and that's no state of mind to be in if you're thinking about mixing your life up with someone else's. And something told me that if anything did start with Hector, it wouldn't be casual. It would be very mixed up.

So, to sum up for the jury...I. Was. Not. Ready.

But I kind of hoped I would be soon.

Now, Voyager
1942

This is one of those movies that I've seen a dozen times and never realized it was all about sex until I tried to write about it. Yes, it's about finding your identity and learning to stand up for yourself. It's about what it means to be a grown woman with choices, and it's even about the redemptive power of proper eyebrow grooming. But at its core, this is totally a movie about sex.

Bette Davis plays Charlotte Vale, and she's a mess. When we first meet her it's because her sister-in-law Lisa (Ilka Chase) has arranged for a psychiatrist (played with quiet warmth by usually-a-villain Claude Rains) to come to the family mansion in Boston for what amounts to an intervention.

Charlotte is middle-aged and beyond dumpy. She wears glasses because her mother thinks she should. She carries extra weight because her mother doesn't believe in slimming. She wears baggy dresses and sensible shoes— you can guess why. Her mother (Gladys Cooper) is a domineering tyrant, who refers to Charlotte as "My ugly duckling." And that's when she's being nice. Charlotte, we learn, is having a nervous breakdown. Who wouldn't? The only thing that gives me hope for her is that she smokes in secret. Rebellion! Yes! (I mean, smoking itself, no, but rebellion, absolutely.)

The horrible mother agrees for Charlotte to go for a cure at the doctor's Vermont sanitorium because she fears the shame that news of Charlotte's crackup might bring to the sacred family name. Also because Claude Rains calls her out. "My dear Mrs. Vale, if you had deliberately and maliciously planned to destroy your daughter's life you couldn't have done it more completely." Go, Claude.

It's during a conversation with the doctor that we find out Charlotte wasn't always a scared, sexless rabbit. Quite the contrary. When she was twenty, she had a shipboard romance while on a cruise with her mother. He was a dishy sailor and all the girls were after him, but he chose Charlotte because "I was so responsive." *Really*. Do tell...Of course the couple is found out—found in mid-make-out session, in what Charlotte calls "the proudest moment of my life." Interesting.

Mother, as you can imagine, brings down the hammer. And the result is the sad old spinster still hiding those cigarettes. Until...self-esteem happens. No, they didn't call it that in 1942, but you know what good therapy and a healthy lifestyle can do for a woman. In a movie, at least. After months of healing Charlotte is ready to leave Vermont. But she isn't going home. No, no, no! She's going on another cruise! This one to South America, and notably without Mother.

This is where we have The Shot, people. The iconic shot of Charlotte stepping off the ship and into her new life. And you better believe she takes that step wearing heels! She's so chic it's insane. The glasses are gone, the eyebrows are perfect, and the lipstick totally on point. The dress is fitted to show off her new slim waist, and this shot is the best argument there will ever be for bringing back hats. Please, can we bring back hats?

There is, inevitably, A Man on the ship (Paul Henreid).

He and Charlotte are thrown together and it's awkward at first because she doesn't know how to act around a normal, but then it isn't awkward anymore because it's perfect. They're perfect for each other. We know they're perfect for each other because of the way Max Steiner's theme music swells every time they're together. (*"Wrong, would it be wrong to kiss? Seeing I feel like this..."* Trust me, it's dreamy.)

The only thing that mars all the perfection is the fact that the man—Jerry—is married. Yup. Unhappily married, as we learn from the wife of a friend, but he's too much of a saint to leave the wife and abandon his emotionally fragile daughter. (Okay, okay, but maybe that wasn't quite as cliché in 1942? Just go with it.)

They're perfect for each other but they can't be together. And it's that *longing*, that just-out-of-reach love that they can see but they know they can't have that keeps me (and thousands of gay men) coming back to this movie. I've never smoked, but when Jerry lights two cigarettes and takes one from his lips to put it on Charlotte's, it's a classic movie moment that's still shockingly swoon-worthy. It's almost a kiss. Almost.

You know how I just said they can't be together? Ha! Not so! Because of a truck accident and a missed ship they get five glorious days in Rio. And Charlotte gets to be all kinds of "responsive" again. They are *together*, if only for a moment, but in the world of this movie adults know that sometimes that's all you get. Sometimes you can only have "that little strip of territory that's ours." Sigh.

And then the trip is over, and Charlotte goes back to Boston, where her new backbone is very much in evidence. Mother is not a fan. But Charlotte, let's not forget, is played by Bette Davis. Do you think she'll crumble again? Not with Max Steiner's music playing, she won't! Not with her memories of being loved to give her strength. She may still be single, but Charlotte Vale is no old maid anymore.

There's more, involving a new boyfriend and a chance meeting with Jerry's daughter (!!) but I won't tell you the rest. Because the last line of this movie is one of the best, most tear-jerking lines in all of movies, and I want you to *earn* it. Bette did.

Beauty thoughts:
Okay, so this movie has a disturbing inclination to equate being pretty with being lovable. How many of us have internalized that message from how many movies? Or, for that matter, from how many makeover shows? Cut it out, Hollywood! On the other hand, Charlotte's pre-Vermont eyebrows were tragic.

Voyaging thoughts:
There has never been a more romantic place to say goodbye than a train station. Fact.

Movies My Friends Should Watch
Sally Lee

CHAPTER 33

A brief article appeared in the Entertainment section of the online *Los Angeles Times* the next morning.

San Francisco's Palace Theater Gets A Second Act

We're spoiled here in the City of Angels. Our collection of landmark movie theaters is second to none. So in this as in many things we might feel a little superior to our chilly Bay Area neighbors. But now one of LA's own is taking a piece of cinema history and giving San Francisco's Palace Theater a second act.

Okay, I should have known that the writer would lead with a little regional snark. And, by the way, I wasn't one of "LA's own." I'd been born in Dayton, Ohio. But that was beside the point.

Nora Bishop—yes *that* Nora Bishop, one-time screenwriter and soon-to-be-ex of A-lister Ted Bishop—has a new project. She's taken over the Palace and is turning it into a glittering reminder of what Hollywood's Golden Age was all about. Cue Busby Berkeley's chorus girls, because Miss Nora Paige (she's already ditched her husband's famous name) is showing nothing but classics at the Palace. Turns out the almost-ex is writing a second act for herself as well. We asked the classic film buff, why the Palace?

"It was made for these films," she told us. "The

theater has been retrofitted and brought totally up to date with the latest in comfort and technology, but it's still true to its original design. So the experience is as close to stepping back in time as you can get—but with more comfortable seats. You may think you've seen your favorite film when you've seen it on TV, but just wait until you see it on the big screen. There's truly nothing like it."

But don't expect her to be showing any of her husband's films any time soon. "We'll have to give them fifty years or so," she said, smiling cheerfully. "To see if they stand the test of time."

We also asked the movie maven about the ghost rumored to be haunting the Palace. Her response was typically upbeat: "I can only quote Gene Tierney, in *The Ghost and Mrs. Muir*: 'Haunted! How perfectly fascinating!'"

Fascinating indeed. A classic film repertoire in a haunted movie palace? Sign me up.

This is the kind of piece that a team of public relations specialists could plant with forty-eight hours and one quick Skype call. I would have preferred if they hadn't mentioned Ted and had concentrated on how incredibly safe and structurally sound the theater was—which is mainly what I'd told them about—but I'd take what I could get. I could only hope the line about it being retrofitted and up to date would help to combat the rumors about the balcony being "faulty." Because passing the inspection was only half of the job. The other half was getting customers back in the theater.

By the time I got to the Palace that morning the piece had been picked up by our local news site, SFGate, and the PR squad had zapped links to it all over social media. Someone sent it to Callie before she'd even had her breakfast.

"I mean, yay," she told me when I found her in the lobby. "Did you give them that picture?"

"Albert had it," I told her. "I just sent it to them yesterday."

Accompanying the article was a photo in glorious black and white of the Palace marquee taken on a summer night at a time when the customers lined up around the block and every person in line wore a hat.

"Albert called a while ago," Callie said. "He said to tell you he's staying home today."

"Good." I moved around the candy counter, drawn to the steaming pot of coffee. "I wouldn't want him out in this rain."

The drizzle had finally turned into something a little stronger. I'd fought with my umbrella all the way from Robbie's guest house.

I was pouring coffee when I heard the blaring trumpets of the 20th Century Fox overture, announcing Marty's arrival. I jumped and spilled hot liquid all over Albert's freshly-polished glass counter.

I looked up at Marty as he shook himself dry by the lobby doors. His resemblance to an aging Saint Bernard had never been stronger.

"Is that the famous soon-to-be ex?" he asked. "I don't recognize her when she isn't smiling cheerfully."

"I take it you saw the story," I wiped at the spilled coffee.

"I did and I *hated* it," he said. "But at least it's an attempt to salvage our tattered reputation, so..." he shrugged.

"I'll take that as a win. And I'm sorry they made it sound like showing classics was all my idea. I would never have said that." They'd been showing classic films long before I'd gotten to the Palace.

"We know you wouldn't," Callie said.

We were interrupted by the ping of a text on my phone. I'd been getting them all morning as people had seen the story, but this one was different.

Nora, we haven't met but I believe we have some interests in common. This is Otis Hampton. Please contact me at you earliest convenience.

"What?" Marty was looking at me closely. "Why do you have that weird look on your face?"

"Otis Hampton just sent me a text."

"Otis Hampton the billionaire?"

Otis Hampton the billionaire who had been dating Priya Sharma right up until she got engaged to my rat of a husband.

"I don't think there's another Otis Hampton."

"That's practically incestuous." Marty got himself a Coke from the soft drink machine. "What does he want?"

If he was anything like me, he probably wanted both Ted and Priya to fall into an active volcano on their honeymoon. Or free-dive into a school of sharks. Or ski into an avalanche, maybe. Not that I'd been indulging in any violent fantasies or anything. "I have no idea."

"I mean, call him." Callie said. "Maybe Ted and Priya broke up again. Or maybe he wants you to help him split them up."

"Oh, God. Not this again," Marty moaned.

I shot him a pointed look. "I'm not the least bit interested in splitting them up. Ted and Priya are none of my concern." Maybe they'd go sky diving.

He gave me a look right back. "Try that again, this time like you mean it."

"You should still text him," Callie said. "I mean, *Otis Hampton.*"

Sure, Otis Hampton, but I had things to do. I had to make sure none of the fire extinguishers were expired before the building inspector showed up. I had to get in touch with that carpenter about fixing the stage, I had to prove that Cora or McMillan or both of them had been behind the murders of Warren and Sam. I had to have a lot more coffee.

I glanced up at the balcony landing and saw someone there. At which point there was only one thing I had to do.

I had to talk to Trixie.

*   *   *

"Nora! Yoo-hoo! Hi, Nora!"

I grunted something in Callie and Marty's direction and dashed up the stairs.

"Nora, I'm so glad to see you! I came back last night, and I don't know how long I've been gone. How long have I been gone? And why aren't there any pictures on the marquee? It says we're closed. Why would we be closed? What—"

She burbled all this while I was on my way up. Knowing Callie and Marty were watching me, I swept past her without a glance, but as soon as we were in the hallway behind the closed door I turned and swept my arms right through her in a cold attempt at a hug.

"Trixie, I've missed you so much. How are you? Are you okay?"

I'd expected her to return traumatized, or at least sobered, by what she'd seen before she'd vanished. Watching Sam fall had shocked her so badly she'd disappeared for days. But now she showed no signs of distress.

"Why wouldn't I be okay?" Her penciled brows came together. "What's going on?"

Looking at her confused face, I thought I understood. "Let's go to the office where we can talk."

Once before, after she'd seen something terrible, and done something terrible, she'd come back from "away" with no memory of it. I'd wondered at the time if her loss of memory was some sort of mental protection, blocking out something she couldn't bear to remember. Now, thinking the same thing might have happened, I hoped it was true. I hoped she had no memory of seeing Sam fall as she herself had fallen.

"Everything's fine," I told her when we got to the office. She perched on the desk, her feet on a guest chair, while I paced and tried to figure out what to say. "You've only been gone a few days."

"Whew! Gee, I was worried. I couldn't tell. But why are we closed?"

"There was an accident in the balcony, so we have to have a

safety inspection, that's all." I looked at her closely. "Do you remember the accident in the balcony?"

She blinked rapidly. "Why? Was I there?"

"I—" To be absolutely honest, I didn't know if she'd been there. If she'd been glued to McMillan, she'd have seen him push Sam off the balcony. That was *if* he'd been the one to push her. "I'm not absolutely sure."

While I was happy that Trixie had been spared the trauma of remembering Sam's death, her blank spot meant I didn't have a witness to what had really happened. "What's the last thing you remember?" I asked her. "You disappeared on Monday, the day all the realtors were here."

"I remember that!" she said eagerly. "I was Mata Hari!"

"You were an amazing Mata Hari." I sat in the second guest chair, looking up at her. "The last time I saw you that day it was lunchtime. You were with Stan McMillan and a bunch of guys at his table on the balcony landing. Do you remember?"

She nodded, curls bouncing. "I do!" Her face clouded. "Oh, Nora. I don't think you should be friends with that man. He says some terrible things."

"I have no doubt." I leaned forward. "What happened when you were at the table?"

She blinked rapidly, and adjusted her little cap. She clasped her hands, then shook them out, scrunching her face in concentration. She fidgeted with the top button of her uniform, biting her lip. I was ready to scream by the time she answered.

"They were all talking, and I was trying so hard to follow because I wanted to tell you everything, but I'm sorry, Nora. I didn't understand a lot of what they said."

"That's okay," I told her. "That's fine. It was probably all about real estate anyway."

"I think one of them is in demolition or something," she said. "He kept saying he was 'crushing' everything."

I nodded. "He's probably in demolition." Or he was just an obnoxious bro. "What happened then?"

She thought, then her expression cleared. "Oh! I remember! Somebody screamed!"

There it was. The confirmation I hadn't wanted. If Trixie had been with McMillan on the balcony when Sam screamed, he couldn't be the killer.

"And you were with McMillan when you heard the scream?" I said, just to be sure. "You saw him?"

She nodded. "I remember because he said, 'What the—'" She stopped herself, her eyes wide. "Oh, Nora, the way he talks."

"I'm sorry you had to hear him," I said. "What happened after the scream? Do you remember?"

"Everybody rushed into the balcony to see what happened," she said. "Not him, not right away, but one of the fellas who was at his table got up to see, and a bunch of other people were already going in." She brightened. "Marty! He came out the hallway door and went past us right to the balcony. Maybe he can tell you what happened!" She looked pleased at the thought.

"That's a great idea. But do you remember anything else?" A thought struck. "What about Cora? Did you see her?"

She blinked. "I don't think I know her. Who's Cora?"

Right. I'd only met Cora that Monday myself. "She's one of the real estate people," I said.

"Oh. Oh!" She sat up. "Then I don't think she went in after the scream. I saw the ladies go in before. It must have been one of them who screamed. What happened? Did they see a mouse or something?"

"Do we have mice? Never mind," I waved a hand. I didn't want to know. "Which ladies went in? Was one of them tall and blonde?" Had Trixie seen Sam enter the balcony?

Trixie nodded eagerly. "She was one of them, but she was with another one. The older one. They both went in together before the scream."

The older woman. Cora.

"Trixie, what did the—"

At that moment the office door slammed open. I jumped and

yelped. Trixie squealed and vanished. Marty stormed into the room. "All hands on deck," he yelled. "David just called. He's on his way here with the building inspector!"

CHAPTER 34

"NO!" I looked around the office, but Trixie was gone again.

Marty thought I was talking to him. "David put some pressure on to get the inspection done early, so he can rule out a faulty balcony in the investigation. We can get cleared by the city and the cops at the same time, but it's happening today. What are you waiting for?"

I was waiting for Trixie to materialize again and confirm that it had been Cora who pushed Sam off the balcony. Then I realized what Marty had just said.

"What? The—When?" I focused. "How much time do we have?"

"None."

"Okay." I thought fast. "You get down and take that snarky message off the marquee. I'll lower the screen to hide the hole in the stage." I was already halfway down the hall.

"Callie! Go outside and send me a text the minute you see them pull up." I yelled this from the landing before opening the balcony doors to make sure the police tape was still up, and everything looked in order for the inspection.

Callie's production equipment was still in place down front, but everything else was normal. I took a breath and told myself there was nothing structurally wrong with the balcony, and that everything would be fine. Then I dashed back out and down the stairs to hide the hole in the stage.

Once in the auditorium I turned the house lights all the way up and took the stairs to the stage two at a time. I went straight to the control panel and nearly knocked the fire extinguisher off the wall in my rush to open the panel next to it. The screen lowered slowly—which was a safety feature—so I spent the next few minutes trying not to ignite in frustration as it inched its way down. It finished just as Callie's text pinged, announcing the inspector was here.

I turned off the backstage lights and hopped back down the stairs for a look. Good. You'd never know there was a potential deathtrap lurking in the darkness behind the screen.

"Showtime," I whispered to myself. Then I went to the lobby to meet my fate.

"Thank you, Vik," I said wholeheartedly. "And thanks again for rushing this. We really appreciate it."

"No problem." Vikram Khatri, San Francisco Building Inspector and my new best friend, had just handed me a certificate that said the Palace was good to reopen. He shrugged into his jacket and looked around the lobby, none too eager to head back out into the rain. "My daughters love this place," he said. "They'd have killed me if I hadn't passed you in time for you to show *National Velvet* next week. It's their favorite. And I wouldn't let them come here if I wasn't sure the building was up to code. This just verified it."

"I hope giving your daughters all the free popcorn they can eat isn't considered a bribe, because I fully intend to give your daughters all the free popcorn they can eat when they come in," I told him.

I'd never loved a human being more. I'd never loved *National Velvet* more. And I loved *National Velvet* (1944, Elizabeth Taylor and Mickey Rooney) a lot. I closed the lobby door behind Vik, thinking nothing but lovely thoughts for one lovely moment.

The only thing the inspector had dinged us on was the rickety wooden ladder Marty used to change the marquee. He'd given the balcony a thorough going-over, but never even glanced at the stage.

I turned around to share the triumph, but I had the wrong crowd. Marty was by the candy counter, glowering as usual. Callie was on her phone, furiously alerting social media that the Palace was back in business. Detective Jackson, standing at the foot of the balcony stairs, was also texting, although with less gusto.

"Hey," I said, "anybody feel like celebrating?"

Nothing.

. "Detective Jackson, I wish I'd known you had so much pull with the building inspector. I could have saved myself a trip downtown." And a promise to read some kid's screenplay.

He glanced up from his phone. "No problem. I've just gotten clearance from the crime scene squad that you can take down the tape. They have everything they need."

"What does that mean?" I asked him. "You're still investigating Sam's death, right?" They couldn't be closing the case. Not when I had a ghostly eyewitness who had seen Cora go into the balcony with Sam moments before she fell. Not that I could tell Jackson that.

"We're still investigating," he assured me. "With the faulty-balcony scenario off the table we're down to Sam's death being either an accidental fall or a deliberate act. But in either case we're confident we have all the physical evidence there is." He pocketed his phone.

"We can reopen," I said. I felt a little lightheaded. "We can really reopen."

Jackson flashed a rare smile. "Eleanor Powell fans can sleep well tonight. There will be Broadway Melodies tomorrow."

At this, Marty made a strangled sound and crossed the lobby swiftly, moving toward the detective with a focused look on his face. I wasn't sure what was happening. When he got to Jackson he didn't slow down, he just swept him into the kind of swirling embrace that can only be described as cinematic. It was Rhett-and-Scarlett level stuff, and it went on for a while.

"Are you two going to, like, get a room?" Callie finally said. "Because Albert wants to know how much champagne he should bring for our grand reopening party." She wiggled her phone. "He's waiting."

Marty released his hold on Jackson, who staggered a bit before clearing his throat and straightening his raincoat. "I think I should go back to work," he said. Then he looked at Marty meaningfully. "I'll see you later."

"That's right you will." Marty watched as his boyfriend (I don't care what he said, I was calling Jackson his boyfriend) made his way out into the rainy afternoon.

"What?" Marty said, looking between Callie and me defiantly. "He remembered about Eleanor Powell."

"I totally get it," I told him.

"I mean," Callie said, waving the phone again, "Albert? Champagne?"

"A lot," I answered. "Tell him to bring a lot." Then I ran after Detective Jackson to tell him about Cora's wristwatch. Because I couldn't tell him what Trixie had seen, but at least I could tell him that Cora had been at the Irish Bank the night Warren was killed.

At least that was something.

I'm so relieved! I knew everything would be fine, but I'm so relieved!

The text was from Robbie, in response to mine telling her the Palace would be back up and running tomorrow night. Another message appeared.

I hope you're celebrating. Are you celebrating?

We're about to open another bottle of champagne.

The Palace break room had never known such revelry. Marty ordered pizza, which arrived just as Brandon came by after school. We made a fuss over his cast and crutches, and he basked in our attention. At least in Callie's. He seemed to find the rest of us embarrassing.

I thought about inviting Hector, but this was a family party.

The only person missing was Trixie. I kept looking over at the open door, thinking she'd be drawn to the fun, but she made no appearance.

My phone pinged with another text.

I understand this may seem odd, but I really do think we should speak.

From Otis Hampton again. I didn't know what I wanted to do about Priya's ex-boyfriend, so I didn't do anything. If there was one thing I was good at, it was ignoring texts.

"Nora?" By the way he said it, I assumed this wasn't Albert's first attempt to get my attention.

"Sorry. What?" I shook my head.

He smiled. "How many shows do you want tomorrow? Can we show all three features twice?"

"Probably not. Nobody will come to anything before noon, so how about we do '38 and '40 in the afternoon, then all three in the evening?"

"Why doesn't '36 get two showings?" Marty asked.

"Because it's the weakest of the three." Eleanor Powell made three *Broadway Melody* movies, *Broadway Melody of 1936* with Jack Benny, *Broadway Melody of 1938* with Robert Taylor, and *Broadway Melody of 1940* with Fred Astaire. No offense to Jack Benny, but everybody knew '36 was the weakest.

"I *beg* your pardon." Marty on champagne was possibly more hair-triggered than Marty on caffeine. "Who says it's the weakest of the three?"

"Common knowledge," I said airily.

"Oh, dear," Albert sighed.

"Are you seriously going to sit there and tell me that '36 didn't pave the way for everything that came after it?" Marty demanded.

"Are you seriously going to stand there and deny that '38 improved on it?" I countered. "Do I have to remind you that Judy Garland was in '38? Do I have to bring up Sophie Tucker?"

"You know I worship them both as the goddesses they are!" he shouted. "Which doesn't change the fact—"

"Can we all simply agree that '40 was the best and leave it there?" Albert interjected. "After all, Fred Astaire. And Cole Porter." He nodded sagely.

Marty sniffed. "Fine. But only because I don't have time for this. I have a date."

"Fine," I agreed. I was not one to argue against Cole Porter.

The party pretty much broke up after that. Marty charged off into the night, Albert offered Brandon a ride home, and I cleaned up the pizza boxes and paper cups while Callie did something on her phone. I'd just put the last of the recycling in the bin when I noticed she was looking at me, her expression speculative.

"What?"

She held up her phone, the screen showing that she'd been looking at IMDb, the Internet Movie Database. "*Broadway Melody of 1938*," she said. "What's Eleanor Powell's name?"

"Sally Lee," I said automatically. Then I got a very bad feeling.

"Uh huh," she said. "Just like that blogger Marty swears by. And what's her name in *Born to Dance*?"

Born to Dance (1936, Eleanor Powell and Jimmy Stewart) had been one of my mother's favorite movies. And my mother had married a man named Paige. I turned to face Callie squarely. "Her name is Nora Paige. Why do you ask?"

More speculative scrutiny. "I mean, if I was named after an Eleanor Powell character, and I found myself needing a fake name to for some reason, like, maybe to blog under, I might think it would be funny to use the name of a different Eleanor Powell character."

"Interesting." I gave the table a wipe with a paper towel. "Are you about ready to call it a night?"

She grinned. "Nora! You're Sally Lee! Admit it!" She slapped the table. "Marty will die! This will literally kill him!"

I sat across from her. "Marty will never know," I said meaningfully. "At least, not until I want him to."

"This is too good," Callie breathed.

I gave her a warning look. "Do you really want his head to explode?"

"It literally would," she said. "But it would serve him right!"

"I'll tell him eventually," I assured her. "I'm just waiting till the time is right." Sure, that's what I was doing.

"Sure you are." Her eyes were dancing. "Please just promise me one thing?"

I looked at her warily. "What?"

"Please, please, please let me be there when you tell him!"

I didn't say yes. But I didn't say no, either.

CHAPTER 35

The next morning it was with a full heart and a somewhat fuzzy head that I rounded the corner and saw the marquee lit up with showtimes for Broadway Melodies.

I hadn't forgotten that Sam had been murdered in my theater, or that her killer was still on the loose. I hadn't forgotten that McMillan had designs on the Palace and the neighborhood, designs that included burning down a business that refused to go along with his plans. I hadn't forgotten about Warren. But standing on the pavement, with everything around me clean from yesterday's rain, I felt a completely unwarranted optimism. Eleanor Powell would dance tonight.

My phone pinged. It was a text from June, finally.

Nora, I'm so sorry I haven't been in touch. I'm sure you understand how difficult this has been. Let's talk soon, okay?

I immediately wrote back.

June, I'm so glad to hear from you!

I started typing another message.

We have to talk about Cora. Do you know where she was when Sam was pushed from the balcony? Or when Warren was killed?

I was about to hit the Send button when something stopped

me. The number I was using to text June was her business line. Would Cora, as her assistant, have access to it? Could she see June's texts? If I sent that note, would it put June in danger? Or tell Cora that I was on to her?

I gritted my teeth and held the Delete key until my words were gone. It was too risky. I had to assume any text I sent June could be read and any voicemail I left her could be heard by my main suspect in Sam's murder. So I sent June another text.

Please call as soon as you can. We need to talk. It's about Warren and Sam.

I saw the three gray dots that told me she was replying, but then they disappeared. I held my breath, hoping the phone would ring with a call instead. Which is how Marty found me when he came out the lobby doors.

"Are you going to stand there taking selfies all day, or are you going to come in here and manage a theater?"

The phone didn't ring. I put it in my pocket and went inside to manage a theater.

We had a pretty good turnout for the twelve fifteen. Mostly regulars, all very happy that we were open again. A few brave souls even sat in the balcony.

I'd gotten two more texts and a call from Otis Hampton during the day, and when I got another, I faced the fact that I'd eventually have to acknowledge him. So I finally responded.

Hi Otis. I know this is difficult. Trust me, I know. But I'm moving on, and I think you should do the same. There's really nothing for us to talk about.

He answered immediately.

Trust me, there is. Please call.

I didn't.

The two-thirty drew a slightly bigger crowd, and even included some people who weren't eligible for the senior discount.

"I told you," Albert winked as the last patrons went into the auditorium. "The 1940 is the best. People love Fred Astaire."

"And Cole Porter," I agreed. I went up to my office while the film was playing, hoping to find Trixie, but she still wasn't back. I checked in with the PR firm and was just about to open my email when Callie burst into the room.

"Nora!"

She was completely freaked out, holding up her phone and pointing to it with wide eyes.

"What?" I immediately thought the killer had struck again. Had Cora killed June? Had McMillan gone after Cora?

"Ted!" Callie managed to say.

My heart plummeted. "What happened?" I'd been wishing all sorts of catastrophes on him, but now I was afraid. "Did Otis kill him?" Why was that my first thought?

She shook her head, her wild hair flying. "He tweeted."

"Who tweeted?" This was getting ridiculous. I grabbed her phone.

Ted had tweeted.

If you're anywhere near the Bay Area tonight you need to get to the Palace Theater where my best friend Nora is showing some amazing movies. Trust me, you do not want to miss out. #filmbuffs #fomo #SanFrancisco #placetobe

I stared at Callie. "Best friend?" I must have looked as shocked as she did. "Why in the world...?"

"He has eight million followers," Callie breathed.

I swallowed. "We better make some more popcorn."

*   *   *

That evening, for the first time since I'd been there—possibly for the first time in decades—there was a line down the block from the Palace box office. When Brandon showed up with his mom, just intending to watch the movies, we got him a stool and put him to work at the espresso machine. Claire and Mike sold popcorn, drinks, and snacks as fast as they could, and Albert greeted every single filmgoer as if they were his long-lost friends.

Marty, true to form, was having none of it. "These people aren't here to see a classic movie," he said when I checked on him in the projection booth. He was scowling down on the crowd from the booth's little window. "They're just here to be part of some stupid viral Internet scene."

"I know," I told him. "And they all paid for the privilege. Isn't it great?"

He snorted, which is all I could really expect.

Before I could catch my breath the six-thirty was about to start. I'd been keeping my eye out for Hector and Gabriela. He'd texted earlier to let me know they were coming. When they finally arrived, they looked around the bustling lobby in amazement.

"All these people are here for a black and white movie about a tap dancer?" he asked. I have to say that wounded me a bit.

"Not according to Marty," I admitted. "But once they're in the door we can make converts of at least some of them."

"Are you sold out?" Gabriela asked.

I blinked. "I have no idea. We've never had to count the customers before."

I went with them to the back row of the auditorium, where there were gaps between the seats to allow for wheelchairs. "Let me get you some popcorn," I said as they got settled, but Hector put his hand on my arm.

"I'll take care of it," he said. "You have several thousand other things to do, yes?"

I felt the heat of his hand all the way down to my toes. He

nodded and left to go back to the lobby, and I realized Gabriela was looking at me closely.

"Um..." I said, brilliantly. My mind had gone completely blank.

"I think my cousin is already one of your converts," Gabriela said.

I could only hope so. I was fast becoming one of his.

Standing at the back of the packed house, listening to the opening strains of "Broadway Melody" over the titles, I felt tears in my eyes. This is what I'd wanted from the first day I'd come to the Palace. All these people sharing an experience together. Sharing something wonderful.

I'd have given anything for Trixie to be able to see it. I kept thinking I saw her in the crowd, just out of the corner of my eye, but then when I looked again, she wasn't there. It was like she was a ghost or something.

And then, before I knew it, everything was over. The six-thirty, the eight-fifteen, and the ten o'clock shows had all had record-setting crowds. By the time the last of the customers had left the building it was after midnight and we were all completely drained. We were also sold out of everything but gummy bears.

Claire and Mike dutifully grabbed brooms and buckets as soon as the lights came up, and Callie had already closed down the cash registers during the final show, so it didn't take long until we were ready to lock up.

"Callie, may I offer you a ride home?" Albert asked gallantly. It was midnight, but the ninety-something-year-old looked like he'd just gotten his second wind. "Nora? Children?"

"Children" was directed at Claire and Mike, who accepted his offer. I wanted to hang back for a bit.

"You guys all go. I want to go upstairs and check my phone. I got a million messages tonight and haven't answered any of them." Which normally wouldn't have phased me, but this time not all the messages were about things I was trying to avoid.

Marty thumped down the stairs. "Well, at least that's over," he said.

"Until tomorrow." I held up crossed fingers.

"Don't kid yourself. Internet fads never last. We'll be back down to the hardcore regulars before the week is out."

He was probably right, but damn.

They all trailed out and I locked up behind them. I could have checked my messages from home, but I wanted to try to contact Trixie one more time.

I went up the stairs, humming "Begin the Beguine," because Cole Porter is irresistible. I pulled my phone out of my pocket when I got to the landing. I'd turned it to silent hours ago because it seemed like everyone in the world had been texting me about Ted's tweet.

"Trixie?" I called when I got to the hallway. "Everybody's gone. It's just me." It's possible that, as much as I thought she'd have enjoyed it, all the commotion might have been too much for her.

I glanced at my texts as I got to the office. The most recent one came up first.

I have to see you. I need your help. I've been in hiding. Don't trust Cora. And don't tell the police. I'll come to the Palace after your last show. Please, Nora. Please help me.

It was from June.

Five minutes later I was back down in the lobby, pacing. I'd sent June a text telling her it was safe to come, then I'd turned off the lobby lights so nobody would see her approaching from the street.

I wanted to call Detective Jackson, but June had said not to. Why? My screenwriter mind went to a dozen possibilities. Maybe June had hurt Cora and was afraid of getting into trouble? Maybe Cora had some sort of connection to the police that June knew about?

That was ridiculous. June had said "the police" but she hadn't said "Marty's boyfriend the detective." I was deep into a message to Jackson when I heard a sound coming from the auditorium. A sound I recognized. It was the screen going up.

"What the..."

"Nora!" I looked up. Trixie was skipping down the stairs. "Oh, Nora, it was wonderful! Why, I haven't seen that many people here in I don't know how long! Gee, how'd you do it? What—"

"Trixie, you were here?"

"'Course I was here. Where else would I be?" Which was a question for greater philosophical thinkers than myself.

"I didn't see you. I mean, I thought I saw you, but—"

"Oh, well. With that many people around I kind of just popped in and out, you know?"

No, I didn't know, but we didn't have time for that right then. Someone was in the auditorium. Someone had raised the screen.

"Trixie, stick with me," I said. "Something's going on."

Her eyes grew wide and she nodded, following me to the auditorium doors.

When I opened them, I saw the stage lights were glowing, the screen was up, and there was a figure sprawled on the stage near the gaping trap door. June stood over the figure, her clothes dirty and torn. She looked up when she heard the door.

"Nora!" she yelled. "Thank God you're here! Cora tried to kill me!"

CHAPTER 36

The figure on the floor, Cora, moaned and moved. June took a step back, holding something in her hand.

"Hurry!" she called. "I need your help tying her up!"

I raced down the aisle and up the stairs.

"Nora!" Trixie called, following me.

"June, what happened? Where have you been?"

The usually-elegant realtor brushed her disheveled hair from her face. "Cora killed Sam," she said. "She's been holding me captive." She spoke quickly, babbling, as I took in the sight of Cora, bruised and semiconscious, at her feet.

"She closed down the office," June said. "She used my email to send everyone but me a note telling them not to come in, and then she attacked me when I got to work."

June looked feverish. Her eyes kept darting back to the prone figure of Cora, who again moaned and moved. June had been a prisoner somewhere in the office when I'd knocked on her door the day before.

They were both near the hole in the stage that Brandon had fallen through. Dangerously close. And the orange traffic cones I'd place at the four corners of the trap were no protection from its edge.

"Nora, it's her!" Trixie said urgently.

"I know," I murmured, only half paying attention because I'd just registered that something was out of place. The wrappings for the rental furniture, the ones Brandon had never fetched from the back of the stage before he fell, were now piled next to the trap.

"Cora was going to burn down the Palace," June said, frantic.

"She was going to leave me in here to die. Thank God I was able to get free and text you. Here, help me tie her up." She kicked the pile of wrappings toward me. The pile of straps and much-used padded blankets that looked greasy and incredibly flammable.

"Nora, that's the real estate lady who went into the balcony with Sam!" Trixie said.

"I know," I said, not caring if June heard me. "Don't worry. I'm going to—"

"No!" Trixie stepped in front of me as I was about to pick up a strap. "Not her! Her!" She pointed at June. "She's the one I saw go into the balcony!"

I froze. June, focused on me, seemed to sense something had changed.

"Are you sure?"

"Of course I'm sure!" June and Trixie both yelled at the same time.

Then I saw what June held in her hand. A lighter.

Cora moaned again and tried to sit up. "Don't move!" I told her. If she rolled over on her side, she could plummet through the trap.

I met June's eyes. She knew I knew.

Trixie stood between us, her arms stretched out in either direction, as if she could hold us both back. She swiveled her head from June to me. "Nora?" Her voice was uncertain. She didn't know what to do. I didn't either.

"Why did you do it, June? Why did you kill Warren and Sam?"

She looked at me for a moment, as if trying to make up her mind. Probably about whether to kill me now or kill me later.

I swallowed. "I thought Cora was the killer. I thought she and McMillan were working together."

June barked a laugh. "Cora? Please. She was just doing what Stan and I told her to do." Her eyes narrowed on me. "You thought he was the big bad mastermind, didn't you? You thought he was the one buying up the neighborhood. I could tell the minute you met him. You gave him all the credit. Well he wasn't. I am. I'm the one in charge of the whole thing."

"In charge?" I echoed. "You killed two people."

"Not because I wanted to!" she shouted. "I didn't have a choice. Warren never should have been at that bar that night. He never should have seen Cora and Stan together. He had only himself to blame!"

"Nora," Trixie whispered. "What should I do?"

But there was nothing she could do. I shook my head.

"Warren thought you'd freak out when he told you he saw them," I said to June. "He thought Cora was going behind your back to work with your competition."

"She was just our intermediary," June said. "Our carrier pigeon. I'm not stupid enough to use texts or emails that could leave a record. So I used her." She looked down at Cora with disdain. "She hated Stan. All I had to do is tell her I was going to set him up for a fall and she did anything I told her to."

"But Warren wouldn't have," I said.

"Warren would have told everyone he'd seen them, which meant someone might start putting things together. I had to contain the situation."

"Contain the situation? By killing him?" It came to me suddenly that all the rumors about a burglary gone wrong had come from June. She'd been covering her tracks from the beginning. "What did you do? Did you follow him home that night?"

"He sent me a video," she said. "He was disgustingly drunk, and the video showed Stan and Cora together in the bar. I had to get that video, and I had to keep him quiet." Her face twitched at the memory. "I thought, as drunk as he was, that I'd be able to do something to him on the street. Take his phone and make it look like a mugging or something. Maybe a hit and run."

"But Other Girlfriend Ingrid was there," I said. "She was with him."

"What did they all see in him?" she asked, exasperated. And just for a moment she was the woman I'd come to think of as a friend.

I shook my head. She was not that woman. "So you waited until Ingrid left in the morning."

"And then I just knocked on his door," she said.

"And killed him."

Her face twitched again. "I did what I had to do!"

"Why you?" I asked. "Why not McMillan?"

She lifted her head. "Oh, come on. You know any man who swaggers that much is going to be completely' useless when it actually comes down to doing something."

I got it, but I wasn't much in the mood to have a sisterly chinwag about useless men. "Does he know?" I asked. "Does he know you did it?"

"He's too much of a coward to face the truth," she said. "When I saw him on Monday, here on this stage, I knew. He couldn't handle it. He just wanted to prance around and take his big bow."

"After you did all the work," I said. "Sam told me that's the way it was. You did all the work and he took all the credit."

"Yes, well." She blinked. "I wouldn't have minded if he took the credit for Warren. And believe me, he's going to take the credit for this."

I shuddered, then something she'd said caught up with me. Something about McMillan prancing around. "You sabotaged the trap door," I said. "You must have known about it from when you worked here as a teenager. But how did you get in? And when?"

She smirked. "It wasn't exactly difficult to slip downstairs during a movie on Sunday." She looked down at Cora, who seemed to be following the conversation groggily.

"Nora!" Trixie whispered urgently. "How do I work your thingie?" She pointed to the phone I still clutched in my hand. I'd been writing a message to Jackson when I'd been startled. All I had to do was press Send. But the minute June saw me do that, she could drop her lighter in the pile of furniture pads and shove Cora through the trap.

But what if I didn't press Send? What if I just put the phone down? Would Trixie be able to muster her strength and concentrate hard enough to hit the Send button? It was hard enough for her to move a physical thing, could she interact with an electronic one?

I didn't see any other option.

"June. Put the lighter down." I held up my phone lightly, between two fingers. "I'll put down my phone. It's just us here. You put down the lighter."

I set the phone gently on the stage. I didn't expect her to put down the lighter, but now Trixie could do her best with the Send button.

June watched narrowly. So did Cora. I spoke quickly, urgently, to distract June. "You wanted McMillan to fall through the trap." I had to keep her full attention. I didn't want her to notice that Cora was more alert. "You just said it—he liked to prance around the stage when he spoke. You took a chance he'd be the one to fall."

"So much for luck being on my side," June said bitterly. "I would have loved it if Stan fell, but you'd have done just as well. I almost wish it would have been you. Then we wouldn't all have to be here now."

Trixie was kneeling over the phone. I could see the look of concentration on her face as she pressed her finger to the screen. It went straight through.

I looked away. "Did you set the fire at the café?" I asked June. "How did that fit in?"

Her face contorted. "I thought Stan would get the blame. If he wasn't going to be helpful, why did I need him anymore? And everyone knew he was buying up that whole side of the street. Who else would try to burn out the only holdout on the block?"

"Were you in on it?" I asked. "Is that the big secret? That you were partners with him in the redevelopment?"

"You have no idea." Her words dripped with distain.

"So tell me. And tell me how you broke in to the café."

"Breaking into a restaurant with no alarm system wasn't exactly a challenge," she said, mustering a bit of her usual poise.

"But you made a mistake," I said. "You couldn't leave by the café's back door after you set the fire, and you had to leave the locks open on the front door."

"Which wouldn't have mattered if you and that gangster hadn't played the heroes and put the fire out," she spat.

What I wouldn't give for that gangster to show up now. But he'd left after the last show to take Gabriela home. We had plans to meet for breakfast. If I was still alive for breakfast.

Cora was now fully conscious. She looked from me to June.

"What about Sam?" I asked June, desperate to keep her attention. "Why did she deserve to die?"

June's face became a mask of anger. "She tried to *blackmail* me! She figured it out because of something you said. Blackmail! Can you imagine? The nerve of some people! She deserved to be pushed off that balcony!"

Trixie looked up from the phone. "What?"

"She expected me to pay her to keep her mouth shut?" June railed. "There was no way that was going to happen. I just gave her one good push and—"

"*What?*" Trixie yelled. She leapt to her feet. "You pushed her off the *balcony*!?"

June didn't hear a thing. "—Then I ducked back into the shadows and blended in with everyone who came rushing in," she finished.

"How *DARE* you?!" Trixie shouted. I'd only ever seen her that angry once before, and something terrible had happened. "*Nobody* should get pushed off a balcony!"

Then everything happened at once. Trixie advanced on June just as Cora thrust out both her legs, swiping June's feet out from under her. June crashed forward, gripping the lighter and igniting it as she tumbled, screaming, through the trap door.

The lighter hit the pile of blankets and flames caught with a whoosh, but I was already moving. I had to get to the fire extinguisher before the flames spread.

I sprinted to the side of the stage, pulled the extinguisher off the wall and turned. I didn't see a theater in flames. I didn't see Cora writhing in fiery agony. I saw Trixie, spread eagled over the pile of blankets. She looked over to me, dazed. "Nora?"

"Trixie!" I dropped the extinguisher and stumbled back to her. Cora was coughing and sitting up, and I didn't care if she thought I was crazy.

"Did I put it out?" Trixie asked, sitting up at the edge of the trap and looking at the singed wrappings. She put a hand up to her head to straighten her cap.

"You did," I told her. "I don't know how, but you did."

"Gee, I'm glad." She brushed off her jacket, not that it had any evidence of the fire.

Cora didn't seem to notice that I was talking to a ghost. She was looking down into the hole.

The room below was too dark to see anything, but June made no sound.

CHAPTER 37

"June knew I hated McMillan," Cora said. "We worked together years ago, and he was a complete pig. I got out of real estate completely for a few years because of him and guys like him. When June asked me to get involved, I agreed because I thought it was all to take him down."

We were in the lobby, sitting on a gurney while once again San Francisco's police, fire, and EMT units went about the business of dealing with something horrible that had happened at the Palace.

June wasn't dead, but her fall had been much worse than Brandon's. The team who'd put her in their ambulance said she'd be lucky to ever walk again. Not that there would be much walking once she was in prison for multiple murders.

"I thought she was trying to get proof that he was crooked," Cora went on compulsively. "So she could drum him out of the business." She closed her eyes. "I didn't know she was just as bad as he was until it was too late."

"She was going to kill us both tonight," I said.

"She was right about me being stupid," Cora said bitterly. "She told me we were going to catch McMillan in the act tonight after the last show. That he planned to set a fire and that we'd get it all on video and expose him for what he is. And I went right along with her, slipping backstage and hiding until everyone left. I didn't even know she'd knocked me out until I woke up with you talking to her."

"She would have burned down the Palace," I said. "She must have known I'd fight any plans to take it over, so she decided to destroy it and get rid of me along with you. And I'm sure she had a way to implicate McMillan for it all."

"I can't believe I was so stupid," Cora said.

There was a lot of that going around.

"June must have been the one telling the press that the balcony was faulty," I reasoned.

"In every interview she gave," Cora nodded. "And she gave one to anyone who'd listen."

I'd thought McMillan wanted to drive the price of the theater down by having it labeled unsafe. I'd had the right plot, but the wrong evil mastermind.

"What about Sam?" I asked. "I know June pushed her, but she didn't die from her fall. She died at the hospital. You told me, in the waiting room that day, that June had never left Sam's side. That she'd brought her flowers."

Cora knew what I was asking. "I don't know." She looked up at the ceiling. "I don't know if she did something to Sam in the hospital. All I know is, either way, June killed her."

There was a lot more I wanted to ask her, like if June had been behind all the social media rumors about Warren, and what she'd done with his phones. But that would all have to wait. The EMTs were ready to take Cora to the hospital to check out her head wound, and just as they wheeled her away, I heard an unmistakably deep and commanding voice.

"Hello, Detective," I said as Jackson approached. "I should probably catch you up."

"Oh, Nora! I'm so glad you're okay! I'm so glad I'm okay! I'm so glad the Palace is okay!"

Trixie was bursting by the time I met her up in the office later. It was after two in the morning.

"We're only okay because you stopped that fire before it got started," I told her. "How did you do it?"

She shook her head. "I don't know. All I remember is being so mad at that lady that I could have spit. How *dare* she push someone off the balcony?" She stamped a petite foot.

"Trixie, you were so brave," I told her.

"And angry," she nodded. "You know something, Nora? I've noticed that I'm a lot stronger when I'm angry. Have you noticed that?"

"I have," I told her. There was a lesson there, somewhere.

"I didn't plan to put out any fires," she said. "I just wanted to slap that lady so hard, or kick her or something, so I started for her, but then she fell, and I fell, and it just...worked out." She dimpled.

"It worked out really well," I told her. I was supremely grateful that the one physical trait Trixie manifested was her coldness. I'd felt it, Callie's mother had felt it, and I knew that if not for her chilly presence falling on the lighter just as it hit the flammable pile of wrappings, I might be sifting through the ashes of the Palace right now. Or worse.

"Gee, it's late," Trixie said, looking out the window. She started to shimmer a little, a sure sign that she was exhausted. "Do you think everybody will be gone soon? I think I could use a rest."

"Of course you could," I told her. "You've earned it. But don't stay away too long, okay?"

She waved a hand. "'Course not. There's too much going on around this place lately. You need me!" She grinned and faded away.

Truer words were never spoken by a ghost.

Jackson gave me a ride home eventually, but I was far too wired to think about sleep. I scrolled through the messages on my phone, marveling at how much could change in a few hours.

The messages were largely similar, most of them from LA people who had dropped me once Ted left. Now that he'd publicly called me his "best friend"—and I still couldn't figure that out—I was apparently back on everyone's call list. I scrolled through them pretty quickly. But one message stood out, both for its length and its subject matter. It was from Otis Hampton.

Okay, Nora. If you don't want to talk I'll just say everything I have to say. First, I want to tell you that I know what Ted did with your money. Beyond that, I think I know how to get it back. And I very much want to get it back because I very much want to thwart any plans Ted Bishop has. I realize it's petty of me, but there it is. Priya is a woman who requires a very expensive lifestyle, and I want her to realize Ted will not be able to provide it. I won't lie. I want to win her back. Even if you've moved on—and I'm happy for you if you have—surely you still want what you deserve. And surely you'll understand if I'm not ready to give up on Priya yet. Consider me your ally, and don't hesitate to let me know if there is anything I can do to make your life easier. If it makes Ted's life harder, so much the better. I have the kind of resources that can solve a lot of problems.

Okay. Well. I should probably call him. But not at four in the morning.

With Café Madeline out of commission, Hector and I had agreed to meet at a diner a few blocks away the next morning. I'd gotten about twenty minutes sleep since confronting a killer and nearly burning to death, but for some reason he wanted to make everything about him.

"Why didn't you contact me? I should have been there! I should never have left you alone!" This is how he said hello. We'd been texting since dawn, but he still wanted to rant in person.

"Don't be ridiculous." I took his coffee and downed it, not wanting to wait the thirty seconds for a cup of my own. "When was I supposed to call you? And, if you'll recall, I did tell you that I didn't need you to take care of me." The waitress materialized with more coffee, bless her. "I can take care of myself." With the help of an extraordinary friend, I didn't add.

"Nevertheless," he said, his face like thunder. "I blame myself.

I should have seen that woman June for what she was."

"None of us did." I was ravenous. Everything on the menu looked amazing. "Why should you be any different?"

He opened this mouth, then closed it.

"I'll have the special," I told the waitress. "Extra bacon, please."

Hector looked at me like I was deranged. "You're just going to sit there and eat bacon like nothing happened?" he said.

"I'd rather talk about everything with you, but not if you're going to be all..." I made a gesture that was supposed to indicate the fact that he was completely wigging out.

He took a deep breath. "Okay. I'll control my..." he repeated the gesture, which involved flapping hands and just looked ridiculous when he did it. "Now, tell me everything that happened."

I gave him much the same version I'd given Detective Jackson the night before. The one that omitted Trixie and said the fire just hadn't caught.

"Just a small patch around the trap door got damaged," I said. "But I'm not kidding myself. It's going to cost a fortune to repair the stage and get rid of both of the traps. And I haven't even checked to see if the screen got any smoke damage. Meanwhile we've got a show scheduled for—" I checked my watch. "—Four hours from now."

"Don't tell me you're planning to show movies today," Hector protested.

"It's what we do," I told him. "Are you familiar with the saying 'the show must go on?' We've got crime scene tape up—again—but only behind the screen on the stage. We're going to be open for the twelve-fifteen."

He stared at me, and a vein on his forehead that I'd never noticed before throbbed. He looked like he'd like to throttle me. Or something.

"What?" I demanded.

He closed his eyes and rubbed his face with both hands. "There are over three billion women in the world," he said. "Over a hundred million just in the United States." He looked at me. "Probably ninety-nine million or so would be easier than you to—"

He stopped himself, and the air around our booth suddenly felt charged with electricity. I swallowed. "To what?"

He looked at me, and he simmered. "To have breakfast with."

I nodded. This man was a former crime lord and a surprise at every turn. And he could turn the air around me electric.

"Right back at you," I told him.

By the time I got to the Palace, Marty had told Callie and Albert everything. Or at least everything Detective Jackson had told him.

They followed me up to the office, peppering me with questions. But since they'd also made extra-strong coffee, I was okay with that.

"I'm fine, everything's fine," I repeated, and then went over it all with them again.

Callie was completely stunned. "I can't believe *June* killed Warren," she said. "She loved Warren."

I put my hand on her arm. There was nothing I could say to explain it.

"Gee, that's rough." Trixie spoke from behind me. I hadn't noticed her appear. And I didn't acknowledge her in front of everyone.

Marty gave us all of fifteen seconds to experience our emotions. Then, "Are we actually going to get the theater ready? Because a million people might show up today if your ass of a husband sends out another tweet."

I stood. "You're right. Not about Ted tweeting, but we've still got a lot to do in case more than the usual handful show up. We sold out of everything yesterday, so I'll go make a Costco run, and Albert, could you give that carpenter a call? I have no idea how we're going to pay for it, but we really need to get the stage repaired."

"Of course," he said, standing.

"Nora?" Trixie had moved to the window. She was waving me over. I moved around the desk.

"Oh!" Callie yelped. "I forgot to ask you. Lisa came by earlier. She gets her new ovens next week, but it's going to take a while for all the repairs. She wondered if she could bake things across the street and have a popup shop here in the lobby to sell them."

"That's brilliant. I'll call her later." I couldn't wait to tell her that, with June under arrest and McMillan no doubt facing investigation for his part in things, the threat to Lisa's café seemed to be lifted. Likewise, the threat to the Palace.

We were safe.

At least for now.

"Nora?" Trixie pointed out the window. "Why is there a moving van outside the theater?"

I went to the window and looked out. I was just saying "Why is there a moving van outside the theater?" myself when there was a loud rapping from the lobby doors below.

We all went downstairs.

"Nora Paige?" The mover asked when I opened the door. "Where do you want this?"

"What is it?"

Trixie clapped her hands and scampered to my side. "A delivery! What is it? Is it a present?"

The mover checked his invoice. "Twenty-two boxes of personal goods." He squinted at me. "Are you expecting it?"

My things. Everything Ted had sent me.

"Your clothes from LA," Callie said from behind me. "Cool. Are they, like, nicer than what you've been wearing?" She saw the look on my face. "I mean, not that—"

"Never mind," I said. "Where am I going to put it all?" Robbie's guest cottage wasn't big enough for twenty-two boxes of anything.

"Bring it in here!" Trixie said. "I want to see it! I haven't seen new clothes in ages!"

"There's always the basement here," Albert said doubtfully.

I shared his doubt. "I need to go through it all. I'm not even sure I want most of it." It belonged to a different person. To a different life.

Trixie pouted. "Aw, come on, Nora. We can play dress up. At least you can."

I shook my head. "Let's take it to Robbie's," I said. "We can store it all in the garage until I figure it out."

"Don't you already have a Tesla in Robbie's garage?" Marty glanced over from the position he'd taken at the candy counter, pointedly not joining in.

I stared at him. I'd completely forgotten about the Tesla. Ted had given it to me, along with a diamond bracelet, when he'd come back into my life three months ago, begging me to forgive him. I hadn't wanted the car or the bracelet, which was probably still in the glove compartment of the car I had never even considered using.

"Nora?" Trixie said.

"Ma'am?" the driver asked.

I held up a finger. "One minute." Then I pulled out my phone and sent Otis Hampton a text.

Otis, how would you feel about buying a Tesla from me? And a diamond bracelet?

It might not cover the cost of all of the repairs, but it would be a good start.

I hit Send. The reply came immediately.

I'll be in San Francisco in three hours. We have a lot to plan.

I stared at the text with a sinking feeling.

What had I just started?

Born to Dance
1936

Okay, sure. There are a jillion movies like this. Movies with a plot about a plucky and talented young thing trying to break into show business—specifically, trying to get into a Broadway show, and getting the One Big Break she needs just in time for the finale. Eleanor Powell made a career out of them. But you might not realize what everyone in 1936 knew: the plot didn't matter.

What matters is the music. What matters is the songs. What matters (a little) is the romance, and when we're talking about Eleanor Powell, what matters most is the dancing. Because—you may get this from the title—that woman was born to dance.

And in the case of this movie, that woman is dancing to Cole Porter songs, and the love interest is Jimmy Stewart. So this is one to watch, my friends.

Eleanor comes to town and for no apparent reason is befriended by the delightful Una Merkle. In the world-building of a 1930s musical, girls who run the desks of hotels and sailors who are in town on shore leave all have talent and are just one number away from starring in the latest hit show. And why not? This is America, after all! Three cheers for the red, white, and blue! (Wait—we don't get to sing that until the extravaganza of a finale.)

Anyway, the three sailors are a short guy from Brooklyn, a tall guy from the hay fields of the heartland, and Jimmy Stewart, looking young and wistful and, as described by a lovesick telephone operator, "A tall sort of answer to a maiden's prayer, on stilts."

Everybody gets to dance. The tall hayseed you may recognize. He's Buddy Ebsen (Yep, from *The Beverly Hillbillies*) and he has a lanky, awkward, comic style of dancing that (and this is just my opinion, but why else are you reading this?) is a tad overdone in this film. But he gets to gambol, and there's a fun number with our six leads singing about being nuts about each other that's just a breezy delight.

All this leads to Eleanor and Jimmy walking through a moonlit park, Cole Porter helping them out with "Easy to Love." Which is a love song for the ages, but the whole interlude is a somewhat misbegotten attempt to have Jimmy croon and Eleanor waft gracefully. She was God's own tap dancer, but wafting was never her thing. Luckily, they're interrupted by a park cop before things can get too uncomfortable.

Hollywood was trying hard to figure out what to do with Jimmy Stewart in 1936. He released *nine* films that year. I think they had him try a little bit of everything to see what would stick. Now, I love my Jimmy Stewart, but I think we can all agree it was for the best that his musical career never really took off.

Back to Eleanor. The number in the park is one of very few I can think of where she actually danced with a partner. And even in this case, they were sort of in the same place at the same time, but not dancing *together*. There was none of that Fred and Ginger stuff. And that was typical for her. Eleanor most often danced without a partner.

And when I say *danced*, I mean she tore up the freaking stage. The way she could tap! She found rhythms where there were no rhythms. She hit that stage and she owned it. Even if you don't watch this whole movie, do yourself a favor and look up the finale online somewhere. Your jaw will drop at her strength, at the athleticism and the speed and the unbelievable *life* she brings to a ridiculously overblown shipboard spectacular.

You may not notice the sequined and spangled sailors in the chorus. You may not see the gigantic guns on the ship behind her (although it's fun to wonder if Cher saw this number before filming the "Turn Back Time" video). You may not register that there's a full marching band on the ship. Because Eleanor's dancing is bigger than all of that.

She had this thing where she'd bring her shoulders up and open her mouth as if she just couldn't contain all the joy that her dancing was giving her. She's not trying to be pretty or feminine or romantic. She doesn't appear to be trying at all. She's just dancing like she was born to.

I've learned a lot watching Eleanor Powell movies. A lot about finding my own rhythm. A lot about staying plucky and trusting that I'll get my One Big Break in time for the finale. But I think there's something more to learn. Something about how she danced. It wasn't as if no one was watching. No self-help adages for her. She knew everyone was watching. They had no choice. She *demanded* them to watch, she demanded them to marvel, because she was up there on that stage and she was doing something extraordinary.

I want to be more like Eleanor Powell. She danced unpartnered. And she danced with joy.

Movies My Friends Should Watch
Sally Lee

Want More Sally?

If you enjoyed Sally Lee's movie blogs, check out the Movies My Friends Should Watch website for more.

Visit moviesmyfriendsshouldwatch.com.
And watch good movies!

MARGARET DUMAS

Margaret Dumas lives in the San Francisco Bay Area, where she reads and writes books when she isn't watching old movies.

**The Movie Palace Mystery Series
by Margaret Dumas**

MURDER AT THE PALACE (#1)
MURDER IN THE BALCONY (#2)

Henery Press Mystery Books

And finally, before you go...
Here are a few other mysteries
you might enjoy:

THE HOUSE ON HALLOWED GROUND

Nancy Cole Silverman

A Misty Dawn Mystery (#1)

When Misty Dawn, a former Hollywood Psychic to the Stars, moves into an old craftsman house, she encounters the former owner, the recently deceased Hollywood set designer, Wilson Thorne. Wilson is unaware of his circumstances, and when Misty explains the particulars of his limbo state, and how he might help himself if he helps her, he's not at all happy. That is until young actress Zoey Chamberlain comes to Misty's door for help.

Zoey has recently purchased The Pink Mansion and thinks it's haunted. But when Misty searches the house, it's not a ghost she finds, but a dead body. The police suspect Zoey, but Zoey fears the death may have been a result of the ghost...and a family curse. Together Misty and Wilson must untangle the secrets of The Pink Mansion or submit to the powers of the family curse.

Available at booksellers nationwide and online

Visit www.henerypress.com for details

PROTOCOL

Kathleen Valenti

A Maggie O'Malley Mystery (#1)

Freshly minted college graduate Maggie O'Malley embarks on a career fueled by professional ambition and a desire to escape the past. As a pharmaceutical researcher, she's determined to save lives from the shelter of her lab. But on her very first day she's pulled into a world of uncertainty. Reminders appear on her phone for meetings she's never scheduled with people she's never met. People who end up dead.

With help from her best friend, Maggie discovers the victims on her phone are connected to each other and her new employer. She soon unearths a treacherous plot that threatens her mission—and her life. Maggie must unlock deadly secrets to stop horrific abuses of power before death comes calling for her.

Available at booksellers nationwide and online

Visit www.henerypress.com for details

STAGING IS MURDER

Grace Topping

A Laura Bishop Mystery (#1)

Laura Bishop just nabbed her first decorating commission—staging a 19th-century mansion that hasn't been updated for decades. But when a body falls from a laundry chute and lands at Laura's feet, replacing flowered wallpaper becomes the least of her duties.

To clear her assistant of the murder and save her fledgling business, Laura's determined to find the killer. Turns out it's not as easy as renovating a manor home, especially with two handsome men complicating her mission: the police detective on the case and the real estate agent trying to save the manse from foreclosure.

Worse still, the meddling of a horoscope-guided friend, a determined grandmother, and the local funeral director could get them all killed before Laura props the first pillow.

Available at booksellers nationwide and online

Visit www.henerypress.com for details

ARTIFACT

Gigi Pandian

A Jaya Jones Treasure Hunt Mystery (#1)

Historian Jaya Jones discovers the secrets of a lost Indian treasure may be hidden in a Scottish legend from the days of the British Raj. But she's not the only one on the trail...

From San Francisco to London to the Highlands of Scotland, Jaya must evade a shadowy stalker as she follows hints from the hastily scrawled note of her dead lover to a remote archaeological dig. Helping her decipher the cryptic clues are her magician best friend, a devastatingly handsome art historian with something to hide, and a charming archaeologist running for his life.

Available at booksellers nationwide and online

Visit www.henerypress.com for details

Printed in the USA
CPSIA information can be obtained
at www.ICGtesting.com
LVHW061654150823
755323LV00003B/133